SINBAD IN THE KINGDOM OF THE DJINN

Gavin Chappell

Schlock! Publications

For Edward Said

CONTENTS

BOOK ONE: THE CITY OF BRASS

1 THE DJINN

Baghdad was in a state of uproar. Men were shouting, women screaming, children sobbing as a thunderous roar tore through the sultry air. The booths of the shops that lined the street had been knocked awry and a litter of merchandise—cloths, brocades, figs, melons, tools and utensils and weapons—lay strewn across the roadway, or were trampled underfoot.

In the distance, where the golden dome of the caliph's palace stood silhouetted against the silver sky, a high whirling vortex of wind towered into the heavens.

Reining his dromedary by the city gates through which he had just ridden, Sinbad looked askance at his mail-clad companions. 'Wait here,' he instructed them.

He dismounted, and approached the booth of a nearby rug shop, whose proprietor stood gazing open-mouthed at the turbulent skies. 'Peace be upon you.' Sinbad made his salaams, adding, 'In Allah's name, what has happened to the city of peace during my absence?'

With one eye still fixed on the strange swirling whirlwind, the merchant cried shrilly, 'And upon you be peace, stranger! But you must have been away many a moon, if still you believe Baghdad warrants such an epithet. There has been little sign of peace in recent years.'

'What makes you say that, friend?' Sinbad asked.

'Why, do you not know that the city has been plagued by evil wizards and ifrits, stranger?' the merchant cried, and he began ticking off recent calamities on his fingers. 'First there was that Yemeni sorcerer Abdul Alhazred, who bore off the bride-to-be of the caliph's son Al-Wathiq. Even though the caliph sent Sinbad himself after her, she never returned, nay, nor Al-Wathiq himself. You have heard of Sinbad, surely?'

The sailor grinned. 'A fellow of little account; an irreligious wine bibber and wastrel by what they say in Basra, a frequenter of immoral ladies, too, who squanders his days sailing the seven seas in pursuit of worldly pelf. No wonder he failed in his quest.'

The merchant looked affronted. 'Surely it is another Sinbad you speak of,' he said disparagingly. 'Although he was, alas, absent when the Grand Vizier attempted to overthrow the caliph! I had thought all that was over, of course, when the vizier was defeated and his co-conspirators arrested, but now...!'

'I heard word of this,' Sinbad mused, 'but it was indeed when I was gone from the city. Since then I have sailed upon the seas of darkness.'

'Then word will also not have reached you,' the merchant went on, 'of the blood drinking imp who terrorises the nobles and princes of the land. It is true! Almost all of the nobility have reported awaking to find strange incisions on their bodies, still sticky with blood—as if some foul creature had been feasting on them in the night!'

'Strange indeed,' said Sinbad. 'But what have such lamentable events to do with this latest pandemonium?

Even as he spoke, the vortex vanished as if it had never been, but now winds began to hurtle across the city. The fleeing mob was caught up by the sudden storm, people thrown every which way, the already torn canopies swirling off into the air. And through the air above them whirled a vast cloud of vapour, crackling with lightning as it sizzled overhead. Unspeaking, the merchant darted inside his shop, slamming the door behind him. Sinbad flung himself down behind his crouching dromedary.

Looking up, he saw a laughing face limned in the cloud, as huge as the sail of a dhow. And sitting apparently upon shoulders of vapour, two figures, a man and a woman. In one crazy instant Sinbad recognised the man's face, and then they were gone. The cloud banked, and soared off across the city, vanishing into the south east.

Sinbad rose, and the dromedary clambered to its feet with a complaining squeal. Looking up and down the street, the sailor saw no sign of anyone stirring. Crushed and broken bodies lay intermingled with spoiled merchandise. The shops themselves were half ruined.

Leading his dromedary by its reins, Sinbad went back up to the gate where he had left his companions. An eerie silence hung over the city and all he could hear was the crunch of his footsteps, and the thudding of the dromedary's hoofs, as they picked their way up the debris strewn street.

'Captain Sinbad!

The cry split the silence. Sinbad's two mailed companions, who had taken shelter behind their own richly caparisoned horses, were now struggling to their feet. Two Christian knights, they had escorted him on his journey from the far-off empire of the infidel Franks, where he had been sent as an emissary to their king.

'Sir Acelin of Gascony,' Sinbad acknowledged, nodding at the tall, fair haired, square jawed knight. 'And Sir Barnard,' he added, turning to the older, bulkier, more rubicund of the two men. 'It seems we reach my city in a time of some distress.'

'Mon Dieu!' said Sir Acelin. 'What in Lucifer's name was that thing?'

'Are such monsters common in paynim lands?' asked Sir Barnard.

Sinbad grimaced. 'Never in my many voyages have I ever seen such a sight,' he said. 'Certainly not in Baghdad! Although the rug seller was right,' he added softly, speaking to himself. 'In recent years we have seen much that is strange.' The two knights were staring at him uncertainly. 'But we shall learn nothing standing and talking,' he said aloud. 'Let us ride to the caliph's palace and learn the truth of what has happened during my absence.'

They trotted through the streets. The citizens were slowly beginning to crawl out from their hiding places or pick themselves up, bruised and battered, from where the storm winds had flung them. Some did not stir, and the streets were scattered with unmoving, pathetic forms. Sinbad and his companions rode through the great bazaar and up the winding streets towards the caliph's palace.

Riding towards the great blue gates, they met no challenge from the guards who would normally be posted as sentries in the entrance way. All was silent but for their hoofsteps as they crossed ornamental gardens whose tinkling fountains had flooded out across gravel paths. Trees had been smashed and splintered. A dead peacock lay spreadeagled across the pathway, and nearby huddled the corpses of two guards. At last they reached the wide, white, sweeping stairway to the main audience chamber, where a despondent man in a huge turban sat upon the lowest step, gazing about him.

Sinbad reined his steed and dismounted. He gestured to the two knights to dismount him, and kissed the ground before the dejected figure. 'Peace be upon you, O Prince of the Faithful!' he called out, rising, his voice ringing back from the battered marble walls that surrounded them.

The caliph Harun al-Rashid—for it was he—drew himself up. His large turban was at a rakish angle, his silken garments were rent, and there was a cut on his brow that wept tears of crimson.

'Upon you be peace, O Sinbad,' said the caliph. 'And upon your companions. You choose an ill time to return from your voyages in the lands of the infidel. We had given you up for lost.'

Sinbad's fame as a sailor had drawn Harun al-Rashid's attention some years ago, and despite a growing desire to retire from the seafaring life, the sailor had found himself despatched on more than one desperate diplomatic mission. This time, he told himself, it would be different, but he knew that it was a hopeless hope.

'Know, O Prince of the Faithful,' said Sinbad, 'that I have carried out my commands, and return now from the court of the Frankish emperor with words of peace. I was delayed on my outward journey when pagan pirates carried me off to a land where the sun never sets, and men battle for supremacy with creatures from another star ...'

The caliph made a curt gesture. 'This is not the time for the telling of fabulous tales, Sinbad,' he told the sailor. 'As you can see, you and your companions return in Baghdad's time of most desperate need.' As he gestured about him, mameluke guards and eunuch slaves appeared from hiding places, and gathered round.

Sinbad introduced the two knights. 'But what has been happening?' he asked, as the caliph led him and the others into the high roofed audience chamber. 'The last time I was in Baghdad I heard that the Grand Vizier had risen against you. You sent me on a mission to far off infidel lands before I heard much more. And now I return and find the city under attack from djinn!'

Harun al-Rashid gave a shudder. The caliph ascended the seven steps to his throne, while his mamelukes took up position along the marble walls, broad bladed scimitars at rest over brawny shoulders. He sat down wearily, and clapped his hands. 'Bring food and drink for my guests, and let us be pleasantly entertained while I tell these newcomers the tale of the disasters that have plagued Baghdad.'

Eunuch chamberlains twittered and flitted about in the background, and tables containing many dishes and flagons of sherbet were set before the guests. A bevy of dancing girls in diaphanous robes and dark skinned musicians entered the hall, and the dancers began to sway to the strumming of dulcimers. Even under these trying circumstances, the far famed hospitality of

Harun al-Rashid was superb.

Sir Barnard's eyes lit up at the sight of food, and he began to munch enthusiastically on balls of falafel, sipping from time to time on a cup of sherbet. Sir Acelin also ate and drank, but strictly in moderation. When he saw that Sir Barnard's eyes were drawn by the delectable gyrations of the dancing girls, he scowled at his fellow knight. Sir Barnard crossed himself and muttered a prayer.

'Your munificence is justly famed, O Prince of the Faithful,' said Sinbad, 'and when my companions return to the court of their emperor, they will have much to speak of. But tell me, please, what is the meaning of the things that I saw and heard this day?'

'And what was it that you saw, Sinbad?' asked the caliph sardonically. 'What was it that you heard? I have seen and heard much this day and others, but little that I could explain.'

'I saw a great cloud shaped almost like a man,' Sinbad said, frowning, 'flying over the city, bringing with it a wind that threw the streets into disarray and flung folk willy-nilly about. And I saw something else. Sitting seemingly upon the shoulders of the cloud man himself, two people—a man and a woman. The woman I could not discern, but the man I knew—as he whom my caliph has forbidden me to name. The man I once knew as the grand vizier. Is it true that he conspired against you?'

'Not only did Ja'afar plot against me,' said the caliph furiously, 'but he succeeded in deposing me by a low trick! And for many moons I was no longer caliph of Baghdad and Prince of the Faithful, but the lowest of the low, compelled to consort with thieves and robbers ere I could regain my rightful throne. When I did so, you can depend upon it, the plotters and all connected with them were righteously chastised, although that scheming vizier had already put himself beyond the reach of my retribution. And now he returns, leagued with the powers of darkness, of Iblis and the djinn, to carry off my beloved sister, the princess Abassa!'

'So it was the princess I saw on the shoulder of that great man of cloud and smoke,' said Sinbad. 'Was that whirlwind a djinn? Does the vizier then command such diabolical forces?'

'Indeed he does,' said the caliph grimly. 'Know you, O Sinbad, that Ja'afar is of the Barmecide clan. Those Persians have been long rumoured to consort with magicians and fire worshippers. Well, now the tales have been proved true.

'But let me begin my own story at the beginning. You may not be aware of this, but it has long been my wont to go out by night amongst my people in disguise. Oft-times was I accompanied by Ja'afar himself, and Masrour the Executioner to guard us, all in disguise, but at other times I went alone. Thus could I learn the mood of the populace without relying on spies who might be unwilling to report news that could arouse my wroth. Due to this subterfuge many an uprising was crushed ere it began, although the vizier warned me that one day I would regret putting myself in danger.

'No doubt he was sincere in his warnings, at least to begin with, but it was this knowledge that he used as the basis of his plot. One day he came to me with a request. A most shameless proposition, for all that he is a powerful man from a powerful family in the city. He requested my sister Abassa's hand in marriage!'

Sinbad could think of few men more eligible, but it would be imprudent, not to say impudent, to voice this thought. 'You declined his request, O Prince of the Faithful?'

'Naturally,' the caliph said with a snort. 'I would not have the proud blood of my royal house sullied by that of a Persian wizard! Not that I knew he was a wizard at that point; he had kept that side of his nature well-hidden.

'The following evening I went out into the city in disguise, as was my custom, and attended a number of underground wine shops, gambling halls, and houses of ill repute—for, do you see, it is in such places that I can best judge the mood of the people. I fell in with a young fellow named Ahmed, who cadged drinks from me all night. In one drinking den, when both Ahmed and I were deep in our cups, a fight broke out between two

Bedouin herders, and the place was raided by the watch. In the confusion that ensued one fighter was slain, the other escaped, while several others waded in and began fighting. But the watchmen laid hands both upon Ahmed and I and we were dragged away to the city gaol as drunkards.

'In the morning I awoke, worse for wear but determined to free myself—and I assured myself that the chief of police's head would roll. I banged on the bars, demanding the gaoler attend to me. He was a long time in coming, and when he appeared he wore the white clothes of mourning. I told him who I was and insisted he free me. In his impudence he laughed at my claims.

'"Besides," he said, "how could a drunkard like you claim to be Harun al-Rashid, prince of the faithful, when this morning it was proclaimed throughout the city that the caliph of Baghdad is dead?"'

2 THE CALIPH'S TALE

To say I was dumbfounded is superfluous, the caliph continued. *I returned to the cell and sat miserably in the corner. My roguish companion laughed, in a not unfriendly manner, complimenting me for my audacity in claiming to be the caliph himself. I tried to make him believe me, but soon saw that it was futile; he thought the knock on my head had scattered my wits. I turned my thoughts to my situation. Ja'afar was at the back of all this, I was certain of it. And yet what could I do? I was a prisoner, and no doubt would remain so for the time being.*

From our cell, we listened to the jubilant din of a city rejoicing. I gathered that Ja'afar was marking his accession with much celebration. A tear trickled down my cheek, hearing so much joy and so little lamentation. Ahmed tried to comfort me with his off colour jokes. What would happen to us? I asked him. He shrugged, and said that we would be hauled before the cadi, sentenced to flogging, and then allowed to go on our way. The very notion of the caliph of Baghdad, scourged in the bazaar under the eyes of the jeering mob! But the worst was yet to come.

The gaoler returned sometime after noon, and we were taken by guards to the cadi, my companion, and myself, now unrecognisable due to the disguise I had adopted and the time I had wallowed in the muck and filth of the gaol. The trial was brief, and we were found guilty. My tender hide smarted at the prospect of eighty lashes. Then the cadi told us that the new caliph had issued his first decrees. Ja'afar was to be a stern, heavy handed ruler, marking a return to the austere reign of the earlier caliphs. There was to be an end to the laxity that had prevailed under recent rulers, he said. And one decree should interest we two prisoners peculiarly.

The punishment for drunkenness was now death by decapitation. The time for the sentence to be executed: the following morning.

We were taken back to the gaol by the guards, some of the more sentimental of whom expressed sorrow at the harsh sentence, but none would listen to my protestations. Back in the cell I faced Ahmed piteously. Eying me with curiosity, he asked me if I could prove that I was indeed the caliph. I told him my story, and he listened. 'What would be the reward for a man who aided you?' he asked idly. 'If you were reinstated, and this Ja'afar overthrown?'

I shrugged. 'He would receive gold and jewels and great palaces and high rank,' I told him. 'But such talk is vain. We are to be executed on the morrow. Better that we made our peace with Allah and resigned ourselves to our unjust fate.'

Ahmed produced a key from the folds of his loincloth. I started up, staring. 'What is that, thief?' I demanded. He explained that he had palmed it from the gaoler on our return, while the man was distracted. Leaving the cell would pose no trouble, as long as we chose our time well. Further escape would be another matter. And as for where we would go, two wanted men who had compounded public drunkenness with a flight from justice...

To make a shorter story of it, we escaped during the hour of evening prayer, when the gaoler was piously prostrating himself in the direction of Mecca. Our luck held until we reached the very gates of the gaol, where we our presence was perceived by a guard, and we were pursued into the streets. Here Ahmed's unrivalled knowledge of winding ways and back alleys came to the fore. Of our flight from Baghdad, and our adventures on the river and in the desert, I need not speak now.

Suffice it to say that after many hair-raising escapades, we reached the city of Basra, where we inveigled our way into a private audience with its governor, an old ally of mine named Ishak; indeed my appointee. At first he was uncertain of my identity, but bathed, wearing fresh clothes, and with my beard trimmed and oiled and perfumed, I was unmistakable, and he listened to my tale in horror. And I was equally horrified by what he told me in turn. Word had reached Basra of Ja'afar's succession to the throne of the caliph, but with it came news that he had celebrated his reign by marrying Abassa!

By all accounts she went to her wedding willingly, which news saddened me beyond bearing. The governor told me of the rumours that said that Ja'afar was widely regarded as a sorcerer. He had used his dark arts to mesmerise Abassa, he suggested. He was said to own a talisman that gave him dominion over the djinn, the marids and the ifrits, and it was the source of his power. If we could replace the ring with another that Ishak had in his possession, one that would turn a sorcerer's power upon himself, we might defeat him.

But how could we hope to make this exchange? I asked. And that was when Ahmed, who had been uncharacteristically quiet, offered his professional services.

'You already owe me, friend,' he said in his rough way, 'for getting you out of clink. But if you want anything stolen, or switched, I'm your man.'

With Ishak's aid we made a secret return to Baghdad, and in the watches of the night we effected a forced entry into this very palace, and, dodging patrols of guards, we entered the caliph's bedchamber, where Ja'afar slept at the side of the princess Abassa. On his left hand glinted a ruby ring. Ahmed stole up to steal it—and replaced it with another ring, seemingly identical; the ring that Ishak had given us. It was at that moment that, due to my cursed clumsiness I knocked over the great porcelain jug that stood upon a small table, and at the sound of its shattering, guards came running and Ja'afar awoke, although my sister slept on as if drugged.

Seeing the two thieves standing over his bed, recognising myself as his great rival, Ja'afar ignored the guards pounding on the door, but instead summoned a djinn to fling us as far as the edge of the world. A figure of smoke and mist burst up from a crack that appeared in the floor, but instead of seizing Ahmed and I, it snatched up Ja'afar and sent him whirling and spinning out of the window through the moonlit skies until he could no longer be seen. At this, my sister awoke from her slumber, and I embraced and kissed her passionately in joy. I flung wide the doors of my bedchamber, and allowed my guards to enter, explaining all that had happened. My first act on being reinstated was to issue a decree making Ahmed my grand vizier. But the cunning thief was nowhere to be found, having fled the palace and all responsibility to return to his dissolute life in the stews of the city.

Sinbad listened attentively. When Harun al-Rashid ceased, he said, 'Ja'afar was defeated by the magic he had thought to control. I had heard something of this, but little of your own adventures, O captain of the faithful. And what of the scenes we witnessed today?'

The caliph looked sombre. 'This day Ja'afar made his return, borne by the same djinn who sent him flying on the wings of the wind, and now he has carried off my sister I know not whither. Not that he took her without a fight! I was with the princess, walking in the palace gardens, when he swooped down, and I drew my trusty scimitar and fought him. But he cut at me with his own blade, striking me on the forehead, and I swooned. He departed, laying waste to my city! But it is his stealing away of the princess that grieves me the most. Sinbad, you have often told me of your adventures with monsters and magicians. I request of you your services one last time. Find my sister and bring her back to Baghdad!'

The knights had also listened avidly. At this, Sir Acelin raised his sword hilt foremost. 'By Mountjoy and St Denis,' he vowed, 'I pledge my blade to your aid, sire. I shall accompany Sinbad and help him rescue the princess.'

Hastily Sir Barnard put down the chicken wing he had been gnawing upon, wiped his greasy fingers on his surcoat, and copied Sir Acelin carelessly. 'I fought the Saracens at Roncesvalles... but if there's a lady needs rescuing, Christian or pagan, Sir Barnard de Bruin is your man.'

'This is all very well,' said Sinbad testily. 'But...'

'You refuse a request from your caliph?' Harun al-Rashid's face grew purple. 'Sinbad, most loyal of my servants?'

The sailor gazed down at the marble floor.

The caliph had promised that his recent voyage into infidel lands would be his last assignment. He wanted to say that he wished only to return to his sumptuous house on the outskirts of Baghdad, to spend his days in bliss with his beautiful wives and his exquisite garden. He wanted to say that he could hardly be expected to find one errant princess in a world that was so wide even he, the far famed sailor of the seven seas, had never seen its edge. But then he found himself troubled by a tinge of that wanderlust, that yearning to seek out new lands and new oceans. Besides, the two knights who had escorted him across the weary miles seemed so eager to experience further adventures.

'Very well,' Sinbad said. 'I accept. But you must understand that it will be a difficult matter. I am a sailor, not a magician. How can I hope to find your sister when she has been carried off into the blue yonder by a djinn? The trail would be hard enough to follow across the sea, but across the sky, hopeless...' He broke off pensively. 'And yet... there is a man who could help.'

'And who might that be?' asked the caliph.

'Jabir ibn Hayyan,' Sinbad told him. 'The Persian alchemist has aided me in the past. He owned a flying machine, a dirigible he calls it. That would be of immense help. I shall go to his house in Kufa and...' He broke off. A stormy expression had appeared on the caliph's face. 'I forgot,' Sinbad added. 'When last I was here, I heard a rumour...'

'That alchemist is no longer welcome at court,' said Harun al-Rashid brusquely. 'He is under suspicion of complicity with Ja'afar. My former vizier financed some of his experiments. No doubt of a darkly sorcerous nature. He is kept under house arrest in his Baghdad townhouse.'

Sinbad shook his head. 'Jabir is a good man,' he said. 'He has no interest in the doings of dark magicians. I shall go to him, and ask his aid.'

The caliph clapped his hands and a group of mamelukes marched forwards. 'You must go with an escort,' he told Sinbad. 'No one can see Jabir without my say-so.' He signed to the mamelukes. 'Take Sinbad to the house of Jabir the Alchemist.'

'Sinbad!' the old man exclaimed, clinging to a staff, limping towards the sailor as Sinbad was shown into his garden. 'How delightful to see you! I have so few visitors these days, and besides, I had heard that you were off on one of your famous voyages.'

Sinbad accepted a glass of Jabir's distilled wine, the old alchemist's own invention, which he called the essential spirits of alcohol. He stood studying his old friend in silence. Jabir wore, as ever, his yellow turban, stained in places with chemicals from his experiments, and his long white beard hung down almost as far as his waist. His kindly eyes met Sinbad's over the rim of the glass.

'I was saddened to hear of your arrest,' Sinbad said. 'What were you thinking of, old friend, getting yourself mixed up in high politics?'

Jabir laughed. 'I had not realised that I had!' he said. 'I accepted some financial assistance from the grand vizier at one point. Many kind people have helped me in that way, and Ja'afar was only one among them. At the time he was one of the richest, most powerful and popular men in the land. I had no notion he would fall so far from grace, nor that I would join him. I know naught of politics but that it is a game played by fools. Extending Man's understanding of the world in which we live is of much greater significance. Speaking of which, did you witness the most remarkable visitation the city was subjected to today?'

'Indeed!' said Sinbad, 'and it was on that very matter that I came to speak with you.' He explained how the princess had been carried off by Ja'afar with the assistance of a djinn, concluding, 'And the caliph has asked me to help him retrieve his sister. I cannot hope to follow the djinn on foot, or even by ship. Then I remembered your dirigible, which came in so useful when I was in the City of Pillars, and later on the Plateau of Leng. Jabir, old friend. Will you lend me your dirigible so I can go in search of the princess?'

Jabir shook his head. 'I'm afraid that's impossible, Sinbad,' he murmured.

3 THE ABYSSINIAN MAID

Sinbad sighed. 'I realise you have known ill treatment at the caliph's hand,' he said in a low tone, so his words were inaudible to the mamelukes who waited nearby. 'But the princess Abassa has been carried off by a flying djinn. The only way in which we can hope to rescue her is if I take to the air myself. So again, old friend, please permit me to make use of your dirigible.'

Again Jabir shook his head. 'It is by no means pettiness that makes me refuse,' said the old alchemist, 'although I have little cause to oblige the Prince of the Faithful. Alas, my dirigible is now out of operation. A crash up in the Zagros Mountains put paid to my nascent aeronautical career. The dirigible was ruined beyond repair; I myself did not escape without some injury.' Wryly, he drew Sinbad's attention to his twisted leg. 'I am not as young as I once was. My flying days are done, and my dirigible is no more.'

'Can the machine not be rebuilt? You still have the plans, surely.'

'I have the plans, but we would need materials we lack. Silks and bamboo, fuel to heat the air that lifts the balloon... All of which would take a long time to gather, and time is at a premium from what you say. And by my calculations, at the rate he was flying the djinn will be out across the ocean by now.'

Sinbad stared at him. 'Your calculations? You mean you know where they have gone?'

'Follow me,' said Jabir mysteriously, and hobbled away.

The two mamelukes watched suspiciously as the alchemist led Sinbad inside. They went up into the small tower that rose from the roof of his house. Wide windows showed a view of the city that surrounded them, and the land beyond. Upon a table sat astrological charts and plans, and a long square tube containing glass lenses was pointed towards the sky. Jabir directed Sinbad to sit on a stool then bustled round, gathering together charts and maps. Making a measurement with a pair of callipers, he added several notations to a piece of paper, then looked up.

'As the djinn passed overhead, I was watching his progress through my optical device,' Jabir explained. 'I followed his progress until he had vanished over the horizon. After a few course corrections he flew south east. Now, if we consult this map...'

Sinbad pored over it. 'Ja'afar was heading for Muscat!' he said triumphantly, pointing at the famous trading city on the Gulf of Oman. It lay directly on the line the alchemist had indicated.

Jabir sucked at his long drooping moustache. 'Perhaps,' he murmured. 'Perhaps. But consider what it is we deal with. Why would a sorcerer or a djinn travel to Muscat, fine city though it is? Where did Ja'afar find his ally? Where did he go when his spell was reversed?'

'He wanted the caliph to be propelled to the edge of the world,' Sinbad said. 'If the spell was reversed, then he…'

'…was sent to the edge of the world in his victim's place,' Jabir finished. 'Have your voyages ever taken you so far, Sinbad?'

Sinbad shook his head. 'I have sailed the seas of the world,' he said, 'but never have I reached its edge. I have heard stories, though. Men speak of the emerald mountains that encircle the world. It is said that amongst them lies the kingdom of Djinnistan…' He halted and stared at Jabir.

Jabir laughed. 'I heard the same tales when I was a child,' he said. 'The kingdom of the djinn.'

'That explains where Ja'afar found his new ally,' Sinbad said. 'Very well, this gives us some notion of where we will find him, and Princess Abassa too, *inshallah*. All we need is to fly south east across the sea until we see the emerald mountains of Kaf on the horizon. Tell me what materials you need, and I will ensure that the caliph provides them.'

Again Jabir shook his head. 'My dirigible could never have flown so far—not over the sea. I flew to the north of China once, as you know, but only in stages. It is necessary from time to time to halt in order to effect repairs and to refuel. It was partly my failure to keep up those repairs that resulted in my unfortunate crash in the mountains. Were you to cross the open sea there would be no opportunity for repairs. Sooner or later, you would pitch into the waters and drown. Besides, my dirigible was the work of science. You deal here not with science but sorcery. Far be it from me to presage a Manichean dichotomy between the two philosophies, but I counsel that you should adopt sorcerous means to travel to a magical land...'

Sinbad was impatient. There were times when he couldn't understand a word Jabir said. 'What sorcerous means do you speak of?'

Jabir smiled. 'Another tale I heard as a child was that of Suleiman and his flying carpet.'

The prophet Suleiman, who ruled over the Hebrews long years before the birth of Mohammed, was said to have been a great wizard commanding many djinn and owning a magical carpet upon which he could fly to any land. 'But surely that's just another children's tale.'

Jabir laughed. 'Some folk doubt the truth of your own stories, Sinbad.' He held up a hand.

'Not I! I saw enough when I was with you to know that the world is far stranger than most marketplace wise men would have it. Equally, djinn, and their country of Djinnistan, are deemed to be a myth by some. But fight magic with magic, say I.'

'Very well,' said Sinbad with a sigh. 'Assuming Suleiman's carpet was real, what happened to it? Was it not taken back into heaven by Allah?'

Jabir shook his head. 'The stories maintain that it came not from heaven but from Sheba. It was a gift from the famous queen of that land, Bilkis, who wove it with the aid of her handmaidens and brought it to Suleiman in Jerusalem. After Suleiman died, it was taken back to Sheba.'

'Sheba, Sheba,' Sinbad mused. 'But where can we find that land? Does it exist outside legend? And where would the carpet be?'

'Sheba lay far to the south, beyond the Red Sea, in Africa,' Jabir said. 'That land is now part of the kingdom of Abyssinia.' He looked weary. 'This is all I can tell you, Sinbad. After that you will have to find Djinnistan. It is said that the emperor of China knows more about djinn than any other man. You might go to him for further guidance; my own knowledge is scant in these matters. You pass now beyond the realms of science into that of stories. But it is there that you will find your solution. Tell the caliph.'

'The flying Carpet of Suleiman?' Harun al-Rashid's face was dark. 'Where can this magic carpet be found, if indeed it is needed?'

From outside Sinbad heard drifting the call to evening prayers from the muezzin. The two Frankish knights were staring at him in wonder. The guards' faces were imperturbable. The dancing girls and musicians played on without heeding his words. But the caliph was angry.

'The stories say that it is to be found in Abyssinia. More than that I do not know, but if I am to travel to Djinnistan in pursuit of Ja'afar, it is my only hope.'

Harun al-Rashid brightened. 'Abyssinia? Why, then this is kismet!' He clapped his hands. 'Come here, Nakeya!'

One of the musicians ceased strumming, rose, and glided forwards to kiss the ground before the caliph's throne. She was a tall, grave young woman, clad in a gown of silk, dusky of face and frizzy of hair like a Soudani or Zanzibari.

'To hear is to obey, O master,' she said in a rich yet sombre voice. 'What is thy will?'

'Nakeya,' said the caliph, 'you are from Abyssinia, are you not? You have often told me tales of that far off land.'

'It is true, O master,' said Nakeya. 'Abyssinia was my home, and my family has dwelt there for many generations.'

'Know ye aught of the Queen of Sheba?'

asked the caliph. 'Or of the carpet she wove for the prophet Suleiman?'

'Indeed I do,' said Nakeya gravely. 'The kings of Abyssinia descend from Menelik, who was son of Solomon, as we name him, and the queen of Sheba. As for the carpet, it is kept in the chapel of a convent atop Mount Abora in Abyssinia.'

'A convent?' Sir Acelin said in surprise, exchanging glances with Sir Barnard. 'Mon Dieu! Surely this distant land is not Christian?'

Nakeya studied him gravely. 'Abyssinia has long been a Christian country,' she said, 'although it lies far away from the empires of the Greeks and the Franks. And as well as the Carpet of Solomon, we possess of the relics of the saints, including a fragment of the True Cross.'

'The True Cross?' said Sir Acelin. 'They keep a fragment of it in the chapel at Aachen, and I saw another in Rome. How did such a relic reach your benighted land?'

'Never mind these questions now,' said Sinbad. 'Could you lead us to the place where they keep the carpet, girl? Would the nuns who guard it be willing to give it to us? To sell it, perhaps?'

'I would pay dearly for it,' added the caliph, 'were it to aid the salvation of my sister.'

'I cannot speak for the Reverend Mother,' said Nakeya. 'She will be reluctant to let it out of her sight. Besides, I cannot journey to Abyssinia. I am a slave in this land.'

'Nakeya,' said the caliph, 'if you help Sinbad

obtain the carpet he needs to rescue my sister from Ja'afar, I swear in the name of the Prophet that you will henceforth be free of my service.'

Nakeya listened solemnly to his words. 'I shall do this thing,' she said, 'if it is my master's command.'

'That is well,' said the caliph. 'Sinbad, you shall sail to Abyssinia with Nakeya as your guide. Go to this convent where the carpet is kept and obtain it as best you can.' He gave Sinbad a heavy lidded look, pregnant with meaning. 'Then fly it to Djinnistan and set free Princess Abassa.'

'I shall go to Basra and ready one of my ships for the voyage,' said Sinbad. 'We must make haste. Ja'afar has a head start on us, and sailing to Abyssinia will only add more time.'

'And we shall come with you!' declared Sir Acelin, indicating himself and Sir Barnard. 'There will be many perils on the voyage, *sacre bleu*, but we shall guard you against them, and fly with you upon this carpet of sorcery to rescue the princess.'

'Very well,' said the caliph. 'But before you depart, there is one other man I counsel you to take, although finding him will be difficult.'

Sinbad stared at Harun al-Rashid. 'Who then is this mystery man? And why should we waste time seeking him?'

'The man I refer to is Ahmed,' the caliph said; 'he who stole the Ring of Ja'afar, and indeed still possesses it. His skills, coupled with that ring, will be invaluable on your quest. You are most likely to find him, as I did, somewhere amidst the crooked alleys of the thieves' quarter...'

4 THE MASTER THIEF

As the shades of night fell upon Baghdad, Sinbad hurried down a narrow, winding street. Despite the sombre events of the day, the poorer parts of town sought solace in merriment. He passed several wine shops that were plying a thriving trade before he reached the street he sought.

A door opened. With it came a hubbub of rough conversation and a spill of ruddy orange light before the departing guest slammed the door behind him. Watching from the shadows, Sinbad waited until the man hurried up the street in the opposite direction before walking up to the peeling wooden door.

He pushed it open and entered the warm, stinking fug of the wine shop. In ill-lit booths, dark figures crouched over roughhewn tables, speaking in whispers as they planned the next day's mendacity. Three musicians played drums and pipes in one smoky corner, their efforts unheeded by much of the throng. Sinbad threaded his way through the drinkers and reached the bar where he bought a cup of raisin wine from the Nasrani who lounged behind it. Sipping it, he leaned his back against the bar and surveyed the wine shop.

Raised voices came from the other end of the bar, and Sinbad saw two big men confronting each other in the shadows. Anger mounted. In the dim lamplight, knife blades flashed, then men came together, and one fell facedown in a pool of his own blood.

The crowd gasped with fear and excitement. Two men dragged the dead man out of the wine shop to dispose of somehow and the wine shop resumed its customary hubbub.

'And what brings a stranger to the House of the Daughter of the Vine?' asked the small man who sat on the stool beside him. 'It is no place for men from the wealthier parts of town.'

'I'm looking for a man called Ahmed,' said Sinbad, regretfully eyeing the threadbare cloak he had pulled over his richer garb. 'Some say he has been seen drinking in this establishment.'

The little man shrugged. 'Many men in Baghdad are called Ahmed,' he said. 'It's a popular name.'

Sinbad saw that he was little more than a youth, and wore dingy, patched garments. His tousled mop of curls was black, as were his button-like eyes. He signalled to the barkeep. Despite his air of poverty, Sinbad saw that he wore on one finger a costly looking ruby ring.

'Another for me, and... what are you drinking, friend?' the little man asked.

Sinbad regarded the raisin wine with disfavour. 'I'll have what you're drinking,' he said hastily, and accepted a cup with thanks. The little man paid for their drinks with a glittering silver dirham that seemed incongruous in that grimy place. 'This fellow who I'm looking for,' Sinbad went on, 'has made quite a name for himself. Even though he has often been on the wrong side of the law, he is the beloved favourite of the caliph, who would have rewarded him with honours and titles had he not vanished into the thieves' quarter before such responsibilities could be heaped upon him.'

'He sounds like a sensible fellow, this Ahmed,' said the little man, looking idly around. 'Do not all men seek to live a life of ease, to make a Paradise on earth where all is joy and delight? Would you not laze in your garden, drinking sherbet, surrounded by silk clad houris?'

Sinbad sipped at his wine and thought about his townhouse, to which he had been so keen to return. But he had earned such luxuries after seven arduous voyages. When he came back to Baghdad with gold enough to buy the place it had seemed that the adventure was finally over. But adventure after adventure had plagued him ever since.

'Such a paradise on Earth is befitting to a

man who has worked hard for many years,' he said, 'but I have heard that this Ahmed shirks work much as he evades responsibility.'

'Is he a beggar, then, this Ahmed? Does he depend on the handouts and charity of richer men?'

Sinbad shook his head sadly. 'Worse than that, I fear,' he said. 'It is said that Ahmed is a thief. The kind of low, saucy fellow who would pick a man's pocket and buy him a drink with his own coin.'

The little man's button eyes danced and he broke out into gales of merriment. 'Such a man would be a thief indeed.' He signed to the barkeep, and called for more wine. 'And what would the far famed Sinbad the sailor want with such a thief?'

'You helped the caliph regain his throne, Ahmed,' said Sinbad, showing no surprise that the little man recognised him. 'He needs your aid once more. Did you see what happened today?'

Ahmed paid for the wine, producing Sinbad's purse from his waist sash. 'I sleep in the day,' he said. 'Last night I found a nice warm place to curl up, beside the walls of a bakery. What with the bakery's heat, the sun, and the wine I'd guzzled the night before, I saw little of what went on. After I awoke, I heard word of what had happened.' He shook his head, and sipped at his cup. 'The sun bakes some folks' brains if they stay out too long at noon. They see all manner of mirages.'

'It was a very real mirage,' Sinbad said, 'that carried off the princess Abassa...'

As he spoke, men entered the wine shop. Two big, hulking men. Ahmed turned quickly to the barkeep and handed over more of Sinbad's gold to hire a private booth. He led Sinbad to the booth and ushered him inside.

They sat across from each other, the stained, scarred expanse of a table between them. 'You can keep my gold,' Sinbad said nonchalantly. 'The caliph will reimburse me. Just as he will reward you richly if you assist me in this matter.'

Ahmed grinned derisively, and drank deep. 'Join you in an expedition to far off infidel lands?' he sneered. 'I've heard all about you and your adventures, sailor-man. And I've noticed one thing about all those tales.'

'And what's that?' Sinbad asked.

'You're always the only one who gets home,' Ahmed said. 'All your fellow shipmates die, eaten by one eyed cannibal giants and worse, and you're the only one who gets back to Baghdad to tell the tale. Oh no, sailor-man, you won't get me to join you on one of your voyages. Besides, I suffer from sea sickness. Even in a barge on the Tigris I'm sick. I'd be a liability. Look elsewhere.'

Sinbad shook his head. 'The caliph himself wants you to accompany me to Abyssinia. There will be some sailing, of course, but the Carpet of

Suleiman is to be found a fair way inland.'

Ahmed laughed. 'I've seen some wonders in my time, but are you truly looking for a magic carpet? That sounds worse than a sea voyage! It would be cold up in the sky, and the clouds would be wet. No, thank you. I helped the caliph when I had no real choice, helped him escape his own dungeon when the sentence of death awaited us both. After that, well... one thing led to another. I got away as soon as I could, and went back to my old life.'

'A life of thieving,' Sinbad commented sourly, 'and of sleeping in alleyways. That ring on your finger. The Ring of Ja'afar. Why have you never sold it?'

Ahmed held up his hand to regard it ruefully. 'I could never sell it. Oh, not for sentimental reasons,' he added, catching Sinbad's sardonic gaze. 'I tried! More than once I tried. But even the most unscrupulous of fences in the thieves' quarter could not hope to find a buyer for so exquisite a gem. I flaunt it openly in a den of thieves, but no one has nerve enough to steal it. It's a curse, sailor-man. A curse. That's what comes of stealing from evil magicians. Ever since I stole it I've had the worst of luck. And now I've met you, and you want me to sail with you on one of your voyages...'

A shadow fell across his face. The light of the lamps that illuminated the wine shop so fitfully had been cut off by two big men. The larger of the two extended a finger in a stabbing motion, straight at Ahmed.

'We knew we'd find you here,' he said in a gritty voice like rocks falling down a pit. 'The thieves' guild knows all your haunts. You're late paying your dues. The sheikh of all thieves is unhappy. And when the sheikh of all thieves is unhappy, he makes everyone else unhappy until they make him happy again.'

'Aye,' grunted the other, resting his bare arms on the table. Sinbad watched in mute fascination as muscle vied with muscle beneath his swarthy skin. 'So pay up this time. Or next time, we'll make you very unhappy.'

'But the Tigris fish will be very happy,' said the first man.

'Now look here, gentlemen,' Sinbad began.

'Keep your lips together,' said the second man in a low voice, not looking at the sailor, 'or kiss your tongue goodbye. We're talking to Ahmed.'

'Do you mind!' said the little man. 'This is a private booth. I've half a mind to call the barkeep and have you kicked out into the street.'

'The guild owns this wine shop, same as all the others,' said the first man. 'Like it owns the whole town. And like it owns you. And you owe the guild. Twelve dirhams it is, and counting.'

Ahmed played with his ring, and the ruby sparkled in what little light sidled nervously round the two hulking figures. 'Only a fool would carry that much in ready cash in a thieves' kitchen such as this. I must speak with my banker. In the meantime, here's a down payment.'

He slipped off the ring and handed it to the first man. Sinbad opened his mouth, but before he could speak, the man snatched the ring and examined it. Disgusted, he flung it down again.

'That ruby's paste, dog,' he said. 'Don't try to fob us off with tawdry trinkets. Give us the money you owe.'

Sinbad picked up the ring and inspected it. The big man knew nothing about jewels; this was a ruby of the first water. The sailor remembered what Ahmed had said. Did it indeed lie under some kind of black spell? With an involuntary shudder, he handed it back to Ahmed.

The little man produced a money pouch from his waist sash.

'Take this, and I'll return here tomorrow evening with the rest.'

Again Sinbad opened his mouth, but Ahmed quelled him with a scowl. The big man unfastened the drawstring, poured out six dirhams in smaller coin, bit at one, then dropped them all back in the pouch.

'We'll take these,' he said. 'But just you make sure you're here tomorrow evening. If not, the guild will scour all Baghdad for you. And when we find you, your next drink will be at the bottom of the river.'

He led his bulky companion from the wine

shop.

Ahmed turned to Sinbad. 'This voyage you mentioned,' he said. 'When do we sail?'

5 THE ROAD TO MOUNT ABORA

Spray dashed over the sides, flooded across the deck in a foaming tide, then receded, leaving only a residue that swilled around the scuppers. Sinbad brushed water from his turban and his neat little beard, then fixed his gaze on the horizon.

All about him the dhow was busy with activity, as the crew he had hired in Basra went about their duties. The first mate, an Arab in his middle years called Omar, looked up from where he was securing a line, and grinned at Sinbad.

'Long journey ahead of us, cap'n,' he said. 'Long way to Abyssinia. Are the landlubbers ready for the voyage?'

A pasty faced figure scrambled up from the cabin, staggered to the side, and hung its head over. Vomiting sounds ensued.

Sinbad kept his eye on the blue green horizon. They were crossing the Persian Gulf, having left Basra on the morning tide, and the waters were thick with shipping. Fishing boats studded the main, casting their nest in hope of catching cobia, grouper, goatfish or barracuda. Traders passed, on their way to the Indies, hope in their hearts, or back from those waters, riches in their holds.

Pirates were not uncommon either; small, fast ships lurking in the lee of coastal islands before boarding solitary craft to plunder them. But Sinbad saw none of the latter as they sailed for the Straits of Hormuz, beyond which they would reach the open ocean. Then, as Omar had intimated, they would have a long, hard voyage.

The man who had been vomiting lifted his head. A dash of spray struck his face and for a moment it was obscured, but as he rose, looking refreshed, Sinbad recognised Sir Acelin.

'How are you finding the voyage, sir knight?' he asked cheerfully. 'Is the sea air to your liking?'

Sir Acelin gave him a piteous look. 'It's like riding an unbroken horse,' he said, grasping a line as the deck lurched under him. Sinbad reached out a hand and helped him across to the stern where he stood, and Sir Acelin clung to the gunwale, looking back the way they had come.

'We are in the middle of the ocean,' the knight said wonderingly.

'Nonsense,' said Sinbad. 'We're only two leagues from Basra. Look there!' He pointed at the eastern horizon. 'See that dark line? That's the rocky coast of Persia.' He pointed in the opposite direction. 'And that way lies Arabia.'

To the Frankish knight, the East was all one, Arab, Persian, Chinese and Indian were indistinguishable. As they rode another swell, he turned and faced it, still clinging to a strut. 'But Abyssinia is our destination. How far away does it lie?'

'Many, many leagues,' Sinbad assured him. 'First we must pass through the Straits of Hormuz, then we enter the Gulf of Oman. From the gulf we sail into the waters of the Arabian Sea, where we veer west south west and follow the coast until we reached the Gulf of Aden, at the mouth of the Red Sea. Then we will make landfall on the Abyssinian coast.'

'Landfall!' said Sir Acelin. Then he looked doubtful. 'And when we are ashore?'

'Then it is up to our guide to take us as far as Mount Abora. How does the lovely Nakeya fare?' Sinbad asked.

'Ask her that yourself,' Sir Acelin said, gesturing.

A tall, grave, dignified figure had appeared from the reed thatched cabin of the dhow and was making its way up the deck, ignoring the looks of the crewmen. Nakeya walked as confidently as if she was ashore, and gave Sinbad a small nod of recognition.

'It is good to be at sea,' she said. 'When I was a young girl I dwelt in a fishing village, and often I went out in my father's boat. That all changed when I was sent to take up my duties at Mount

Abora.'

She settled beside them, and Sinbad took his attention away from the rolling waters to study her. Her long face was as serious as ever, but something else tinged it. Surely not trepidation.

'You were a novice?' Sir Acelin murmured. 'Mon Dieu! Why then did you not become a nun?'

She did not reply directly. 'The long hours in the sanctuary were a burden to me,' she said. 'I, who had known the open sea and the shore, cooped up between walls, high in the mountains. Sometimes I would play my dulcimer, but Reverend Mother did not approve of music unless it was in praise of the Lord. It is little surprise that I did not become a nun.' She looked at Sinbad. 'Why did you bring that servant of yours with us?'

'Ahmed?' Sinbad said, surprised. 'Why, I am sure he will come in useful. Besides, he comes at the caliph's behest.'

Nakeya looked away. 'He is irrepressible in his levity,' she said disapprovingly. 'Forever he is trying to make me laugh at one of his foolish jests. I do not enjoy his company.'

'He only wants you to be happy, girl,' said Sinbad. 'You must admit, you tend towards the serious.'

Nakeya did not meet his gaze. 'I have small reason to rejoice,' she said, and crossed the deck to the prow where she stood looking out to sea.

It seemed curious to Sinbad that a girl who

had not had the severity of disposition to dedicate her life to her god could yet be so lacking in levity. He told Omar to take the tiller, and went for'ard to the cabin. Inside, Ahmed and Sir Barnard were gaming. In front of both of them sat a pile of belongings, but that before Sir Barnard was much smaller than Ahmed's. The big knight was scowling.

'Let me see those dice,' he was saying in a dangerous voice. Ahmed looked up, and grinned.

'Sailor-man!' he said. 'How is the sea looking?'

Sinbad squatted down beside them, and picked up the dice from the deck. 'The sea is as calm as any canal, Ahmed. I thought it was you who suffered from sea sickness?'

'Miraculously, I'm cured,' said Ahmed, looking anxiously at the dice Sinbad held. 'Sir Acelin still needs to get his sea legs, although this big old ox betrays no indication of biliousness. May I have those old knucklebones back? They're not worth much but they have a sentimental value...'

'Nakeya tells me you've been very attentive,' Sinbad went on, ignoring his plea. 'Don't try to lighten her mood, she's of what Jabir would call a saturnine disposition. These dice were very badly made. See?' He rolled them on the deck and they came up with double sixes. 'Sir Barnard, you roll your own dice.' They danced across the deck and came up with a two and a one. 'Play with Sir Barnard's dice, Ahmed. They're better made. I'll dispose of these overboard.'

'But... but...' Ahmed was still spluttering as Sinbad left the cabin.

After disposing of the loaded dice, Sinbad crossed over to Omar and took the tiller. Sir Acelin seemed happier now, and they spoke for a while before he went below, followed by the unspeaking Nakeya. At nightfall, they anchored off a small offshore island.

Sailing on in the morning, they continued their uneventful journey across the sparkling waters. Seeing that Ahmed needed to be kept occupied, Sinbad had Omar and the other sailors take him on as a deck hand, and he spent less time teasing Nakeya or swindling Sir Barnard, being too busy shirking his duties to make mischief. Passing through the straits, they hugged the Arabian coast as they followed it to the west, proceeding towards their mysterious destination, this remote kingdom.

Twice along the way their ship was surprised by pirates, but on each occasion the appearance of mailed knights encouraged the rascals to change their minds and sail in search of easier prey. The seas grew rough as they neared the Horn of Africa, and they spent two days flying before a storm before they sought shelter in a cove on the Hadramawt coast.

Once the storm had blown itself out, they set sail once more, and on the fifth day out from Hadramawt the lookout sighted land. Sinbad climbed the mast and studied the shore that he could see on the distant western horizon. Craggy mountains lifted to the cobalt heavens, cliffs like walls built by some long forgotten race of giants. As they drew closer, he spoke with Nakeya.

'The Negus, who claims descent from Solomon and Sheba, rules over the highlands,' she told him. 'Mine is a warlike race, and the valleys are often the scene of valiant fighting for supremacy. Settlements are sacked, fields are torched, and captives are led off to be sold as slaves.'

She spoke so bitterly that Sinbad wondered if that been her own fate, but he kept his idle curiosity to himself. 'How far will we have to travel through your country to reach Mount Abora?'

She shrugged. 'It is a two week journey by the shortest route,' she said. 'But if war rages, it could be much longer. Even in peacetime, we are likely to meet with delays as we pass through the domains of various barons and knights.'

'You have knights in your land?' asked Sinbad. 'Christian warriors like Sir Acelin?'

She nodded. 'Ours is a Christian kingdom, for all that league upon league of paynim country lies between us and our co-religionists.'

They came ashore in a rocky bay. Here the dhow was moored and Sinbad left several crew members to effect repairs and guard over her in case they needed her to return to Baghdad.

'You have supplies for another month,' Sinbad told Omar, who was in command. 'If I do not return, one way or the other, sail back to Basra and pay the men off there. If I find the carpet, I will do what I can to inform you. Otherwise, make your own judgement.'

'Good luck on your journey inland, cap'n,' Omar said, looking anxious. 'It is not my place to say so, but it seems to me you meddle with dark forces. Go with Allah! You will need his guiding hand.'

They mounted dromedaries purchased from local villagers—at a knockdown price after Ahmed had conducted the bargaining—and trotted away into the hills. The road to Mount Abora, even following the direct route, was a long and winding one leading through mountainous country that in places was lush and fertile, but otherwise was barren and rocky.

Castles frowned down from craggy eminences as they rode, and on one occasion they turned a corner to find a pavilion, where an Abyssinian knight clad in mail like Sir Acelin's, challenged the knight to a joust before he would permit them to ride on. Sir Acelin knocked the man clean off his horse on the third round, and once he had recovered, the Abyssinian knight welcomed them into his pavilion and plied them with meat and drink.

Some days later they crossed a ridge. A high mountain stood at the far end of the valley.

Nakeya called to Sinbad.

'We are almost there,' she said. 'Behold, Mount Abora.'

Sinbad studied the peak. High up on the cliffs great walls were visible, and at the far end was a collection of buildings. 'There is the convent,' Nakeya said, 'and beside it is the chapel in which the Carpet of Solomon is kept, with many other relics.' Her face looked troubled. 'I wish I did not have to return here,' she added. 'But the caliph promised me my freedom. Besides, how can I refuse a command from my master? And yet I do not anticipate that Reverend Mother will yield the carpet willingly.'

Near dusk they reached the foot of the mountain. A long stairway wound up the ridge towards a distant gateway in the great walls. Up here, Nakeya told them, pilgrims went to make their obeisances at the shrine. But no pilgrims could be seen this evening. All was bleak and desolate, and a mournful wind wailed amongst the rocks.

'We'll set up camp here,' Sinbad decided, 'and climb the mountains tomorrow.'

Ahmed took the third watch, which would last until sunrise. After a few moments sitting by the fire, stirring the embers with a stick, he rose restlessly, shivering in the night cold, huffing and blowing like one of the dromedaries that stood in a piquet line on the edge of camp. From the tents came nothing but the gentle sound of snoring.

He approached the stairway. In the darkness, it was impossible to see it they ended. Only the fitful light from the campfire showed the first few steps. Ahmed began to ascend.

The wind buffeted at him as he went, as he climbed higher and higher above the valley where they had camped. Above him was a bowl of stars, darkness shrouded the land on every side. The campfire was now only another star, fallen from above. The air was bone chillingly cold. He wished he had remained by the fireside.

By the time he had reached the great gateway, his feet were numb and his hands felt like ice. His brain had gone to sleep. It was only a glimmer of hazy light from the moon as it rose over a shoulder of the mountain that betrayed a sight that made him stop in his tracks. Just within the gateway lay a huddled, unmoving form.

He turned it over. Two sightless eyes met his gaze in the moonlight; a dark skinned girl dressed in dark robes. She was dead; but her flesh was still warm. Ahmed let the corpse slump to the ground, rose, and went further up the hill. Something bulked against the stars. He drew closer. It was a building, a small, long building with a spire at the far end. In front of him stood a wooden door that had been forced open. Silently he crept inside.

As he halted just within the doorway, his eyes widened in dismay.

6 THE RUINED CHAPEL

Groggily, Sinbad awoke. There was a thudding on the exterior of his tent and he saw a dim silhouette by the tent flap. Sunlight streamed in through a chink. He crawled to the opening on hands and knees and pulled back the flap. A figure stood there, black against the morning sky.

'Ahmed,' he muttered. 'You got it...?' He broke off. It wasn't Ahmed.

'How did you guess?' asked Nakeya. 'Sir Acelin sent me to wake you, since you'd overslept. Ahmed is gone.'

'Gone?' Sinbad said in confusion, squinting up at the risen sun. 'He should be back by now...'

Abruptly he bit off his words. Closing the tent flap, he dressed hastily, then crawled out.

Sir Acelin and Sir Barnard stood by the ashes of the campfire, speaking with the Arab sailors. They turned as Sinbad and Nakeya joined them. 'Captain Sinbad,' said one of the sailors, a barrel chested man in his thirties called Jassim. 'Your servant is missing.'

'When I awoke, the camp was unguarded,' said Sir Acelin. 'Jassim is right; it was Ahmed who had last watch. And he is gone. Beast or bandit carried him off, or...'

'Or he has deserted us,' said Nakeya. 'I knew he was not to be trusted.'

Everyone started talking at once. Sinbad held his hands high and called for quiet. Eventually he got it, and a ring of silent faces surrounded him.

'I sent Ahmed up the mountain,' he confessed.

'You did?' Sir Acelin asked, incredulous. 'Leaving the camp unguarded?'

'I did not think that he would be absent so long,' Sinbad said. 'I was waiting for him in my tent. I...' He looked crestfallen. 'I must have fallen asleep.'

'And your servant has not returned,' said Nakeya, watching Sinbad mistrustfully. 'But why did you send him ahead?'

Sinbad was silent. He could hardly tell her, or the two knights, that he had despatched Ahmed on the mission that the caliph had intimated; to steal the carpet rather than haggle hopelessly with these unbelievers. What had happened to Ahmed he could not guess. If he had been surprised in the act of stealing it, Sinbad's job would be all the harder. He had money with him, the caliph's gold, with which to purchase the carpet if it came down to that. But if Ahmed had already stirred them up, that recourse might prove futile.

'I sent him to scout,' he said, 'and to speak with the Reverend Mother, to tell her what brought us here.'

'You should have sent the girl, cap'n,' said Jassim. 'After all, she is known in these parts.'

Sir Acelin was outraged. 'Send the girl? Better that you sent a knight!'

Nakeya grimaced. 'I was asked only to guide you here,' she said. 'I had no intention of meeting Reverend Mother again. It was she who had me sold into slavery.'

'Why in Allah's name did she do that?'

'Can we not speak of this in private?' the girl asked.

Sinbad nodded. 'Jassim, Zahid, the rest of you—strike camp and get ready for the ascent. Sir Acelin, Sir Barnard, help them.' He led Nakeya as far as the bottom of the flight of steps.

'Tell me,' he said commandingly. 'How did this come about?'

Nakeya looked solemn. 'Very well,' she said after a hesitation. 'I will tell you my tale.

'I was sent to the convent to train as a novice when I was a maid of fifteen summers,' she explained. 'Until then my life had been happy and carefree, but it has long been a tradition in my clan that girls at that age go to serve in the convent; the best become nuns. The lot fell to me, and so I left my village by the seashore, and went to Mount Abora with naught but my dulcimer to remind me of my girlhood.

'That instrument met with the disapproval of Reverend Mother, a harsh, stern woman, who had no time for levity, and severely instilled sobriety and a serious demeanour into girls in her care. Yet I was wilful, and when it was my turn to hold solitary vigil in the chapel, I amused myself by playing upon my dulcimer rather than spending my time in prayer. When she learnt of this she flung my instrument away and it went clattering down the cliffs, smashing itself to pieces. But in secret I made myself another one. My act of rebellion. And perhaps it was this that brought him.'

'Brought who?' Sinbad asked.

She looked up. 'A young, handsome man appeared in the chapel. Where he came from I did not know, and he watched me unspeaking, but he seemed entranced by my playing. I put down my dulcimer and addressed him, but at the sound of my voice he vanished. The next time I held solitary vigil, I played my dulcimer again, and again he appeared, this time more handsome even than he had seemed in the dreams that had haunted my every night. This time he took me in his arms and kissed me passionately before vanishing again. He came to me a third time, and what followed was inevitable. I was a girl and he was a man. But he did not vanish until we were surprised by the Reverend Mother, who found us lying together beside the altar.'

Her face was stricken with horror. 'My sinister lover vanished, leaving me to face Reverend Mother's wrath. She was angry with me. I had fallen into temptation, she told me, and allowed myself to be seduced by one of the djinn of the wastelands, there in the chapel itself. When it became clear that my demon lover had conceived a child, there was to be no forgiveness. I was banished from the convent, sold as a slave to a passing merchant, and at last I was bought by one of the caliph's chamberlains.'

Sinbad could see why she would not wish to return here. 'But you are needed,' he said. 'Only you know the ways of your people. It is imperative that you accompany us.'

Nakeya looked sombre. 'I must,' she admitted. 'It is my master's command that I aid you; besides, it is the price of my freedom. But I shudder to think of returning to the place of my greatest shame.'

'Nevertheless,' said Sinbad, 'return you must.'

The two knights and the Arabs joined them, leading their dromedaries, and Sinbad turned and led them all up the steps, Nakeya at his side. Over an hour later they reached the top of the steps. All around them the mountainous land rolled away, peaks lost in the clouds. The wind moaned and sobbed like a lachrymose phantom. Straddling the stairway was a stone gateway, whose wooden doors stood open. Sir Acelin, who was in the lead now, halted in the doorway, hand on his sword hilt.

'Tread cautiously,' he instructed the others. 'Something is wrong here. I hear no sound of prayers, see no sign of life…' He broke off, pointing. 'And what is this!'

Just inside the gate, where more steps led up to the buildings of the convent, lay the corpse of a middle aged woman. She wore the habit of a nun.

'It is Sister Maryam,' Nakeya said in sick horror. 'I remember her. She was kind to me when all the rest were hateful. Who has done this?'

'No man could do this,' said Sir Acelin after examining the corpse. 'Every bone in her body is broken. It is as if something beyond human strength flung her against the wall.' He rose and examined a dark smear on the wall.

Sinbad brooded. 'Something has happened here. Maybe this is why Ahmed did not return.'

They reached the chapel shortly afterwards. In the morning light it was possible to see that the building lay in ruin, its roof staved in, its brightly coloured windows smashed. Hand on the hilt of his scimitar, Sinbad led the others to the half open doors, and peered inside, unable to imagine the horrors he might see.

'Ahmed!' he cried suddenly, and sprinted into the chapel.

The others followed at a run. Sitting on the ground before the desecrated altar, cradling the body of a woman in his arms, holding a water skin to her lips, was the Baghdadi thief.

He looked up as they entered, and motioned them to be quiet. 'She is fading fast,' he said, looking down at the woman's lined face. 'She still lives, but not for long.'

'What happened to this place?' Sinbad looked around the narrow chamber. Pews had bene flung aside, wall hangings ripped down. More dead nuns lay dotted about the floor.

Nakeya ran forwards, crying, 'Reverend Mother!'

She knelt beside Ahmed and together they tended to the old woman. 'I saw her lying before the altar when I entered the chapel,' Ahmed said. 'The rest of the nuns were already dead, and she was dying. She must have been like this for a day or more. It must have attacked shortly before we reached the mountain.

'It? What was it?' Sinbad asked, joining them. 'What killed them?'

'When she was conscious,' said Ahmed, 'she said something about... a djinn.'

'A djinn?' Sinbad and Nakeya chorused. A croak issued from the Reverend Mother. 'She's trying to speak,' said Sinbad. 'Give her more water.'

Ahmed trickled a few drops on the old woman's lips. 'What happened here, lady?' he asked in a low voice.

The Reverend Mother was having trouble focussing. 'He came again,' she muttered. 'He had already defiled the sanctuary, led my nuns astray. He came again, but this time to kill. He killed them all, and even I am dying. And he came to steal! He took the Carpet!'

'Suleiman's Carpet?' Sinbad cried. 'Who was it? Who took it? Where have they taken it?'

'It was him!' the Reverend Mother slurred. 'He who dwells in the City of Brass, far to the west across the endless sands. That evil djinn who is of the blood of the prince of darkness; he whom the Arabs call Iblis but we Christians name Satan. It was he who they call Hadana!'

Nakeya cried out in horror. The Reverend Mother's eyes opened suddenly, and she focussed on the girl. She gave a sharp intake of breath.

'So you return now?' the Reverend Mother cried. 'At this time? Surely you are in league with... with him...' She threshed in Ahmed's arms, then coughed. Blood trickled from her lips. Her head fell back.

Ahmed laid the corpse down on the ground before the overturned altar and glanced at Sinbad. The sailor was staring at Nakeya. Soon everyone in the chapel was looking at her.

But her eyes were on a distant horizon that only she could discern.

7 THE PALACE OF DEATH

Mercilessly the sun beat down from a sky the colour of brass. All around, the sand lay unmoving, mountainous dunes rolling away to the distant horizon. Nothing moved, nothing stirred. Not so much as a breath of wind disturbed the somnolent grains of sand. Nothing could be heard but a deafening silence.

It was broken by a distant thudding. As the sound began to grow, dust became visible, rising into the air, a great train of dust pluming down over the dunes. It was stirred up by the hoofs of a group of dromedaries, the so-called ships of the desert, upon whose backs sat several men and one woman. Across the desolate landscape they plodded, the sun like a blazing ball of fire in the brassy skies above them.

At their head was a tall, slender man clad, who wore a white turban, a crimson jacket, and green trousers. His face was slender and striking, and he had a neat little beard. His eyes brimmed with intelligence as he took in his surroundings.

'The sand continues unabated,' he commented. 'It is like this in the Kara Kum and the Kyzyl Kum and the Rub' al Khali. Endless sand.'

'But will we ever see this brass city, Sinbad?' asked the small, ill clad young man with the button eyes who rode at his side.

'The City of Brass,' the dusky skinned woman on Sinbad's other side, 'lies many leagues to the west, if the stories are to be told. On the far side of this desert waste.'

The sand stretched ceaselessly ahead of them. Not a drop of moisture darkened the sand, not a hint of life was to be seen. Sinbad shaded his eyes, but he could see nothing. Or could he?

'What is that I see?' he asked suddenly. 'There, on the skyline.'

They halted their beasts and strained to see what Sinbad's eyes had been able to discern, accustomed as they were from years of sea travel to making out the smallest details from a long way. Sir Acelin trotted up, Sir Barnard behind him. Behind them the Arab sailors sat their dromedaries.

Both knights were sweating in their mail, which grew scorching hot in the desert sun. 'I see some black thing,' Sir Acelin murmured, 'high and black, and in the midst of it something as grey as smoke.'

'It is not a part of the desert,' said Sinbad. 'And smoke could be a sign of occupants.'

Sir Acelin coughed politely. 'Who would dwell in such a barren waste?' he said. 'There is nothing here even for nomads, no way to scratch out any kind of living. Whatever it is, I misdoubt me that it would be any kind of habitation. This is a dead land. It is as if some war of the angels stripped it of life long ago, leaving naught but sand and dust.'

'We know that dwellings are to be found in this direction,' Sinbad argued, 'whether they are lived in today or otherwise. We know that the djinn Hadana haunts these desert wastes; that is why we are here, in the hopes of finding both him and the carpet he has stolen. What else would bring us out here, after all?'

'Then do you think what we are seeing is Hadana's home?' Sir Acelin asked. 'Why would even a djinn dwell out here in these lifeless lands?'

'Who can say?' Sinbad said. 'The question does not concern me. All I want to do is to track him down and take from him the carpet he has stolen.'

While they spoke, Ahmed slid down from his dromedary and walked out across the sand, his gaze on something he had seen. He crouched down beside the small hump that broke up the monotony.

'Here is something else,' he called. He reached out to touch the thing that lay almost entirely buried by the sand, and winced with pain, whipping back his fingers as if they had burnt. Ruefully he sucked on them, then circumspectly brushed the sand away. The sun winked upon the sides of a vessel made of brass.

Nakeya came to join him. Together they unearthed the vessel. It was shaped not unlike an oil lamp, and had a stopper of lead, strangely carved. Nakeya reached out to pull out the latter.

'Wait!' Ahmed said anxiously. Nakeya looked at him curiously, then shook the vessel without opening it. It sounded hollow.

'It is empty,' she said. 'It is as if nothing has been kept in it since the day it was forged.'

'What is this symbol on the stopper?' Ahmed said, tracing out a pentacle. 'And this writing?'

'A five pointed star,' she said. 'Some say that Solomon's seal was a five pointed star. As for the writing, I cannot read it, but it resembles Hebrew script.'

She picked it up and went back to her dromedary, placing it in her saddlebag. Ahmed inspected the ruby ring he wore.

'If you like that supposedly sorcerous artefact,' he said, hastening after her, 'you're sure to like this ring too.' He held it out to her. 'Go on, take it. It's a gift.'

'I wouldn't deprive you of your prized possession,' said Nakeya coldly, and mounted her dromedary.

Sinbad had been watching impatiently. 'Never mind scavenging in the dust,' he said. 'We think we have found the City of Brass.'

'That smudge on the horizon?' Ahmed mounted his own dromedary. 'Is it a city, then?'

Nakeya rode up. 'It cannot be the city,' she said dogmatically. 'I told you. All the stories say it lies further to the west.'

The City of Brass, home to a long lost civilisation—now haunted, it was said, by evil spirits—appeared in many Abyssinian folk tales, and Nakeya knew them all. Her knowledge of folklore had steered them thus far across the desert; it was the only map they had to guide them in their continuing quest for the Carpet of Suleiman. How Princess Abassa fared, and what the further delay would cost them, Sinbad did not know. But there was no other choice for them but to cross the sands until they reached the city, and search for the carpet within its fabled walls.

'Then what is that I see?' Sinbad said, but no one answered him. 'Let us ride closer!'

The sun seemed locked in at eternal noon, blazing down from the remorseless sky, so high overhead that their shadows and the shadows of the dromedaries were almost non-existent, and even when they were visible they were pools black as midnight. All that could be heard was the patient plodding of the dromedaries, all that could be seen was the neverending sand and the enigma on the horizon.

As the hours passed, and the sun slowly began to descend ahead of them, the enigmatic shape on the skyline began to resolve itself, until they saw that they were approaching a great castle or palace made of black stone, at the top of a seemingly endless flight of steps. A door of steel winked in the sunlight, and the palace was crowned with a dome of grey metal.

Onwards the dromedaries plodded until, as the sun began to descend, they reached the sand strewn foot of the long stairway. Up this the dromedaries gamely trotted, striking sparks from the stone from time to time. The palace loomed like a mountain above them, its crenellations frowning in stony disapproval at these insolent interlopers.

The silence pressed down on them like a palpable thing, lowering their spirits as they ascended steps that seemed to have been constructed by giants. They were tiny insect like specks of life journeying slowly and painfully across inimical stone. At last they reached the wide landing at the top of the final flight of steps, and the metal gates to the palace towered high above in the black stone wall.

More steps, these of some red marble like porphyry or chalcedony, led up to that gate, which was set around with high columns and a lofty portico. Above the door was a tablet engraved with characters that none of them could read. There was no indication of any inhabitants, not so much as a guard patrolling the battlements.

Sinbad dismounted, and ascended the steps

to the steel door. The others followed, Nakeya looking grave, Ahmed peering around avariciously, the two knights superstitiously silent, the Arab sailors uncharacteristically tongue-tied and abashed.

Sinbad set his hand to the door, which was warm but not too hot to touch, and pushed idly against it. To his surprise, the towering door swung silently open at his touch.

Beyond it lay a court in which tinkling fountains played, and the surrounding walls were of sculpted marble, with frescoes depicting men and women in costumes of long ago, hunting and trading, sailing and warring in a champaign country that was lush and well wooded, with many fields and farms—a stark contrast to the lifeless desert that lay outside the walls.

The travellers led their dromedaries inside and made a camp of sorts beside one of the fountains, whose waters both beasts and men gulped down gratefully. The sailors lit a fire beside the wall and they cooked their meagre provisions. Everyone was hot and weary after the ride, and no one wanted anything other than to eat and rest in the shade. No one except Sinbad betrayed any curiosity about the mysterious deserted palace in which they had sought shelter.

By now the sun had set, the cold desert night lay upon the sands beyond, and although they were out of the wind, the chamber grew cold as death. Though as weary as the others, and grateful for the chance to relax, Sinbad was restless, and walked up and down the halls and galleries of the building, a blazing torch in one hand, peering at the frescoes and the unreadable inscriptions.

Who had built this palace? How long ago had it been inhabited? So long ago that this featureless desert had then been fertile farmland. Sinbad shuddered at the notion of so many long ages stretching back into eternity. Had the builders been men? Had it been the palace of one of those pre-Adamite sultans of whom tales whispered? Or had it been the home of the djinn?

He paused by a fresco that seemed to represent some long ago war. A mighty wizard, who flew through the air, led one side, which was made up of chimerical figures, but none as monstrous as the demonic opponents ranked against them. These latter had the wings of bats, and four arms, two like a man's, two like the forelegs of a lion…

Sinbad walked on. In the middle of the palace stood a rotunda topped by the grey metal dome that they had seen outside. Surrounding it on all sides were elaborate tombs of stone, more sepulchres than Sinbad could count. In the air hung a whisper of death. The rotunda itself had eight doors of wood, studded with precious stones. He tried one door and it opened easily, and he stepped inside to find a single tomb in the middle of the floor. Upon it was another inscription, but still Sinbad could not read it. But beneath it, in Greek letters, which Sinbad could read, was another inscription:

If thou ask my name, I am Kush, the son of Shaddad son of 'Aad the Great.

Sinbad's adventures had brought him some years before to Irem, the mysterious city of pillars lost deep in the Arabian Desert, where he had been set upon by the ghouls of the wastelands. That city was rumoured to have been built by Shaddad, a long ago ruler whose empire had encompassed the entire earth, long ago, long ages before even Alexander the Great. This palace in the depths of another desert, it seemed, was the final resting place of his son.

Sombre in mind, Sinbad returned to the first court. Ahmed was still awake, and he grinned lazily.

'What did you find, sailor-man,' he asked, 'that has you wearing that long face? Not treasure, I'll be bound. Did you meet our host, and did he tally out the reckoning?'

Sinbad shook his head. 'We have no hosts,' he said sombrely. 'The only other dwellers in this palace were long ago claimed by Death.'

8 WHAT THE IFRIT SAID

The following morning saw them riding into the west. The mysterious palace, last resting place of a race long forgotten, receded into the distance behind them as they made their slow progress across the blasted landscape. After three days of further travel it was little more than a dot on the horizon, and the endless rolling monotony had been broken by something else that caught their attention.

The ground grew more broken, with immense rocks and boulders lying scattered about. In the distance was a line of hills. On top of one peak an uncertain form glittered in the morning sunlight.

'A man mounted on a steed,' said Sir Acelin, shading his eyes. 'A man in armour. He bears a lance.'

'He waits for us,' said Sir Barnard. 'Another knight? Is he there to help or hinder us?'

Sinbad peered at the distant form. Something was not right. How far away was that hill?

'That's not a man in armour,' he said suddenly. 'Look how far away it is! It's too big to be any man of normal kind.'

'A giant?' suggested Ahmed. 'A man-eating one like the ones in your story, Sinbad!'

Sinbad threw the little man an impatient look. 'I don't believe that it is a living being,' he told them. 'See how motionless it is? This is something else. A statue, perhaps.'

Nakeya shivered. The landscape was barren and rocky. 'Who would build a statue out here, of all places?' she murmured.

'The same people who built that palace we stayed in, perhaps,' said Sinbad. 'The people of Kush, son of Shaddad. I think this was a fertile land once. Well, enough speculation. Let us ride up there and see what this new wonder really is.'

They cantered up through a rocky defile. The further they went, the greater the figure grew, until it was clear that it was indeed a metal statue, taking the form of a mounted man carrying a lance. A winding path led up the dusty flank of the hill and as the sun climbed steadily higher Sinbad and his companions rode up it. At last they crested the rise and the statue stood in front of them.

It was truly immense, towering high above them and blocking out the sun so they shivered in its shadow. Sinbad and Ahmed rode up to the monumental plinth upon which the horse stood. The whole statue, plinth, horse, and rider, had been beaten out of brass.

Sinbad dismounted and climbed up with Ahmed's aid. Gazing up at the mounted figure, he saw an inscription in Greek characters on the lance. He deciphered it gradually, lips moving soundlessly.

'O thou that comest unto me,' Sinbad read out loud, 'if thou know not the way to the City of Brass, rub the hand of this rider and he will turn round and presently stop. Then take the direction whereto he faceth and fare fearless, for it will bring thee, without hardship, to the city aforesaid.'

'So that's what it says,' said Ahmed. 'How convenient! Well, you'd better start climbing.'

'Yes,' said Sinbad. 'And you're coming with me.'

Nakeya watched as the two men began to climb up the brass leg of the horse. Sir Acelin stood beside her.

'What do they now?' he asked.

Nakeya shook her head. 'I cannot say,' she said. 'Folklore says nothing of this statue. Perhaps they hope to see more of the country round from atop it...'

Sinbad and Ahmed reached the rider himself, and climbed up onto his arm. The sailor rubbed at the great metal hand. Suddenly, with a grinding, wrenching sound like the death agony of some horrific djinn, the statue began to move.

Nakeya cried out, certain that it was a trap.

The dromedaries panicked, and it was all their riders could do to quiet the beasts. The shadow began to move, mimicking the statue, which flashed like lightning as it turned on its base to face southwards. With further grinding sounds, it reached a shuddering halt. With a cry, Ahmed fell off the statue's hand and landed with a thud that knocked the breath out of him on the mane of the brass horse.

Sinbad jumped down after him and help the winded little man to his feet. Together, they descended from the statue, and hurried to meet the others.

'What happened?' Sir Acelin asked. 'This statue. Is it alive? Is it possessed by demons?'

Sinbad laughed. 'It's an automaton,' he said. 'I saw similar contrivances when I was at the court of the Byzantine emperor. A tree of singing birds, roaring lions of metal, and a throne that rose upwards so the emperor towered above the courtiers. Nothing on this scale, of course. This surely must have been made by the lost race of Kush. The inscription says that the statue shows the way to the City of Brass.'

'The City of Brass,' echoed Zahid, one of the younger of the Arab sailors, on whose swarthy brow danced a single black kiss curl. 'Then it truly exists?'

'I never doubted it,' said Ahmed cheerily. 'Now all we need to do is get down off this hill and ride southwards until we get there.'

'And then our troubles will truly begin,' Sinbad forecast gloomily.

They rode back down the path. Once they were on the level again they found another trail leading away through the rocks to the south. This they followed as it wound its way through the hills. The land began to show signs of fruitfulness, with green vegetation growing in the valleys, and trickling streams running down through the rocks on either side.

The path joined a paved stone roadway that also led southwards, and they followed this over a rocky ridge where sparse trees and scrub grew, as far as where it began to dip down into a huge, wooded valley. In the middle, where the woods gave way to meadows, stood a solitary black column. And jutting out of the column itself, sunk up to its armpits, was a black and sinister figure.

At first Sinbad thought it was another statue of some kind, with its wings and its four arms, two like those of a man, two like the legs of a lion. But as they drew closer, he saw that it moved, flapping its wings as if in hopes of taking to flight, or heaving futilely at the black stone in which it was imprisoned.

It had long coarse hair like a horse's mane, and two eyes that glowed like coals in its swart face. A third eye like that of a lynx blazed in the centre of its forehead. On seeing their approach, it ceased its impotent struggles and watched them warily.

'Glory to Allah!' it cried out as they came within earshot. 'He who has condemned me to this imprisonment until Judgement Day!'

Sinbad trotted his dromedary towards to the pillar. 'What are you doing?' Ahmed cried. 'Don't go near that thing!'

Sinbad looked back over his shoulder. 'I think it's harmless. And besides, you heard its piety. Why would so devout a fellow be a threat?'

'It's a trap,' Ahmed said.

'I fear your servant may be right,' said Sir Acelin, and the others agreed vehemently.

Ignoring them, Sinbad drew closer to the prisoner, who watched warily. 'Peace be upon you,' the sailor said. 'What is your name and why are you here?'

'And upon you be peace, O Son of Adam,' said the black prisoner. 'Find it in your heart to pity me, mortal. My name is Dahesh, and I am an ifrit of the djinn. It was Suleiman himself who imprisoned me here, locked me in this black pillar until the end of days. Praise be to Allah, the merciful, the compassionate!' he added, shouting the words so loudly the dromedary put its ears back in dismay. 'He doesn't listen to such as me,' Dahesh confided in Sinbad, 'but it's as well to make it clear to all who might be hearing that I have renounced my former allegiance.'

'What allegiance would that be?' Sinbad inquired. 'You say that Suleiman imprisoned you here? Why?'

Dahesh rolled his bone white eyes at Sinbad. 'It was all long ago,' he said. 'This was a beautiful land in those days. It is no longer, has not been since Suleiman went to war against the marids and the ifrits.

'Know, O Son of Adam,' he went on in deep, rolling, resonant tones, 'that the djinn are divided between those who acknowledge Allah and his prophets, and those who follow Iblis. Long, long ago they fought a war, and Suleiman led the djinn whose sultan was Ad-Dimiryat. Many men and many djinn and many beasts swelled his ranks, and he went in the vanguard on his magic carpet, the work of the Queen of Sheba.

'It all began when the people of this land received a message from Suleiman bidding them renounce the Idol of Red Carnelian who was their god, and bow to the God of Suleiman instead. It was I, Dahesh, son of Al-A'amash, who entered the idol and forbade them to take this course. And there was a princess of the Kushites who loved me greatly, and worshipped me with libations and sacrifices. But Suleiman desired her, and he sent them with this insulting message, and the demand that the princess become but one of his many wives. My loyal people obeyed me, and they defied Suleiman, and would not yield up the princess. And so war was declared. And Suleiman came down with his hosts, with Ad-Dimiryat and all the warriors of Djinnistan, and with them fighters from the birds and the beasts, and from the Sons of Adam. And yet the marids and the ifrits, who did not acknowledge Ad-Dimiryat as their lord, and who were worshipped as gods by pagan people, ranked against them. Terrible was the war that ensued. I fought valiantly in the ranks of the marids and the ifrits, and went many times through the enemy, slaying on either hand until my arms were red with blood to the shoulders.

'At last I met with Ad-Dimiryat himself and we fought. O, how we fought! Our struggle shook the mountains from their roots and the seas from their courses. O, it was a long fight, and a hard, and a mighty. Alas, it came about —for all is in accordance with the will of Allah and none know greater nor better than Allah— that I was vanquished, and led in chains before Suleiman. That great prophet waxed wroth and pronounced judgement upon me. And so I was imprisoned. And long aeons ago I saw the error of my ways and repented, and I cried up to the heavens for forgiveness, but the heavens are deaf to my entreaties.'

'What do you know of a djinn named Hadana?' Sinbad asked when the tale was told.

The ifrit rolled his eyes. 'O Son of Adam, Hadana is one of the worst of the marids. If the ifrits were rebels against the majesty of Allah and his prophet Suleiman (peace be upon him!), the marids were worse. And while I received just imprisonment for my rebellion, and many of my kind were imprisoned in vessels of brass, and cast into the sea, Hadana roams the wastes like a lone lion, free to work his mischief, and free to trouble me and taunt me in my durance. Many a time has he come from the City of Brass that is his dwelling place to speak words of derision to me…'

'The City of Brass! Where lies the City of Brass from here?' Sinbad asked.

'It is nearby, O Son of Adam,' said the ifrit. 'Follow the road on which you travel to the southward, and soon you will reach the place that you seek. But beware, for Hadana is cunning, and all who go in search of him fall prey to the sorcery of his foul spells. Say a prayer for me when next you can, O Son of Adam, I, Dahesh, son of Al-A'amash, who has guided you on the road…'

He fell silent, his words echoing from the stones like a mockery. Sinbad and his companions were already riding south.

9 THE CITY OF BRASS

Two days later they crested another rise and the City of Brass lay before them.

It occupied a huge valley, and was girdled round by high black walls of stone. Two towers of brass stood in the walls, gleaming in the sun. Sinbad guessed that they were the origin of its name. The place was immense. Spires and domes could be seen beyond walls that stretched away on either side, and it was impossible to see where the latter terminated. Only the high hills rose higher aloft than the black stone walls. In them, as far as Sinbad could see, was no sign of any gateway.

'What's the good of a city wall without a gate?' Ahmed asked.

'The entrance must be elsewhere,' said Sir Acelin.

Reaching the walls they dismounted. The wall was made of some black stone, but there was no sign of any crack to show where one block fitted against another; it was as if the entire wall had been hewn from a single piece of stone. In the very distance, it seemed that the walls curved round. On another side of the city perhaps there was a gate. Must be a gate. After all, how else did the inhabitants get in and out? Did they fly?

Sinbad shaded his eyes against the glare of the sun and searched the walls for guards. There were none visible. And there was not a sound from the city. It stood there, immense and splendid and shining amidst an endless wilderness, and it was silent. There was no sign of life. No sign of habitation. And most of all, no sign of any entrance.

'Jassim, Zahid, Hussein,' he addressed the Arab sailors. 'Pitch camp here outside the walls. I will ride around the city accompanied by Sir Acelin and Ahmed, and we will seek a means of entrance. The rest of you, remain with the camp until our return.'

'Me?' said Ahmed in surprise. 'Why do you want me?' He patted Sir Barnard's brawny, armoured shoulder. 'You want a big fighter like Sir Barnard here on a dangerous mission like this one.'

Sinbad grinned sardonically. 'That's why Sir Acelin is accompanying me. But if I find a door that can't be opened, who should I want but you? Get back on that dromedary.'

Muttering disconsolately to himself, Ahmed obeyed. Sinbad and Sir Acelin mounted, and Sinbad led them along the line of the city wall. Behind them, the others busied themselves erecting tents and preparing the camp. Sinbad looked back to see Nakeya watching their departure, a sombre expression on her dusky face.

The sun beat down. The three men rode in silence. On one hand the endless black wall gleamed in the desert sun, resembling some vast mirror of obsidian. On the other hand, the dusty plain gave way to scrub and the foothills of the surrounding peaks. All that could be heard was the thudding of their mount's hoofs.

The blue vault above them was empty but for a few birds wheeling overhead. They were too high up for Sinbad to make them out, but something about the way they circled told him that they were vultures.

'They must think it's their lucky day,' Ahmed commented, pointing at them. 'Three fools riding to their deaths!'

'They will learn that they are mistaken,' said Sir Acelin. 'We do not ride to death. Look ahead!' He gestured forwards, in the direction of the nearing corner of the wall. Jabbing his spurs into his dromedary's flank, he galloped faster.

Back in the camp, Nakeya sat in the shade of her tent, playing plaintively on her dulcimer as she watched the distant riders making their slow progress along the side of the wall. What would Sinbad and his companions find when they reached the corner? Another endless stretch of wall? And would they find the gate they were looking for? Somehow she thought not.

She shivered. Sir Barnard, who was attending to his dromedary's harness nearby, came to sit beside her. 'Don't worry, girl,' the older man said gruffly. 'If they meet any enemies, Sir Acelin will defend them.'

'I'm not afraid of that,' she said, striking two more mournful chords on the dulcimer. 'More that they are wasting their time. Many days have passed since Ja'afar abducted Princess Abassa, and who knows what has happened to her in the meantime? Will Sinbad ever find the Carpet?'

'I can't tell you,' said Sir Barnard. 'But I know that he has chosen a good companion in Sir Acelin of Gascony, who was once a paladin of the court of Charlemagne, you know. Although I'm not so sure about his servant...'

'Ahmed must have his virtues,' said Nakeya, 'although I have yet to recognise them. However, I trust Sinbad as a judge of men. If he takes Ahmed with him, it is for a reason, a good reason. Sir Acelin is also a good man in his own way,' she added, with a quiet smile. 'Have you known him long?'

'I first met him in battle with the paynim in Spain,' said the knight. 'I agreed to accompany him when Sir Acelin was sent by the Emperor Charlemagne to escort Sinbad back to Baghdad. It was intended as a punishment, a journey from which he would never return. You see, he slew one of the emperor's kinsmen—in fair fight, I might add, and with dire provocation. Whatever his past crimes, I know he is a valiant knight and I have followed him loyally since the war with the Saracens.'

Intrigued, Nakeya ceased playing and turned to Sir Acelin, but by then the three riders had vanished around the corner.

Sinbad and his two companions did not return that day. Nor was there any sign of them when Nakeya awoke in her dew studded tent the following morning, and for three more days they all awaited his return with growing alarm. Sir Barnard was also betraying anxiety.

'I shall ride after them,' he said on the third morning. 'Something has happened! Wild beast or wild men have found them, or demons of the wastes! I should have been at Sir Acelin's side! I pray that I am not too late.'

He mounted his dromedary and drew his sword, but as he did so the sailor named Zahid held up a hand for quiet. 'Listen!' the Arab said, and he pointed in the direction of the other corner. A distant drumming of hoofs was audible.

A plume of dust grew visible, and Nakeya saw three dromedaries galloping towards them along the line of the wall. After half an hour, it became possible to make out the three men who were riding them. One was a small man who wore an untidy turban, another was taller and neater, while the third wore mail that glittered in the sunlight.

A despondent expression on his face, Sinbad led his two companions into the camp. All three were lean and hungry looking, and looked haggard and defeated. Sinbad dismounted and Nakeya ran forward to steady him as he almost fell.

'My thanks, Nakeya,' he muttered. 'We have been riding for more than three days, with barely a halt.' He directed the Arabs to tend to their dromedaries and the three men sat down by the campfire. All looked exhausted.

Nakeya watched them. 'Did you find the gate?' she asked.

Sinbad looked up at her sardonically. He gave a bitter laugh. 'We found nothing!' he said. 'Nothing but endless black walls. We have traversed the entire city, and at no point anywhere is there any sign of a gate.'

'Sinbad is right.' Sir Acelin gazed wearily up at the towering walls. 'There is no way over them and no way through them.'

'But we must enter the city,' Nakeya said, 'or we will never have a hope of finding Solomon's carpet.'

'Too true,' said Sinbad. 'But none of us can fly, and it seems that only those who can, like those birds who are waiting so eagerly for our deaths'—he pointed at the vultures that still circled high overhead— 'have a hope of entering.'

'And yet,' Nakeya murmured, 'they do not. Not even the vultures enter the city. It is as if there is a spell upon it.'

'Who needs a spell,' Ahmed said, 'when they have walls of such an impossible height? It's not magic that defeats us but architecture.'

Sinbad considered the hills that overlooked the city. 'Perhaps we will gain a better perspective on the problem from up there,' he said thoughtfully.

'Don't you know when to give up, sailorman?' Ahmed complained. 'We've spent days circling that cursed place and seen not a sign of any entrance. You think things will be better if you look down on the city from the hillsides?'

Sinbad shook his head. 'You're right, I don't know when I'm defeated,' he agreed. 'That's why I'm never defeated. In the end, I always find a way. You can stay behind and doze by the fire, if you wish. Who wants to come with me on a climb?'

Sir Acelin looked stricken. 'I...' he said.

'You don't need to,' Sinbad said. 'You've proved yourself enough. Jassim? Will you come with me? Zahid? Hussein? You've all sat on your backsides for three days. You can come with me.'

'I would join you,' Nakeya said. 'I am a competent mountaineer, like all my people, and I too have been idle for some days.'

Sinbad looked doubtful, but allowed her to

accompany them. They left Ahmed and the two knights to guard the camp, and made their way through the brush towards the steep slopes of the nearest hill. A narrow path, perhaps made by the wild goats who could be seen on the cliffs, trailed up its flanks, and they followed this for some time before it petered out.

Then they had to climb from ledge to ledge. Sinbad forced himself onward, although it was clear that he had had more than enough exertion recently. Nakeya easily outstripped the others, and when Sinbad reached the hilltop she was waiting there for them, solemnly regarding the city below.

Sinbad sat down on a rock, mopping at his brow with a fold of his turban. 'What do you see, Nakeya?' he asked at last. 'Anything of any help?'

'I can see why you spent three days circling the city,' she told him gravely.

The entire place was spread out like a map. Many streets led between houses and shops and temples and palaces. Even from up here, the furthest side of the city was obscured by haze. No birds flew over the city, and the vultures Sinbad had seen appeared to be content with its periphery. Atop the black walls ran a long parapet, wide enough, it seemed, for a patrol of guards to march along. But there were no guards. Nor did there seem to be any citizens at large in the streets.

'Captain Sinbad,' said Jassim. 'There is no

way into the city except over the walls. We must build a ladder, and climb up to that parapet. Then follow it. You see how it leads to those two towers of brass? I think we would be able to get down to street level that way.'

Sinbad had risen to his feet by now, and was studying the city intently. He nodded. 'Good thinking, shipmate. We shall rest and then climb back down to the others with the news.'

The following day the ladder was ready. The Arab sailors were skilled carpenters, and Zahid, who was the best of them, went nowhere without his tools. Although the wood provided by the scrub bushes was not ideal, there was plenty of it, and they cobbled together a ladder long enough to reach the top of the wall when, with much puffing and blowing, they lifted it up until it was vertical. It clattered against the parapet between two merlons, and was still.

Nakeya looked up at it. 'How safe is it, I wonder,' she murmured.

'Don't worry yourself,' Sinbad told her. 'I can climb any ladder. All it takes is one man to get over the wall and then perhaps they will be able to find a better way to get inside.'

He gripped the rungs and was about to climb when Sir Barnard laid a hand on his shoulder. Looking round at the older man, Sinbad frowned. 'What is it?'

'Let me go,' pleaded the knight. 'We do not know what a man might risk, climbing up there.

All manner of peril may await.'

'All the reason why I should go,' said Sinbad. 'I would not send a man into a place I feared to go myself.'

Ahmed chipped in. 'The knight is right, sailor-man,' he said. 'You're too valuable to us all for you to risk throwing away your life. Let Sir Barnard go, if he really wishes.'

Unwillingly, Sinbad stepped away from the ladder and let Sir Barnard climb.

They watched for many long minutes as the knight ascended the ladder. At last he reached the top. Ahmed grinned. 'The old fool's made it!' he said.

Sir Barnard's voice floated down to them. 'Oh, you are most beautiful!' he cried, addressing someone out of sight to the watchers below, and leapt over the wall. A whistling sound was followed by the distant thud of a body hitting the ground from a great height.

10 GETTING INSIDE

Sinbad stared up the ladder in horror. Sir Barnard had fallen to his doom, it seemed. But what had possessed him?

Or were there indeed evil spirits in this place? It was well known that Hadana the marid, of the lineage of Iblis, haunted this lost city. Had some malign influence from the evil djinn inspired the knight to throw away his life?

'He must have been mad. Mad!' Sir Acelin was white with shock. 'What did he say?' he kept asking. 'What was it that he said?'

'*You are beautiful*,' Sinbad said in a voice that shook. 'I... think that is what he said. But who was he talking to? Who is beautiful? Why did he fling himself off the parapet and into the city? Why did he throw himself to his doom?'

'He's dead,' Ahmed said savagely. 'He's dead, sailor-man, and we will all die too if we spend any longer in this uncanny, chancy place. We'll die, I tell you!' He turned to go—as if there was anywhere within hundreds of miles where they would be safe. Sinbad laid a hand on his arm.

'We're staying, Ahmed,' he said warningly. 'Remember the princess! Remember the caliph! Remember our quest! We were sent here to find the Carpet of Suleiman. The carpet that the marid spirited away. We must get inside, and we must find the carpet. Only then will we have a hope of following Ja'afar and the princess to Djinnistan on the edge of the world.'

'I helped the caliph one time,' said Ahmed with a shrug. 'I don't have to make a career of it. I'm beginning to think it was the biggest mistake of my life.' He grimaced. 'Climb the wall yourself, sailor-man, if you're so eager to die.'

Sinbad glared back. 'I shall,' he said defiantly.

'No!' said Zahid, interposing himself between his skipper and the ladder. 'Captain Sinbad, you mustn't risk your own life. Let me go!'

'Why should you go rather than me?' Sinbad argued. 'I would go down with my ship if she were sinking. I would not expect one of my crew to die in my place. I shall take this risk rather than let another man die.'

'We cannot let anyone throw away his life,' Sir Acelin said. 'But we must get inside the city. Let me go. It seems to me that Sir Barnard was concealing some kind of madness. Even I knew naught of it. A desire to take his life! There is a place in Hell for folk who take their own lives. Their future is worse than their present....'

'It seems to me that he fell for the temptations of the flesh,' said Nakeya thoughtfully. '"O, you are most beautiful," he said. I believe that he saw a woman. That she was somehow his downfall. Let me go,' she added, turning to Sinbad. 'I shall not be so affected.'

Sinbad shook his head. 'There were no women to be seen within the city when we looked down at it from the hill,' he said. 'No women, no men, no children. No beasts, no living things. Nothing moving.' He pointed up at the circling dots. 'The vultures still do not enter, even though Sir Barnard lies dead on the far side of this wall.' For good measure he thumped the black stone. 'I do not believe any are women within, beautiful houris or repellent hags. It is a dead city.'

'Perhaps the women were indoors,' said Zahid. 'We could not see much detail from up on the hillside. Well, I shall find them.'

Without waiting for Sinbad's assent, he began climbing the ladder. Sinbad called for him to stop and come back down, but Zahid ignored him and kept climbing.

Sinbad watched his ascent, angry and fearful for his crewman's safety. Hand over hand, foot by foot, rung by rung Zahid climbed, until he was at the level of the parapet. Laughing out loud, he seized the merlons on either side and hauled himself through the embrasure, out of the sight of the watching people below.

'I am coming, O my sweet darling!' Zahid cried, and then they heard him falling with a shocked shriek through the air.

Sinbad looked away in anguish and pain as he heard the distant thud of the man hitting the paves on the far side of the wall. He dashed the sweat from his brow, loosened his scimitar in its scabbard and seized a rung of the ladder.

'No, captain,' said Jassim, marching up to join him. 'This was my own foolish idea. I shall go up, and this time it will be different. I have a wife in Basra and another in Hormuz, and I am not wont to have my head turned by giddy young girls, or whatever it was that Zahid saw, and Sir Barnard.'

'Nay, captain,' cried Hussein, pushing his fellow crewman aside. 'Let me go, rather than him. I am made of stronger stuff than Jassim. Wives or not, every time we go ashore he drinks strong drink forbidden by the Prophet and permits himself to be ensnared by the blandishments of women. I shall not fall for this she, whoever she may be.'

'Better to fall for women than for boys!' Jassim growled.

Hussein's dagger leapt from his sheath, and Jassim drew his own knife. Crouching low, they confronted each other. 'I'll not take that from you,' Hussein growled.

'Nor I from you,' Jassim snarled.

'Stop this at once, shipmates!' Sinbad cried,

striking the knife from Hussein's grasp. 'Fighting like feckless boys! If both of you are as averse to fleshly temptation as you maintain, you can both go up! We'll see how upright you are at the top of that wall!'

Eagerly, Hussein went first, Jassim following close behind. The makeshift ladder swayed visibly under their combined weight, but they went higher and higher. Both were men accustomed to climbing in worse conditions than these; Sinbad had seen them trotting unconcernedly along the sailyards in the middle of a storm, and the ascent would mean little to them. It was what awaited them at the top that concerned him most.

He repented his angry words. He was about to shout up to them to come back and he would make the ascent himself when Hussein reached the merlons and hauled himself up, followed almost at once by Jassim. There was silence.

'O my sweetheart!' came from Jassim, and 'Come to me, darling!' wailed Hussein. And all went as it had before.

Sinbad was shaking with horror. 'I shall not stand here while men leap to their doom. I shall climb.'

'And go to your own doom?' Ahmed shouted up. 'The heat has baked your brains, Sinbad! Come back down here!'

Sinbad was already eight or nine cubits

above his friends. He glanced back down to see Ahmed, Sir Acelin, and Nakeya all watching in concern. Dismissing their fearful faces from his mind, he turned his attention back to the climb.

Hand over hand he went. The wind buffeted him, and he grew cold despite the sun that glowered resentfully down at his slowly moving figure. Halfway up the wall he stopped again, mopped his brow with a fold of his turban, one arm crooked round a rung of the ladder. He took a deep breath and continued his climb. It seemed neverending.

But when the end finally came, it was a surprise. So accustomed had he become to the business of climbing that when he reached up for the next rung and found his hands clutching at empty space, he almost slipped and fell. Laughing at his folly, he grabbed tight hold of the highest rung and looked up to see the two merlons, foursquare and dauntless. Between them was the embrasure, the same embrasure the other men had scrambled through—to their seeming doom. For a long while he stood there, feet on one rung, hands gripping the other, his eyes on the embrasure.

At last, he nerved himself for the final stage. He climbed up to the level of the merlons, seized a hold of either one, and pulled himself up and up until he was kneeling in the middle of the embrasure. Beneath him he saw the great expanse of the City of Brass. A little wind stirred the dust amidst the sea of rooftops, spires, and temple domes, but otherwise all was still. Down in the winding streets he could see no sign of movement.

Awkwardly, he climbed down onto the parapet, and looked to his left, then his right. To the right stood the first of the great towers of brass. To his left the parapet ran for as far as Sinbad could see, curving round until it was hidden behind the rooftops of the city.

Sinbad looked downwards. He was astounded. How could he have been so foolish! There was no city here. No streets or buildings. Instead a pool of limpid water sparkled in the sunlight. Surrounding it were green reeds and bulrushes, while long legged water birds strode through the shallows, catching fish or frogs in their beaks. Beyond the pool was a rolling countryside of wooded hills, where herds of deer roamed. The blue vault of the sky was tranquil.

On the bank of the pool stood ten slender maidens, none more than eighteen years of age; shapely, supple, and clad scantily in diaphanous silken garments that accentuated rather than concealed their physical charms. Each had creamy breasts like full moons, a slim waist, wide hips and long, slender legs. Each wore a veil upon her face, above which sparkled two big kohl-rimmed eyes like the most mysterious and inviting of stars in the heavens. Each one was beckoning to Sinbad with long slender fingers on long slender hands on long slender arms that rang like cymbals, weighed down as they were with bangles and arm rings of glittering gold.

'Come, Sinbad, come!' they cooed like doves. 'Come and sport with us here on the bank! We are burning with hot desire to hear the tales of your adventures, to cover you with our kisses and soothe you with our embraces. Come to us, O Sinbad! Each one of us is a virgin, who has waited all her short life for you to come and reave her of her maidenhead! Come to us, O Sinbad, world famed traveller! Come!'

Sinbad stepped forward to the edge of the parapet.

'*Bismillahir Rahmanir Rahim*!' he cried out in a loud voice. Hearing his words, the maidens wailed in harsh, shrieking tones more like crows or rooks than doves. And they twisted in Sinbad's vision, humps growing on their backs, their long painted fingernails curving into claws, their marble white skin turning black as pitch and suddenly they vanished.

The pool vanished. The entire vision of the wooded landscape vanished from Sinbad's sight. In its place stood the City of Brass, and the street beneath the parapet far below where lay the broken and twisted bodies of Sinbad's companions.

11 THE HORROR BEYOND THE WALLS

This, then, explained what had happened to the others. Only Sinbad had been strong willed enough to withstand the lure of these houris, these evil spirits, these phantasms of sorcery!

He heard Ahmed's thin voice drifting up. 'Sinbad!' the little man was crying. 'Sinbad, are you alright?'

Sinbad thrust his head out between two embrasures.

'Of course I'm alright!' he shouted back down. Ahmed stood at the foot of the ladder, Nakeya and Sir Acelin behind him. The Baghdadi's hand was gripping one of the first rungs. 'Stay below! With the words of the Prophet I have broken the spell that lured the others to their doom, but I do not yet know what other horrors await. I will go down to street level now and see if I can secure a way to let you inside.'

Ahmed let go of the ladder as if it had stung him, and looked round at his companions. They waved at Sinbad in farewell.

Sinbad withdrew from the embrasure and looked up and down the parapet. It stretched into the distance on his left, but terminated at two metal gates in the side of the first brass tower, only a short way away on his right. He hurried in this direction.

The brazen tower gleamed in the sunlight, and as Sinbad drew closer he felt that it was emanating heat. The gates, he realised in wonder as he drew closer, were cast from solid gold. On a plinth between them stood a large equestrian statue, a smaller version of the brass horseman that stood atop the hill in the desert. Its metal hand was outstretched as if it pointed at Sinbad.

The sailor saw something inscribed on the statue's palm. Closer inspection proved it to be Greek characters that said, 'O thou who comest to this place, an thou wouldst enter, turn the pin in my navel twelve times and the gate will open.'

Sinbad climbed up onto the plinth and found the statue's navel, complete with a projecting pin of gold ornamented with garnets. Gripping hold, he began to turn it.

Once he had turned it twelve times, there was a rumbling sound. He jumped down from the plinth as the statue revolved on its axis, its metal skin glittering blindingly in the sun, and as it did so, the left-hand gate of gold swung silently open, revealing a long passage at the end of which Sinbad found a flight of steps leading downwards into darkness.

A strange odour hung within, a spicy yet sour scent that reminded him of the tombs of long dead infidels in Egypt. He began descending the stairway, hands outstretched to trace the warm metal wall at his side. Several times he stumbled in the gloom, wishing that the ancients who had built this place so miraculously from so much brass had also possessed a means of illuminating it. He had heard of a stone called the carbuncle, said to be found in the head of an adder, and glowed with its own light. Had the folk of Kush lacked such wonders, when they had all this?

He began to see a dim glow of light filtering up from below. Soon he could see well enough to be able to make out the steps beneath his feet, and his progress grew more confident. The steps ended and an archway led him out into a large room. A guardroom, he realised, when he saw the armoured figures that sat along the long benches that lined either wall. On the far side lounged another figure in armour, and beside him was a door.

On the walls above hung shields and bows and other warlike accoutrements. But as Sinbad entered the guardroom, not one of the helmeted figures stirred. Drawing close to one of them, Sinbad saw from its withered skin that clung like parchment to a yellowing skull, from the teeth that grinned from between withered lips, from the skeletal hand that gripped the pommel of a short sword, that this guard was dead. All the guards were dead.

Shaking himself to rid himself of the shudders crawling across his flesh, Sinbad crossed over to the doorway. Setting his shoulder to the door, which was hewn of black oak brought from some far distant land, Sinbad shoved it open. With a dramatic creaking it slowly opened, and desert sunlight filtered into the silent guardroom.

Stepping outside, Sinbad found himself at one end of a broad thoroughfare. Directly in front of him stood another gate, this one tall and huge, set in the great black city wall. He had seen nothing to suggest its presence from outside. Examining it closely, he discovered a large keyhole in its face. But there was no sign of a key.

Inspiration struck him, and he turned back to the guardroom. Returning into the eerie hush of the strangely scented chamber, he crossed over to the corpse in armour that sat alone beside the door. This man wore a helmet chased with gold, and emblazoned on his breastplate was a red carnelian. Hanging on a leather thong from the skeleton's neck was a huge metal key.

Grinning with satisfaction, Sinbad took

hold of it and lifted it up over the man's head. The thong caught on one of the helmet's ear flaps. Sinbad tugged impatiently, then leapt aside as the man's skull inclined forward, and fell with a crash, hitting his bony armoured knees and then rolling, with a great clatter that awoke echoes in the chamber, still encased in the helmet, until it came to a rest halfway across the guardroom floor.

As the echoes died away, quailing inwardly under the dead yet somehow scathing gaze of the skeleton guards, Sinbad took the key and went out into the street again.

'What do you suppose he is doing?' Sir Acelin was asking as the three stood beside their camp, gazing anxiously at the stone walls.

'Something foolish, if I know Sinbad,' said Ahmed.

'You are not a very loyal servant,' Nakeya observed in haughty tones. 'You should speak of your master with more respect.'

'Master?' Ahmed sneered. 'Sinbad? Sinbad couldn't master a ship without getting wrecked in some exotic foreign clime jam-packed with cannibal monsters. Why the caliph wanted him to follow Ja'afar is beyond me. Sinbad has probably suffered the same fate as all the others, or something worse. If I was in charge of this expedition, the first thing I would do would be to...'

He broke off. A huge door had materialised silently in the black wall between the two great towers of brass and was moving slowly outwards. Silhouetted in the crack between door and door jamb was a turbaned figure.

'Sinbad!' cried Nakeya, rushing forward. 'You're alive!'

Sinbad laughed shakily. 'Why, yes, I suppose I must be,' he said. His face grew as grave as hers. 'Which is more than can be said for my crewmen. And for Sir Barnard.' Looking at Sir Acelin, he pointed along the line of the wall. 'Their bodies lie somewhere in that direction. We must ensure that they receive decent burial.'

They rounded up enough dromedaries and rode through the gateway and into the street beyond. Sinbad explained how he had got down to street level. Then he broke off, gazing along the street that led deeper into the city.

Shops lined it. Through each open doorway or entrance they could see racks and bales of ancient merchandise. Strewn amongst them were fallen, withered bodies. All along the street it was the same story. Every shop contained at least one corpse, that of the shopkeeper, sitting cross-legged amongst his wares. In the more frequented shops shoppers also lay, withered to bones and dust. The four newcomers rode down the street, their spirits, even those of Ahmed, oppressed by the gruesome sight.

'You were right when you said this was a dead city, Sinbad,' said Ahmed. This was the closest to his customary levity the little man could muster. The rest rode on, unspeaking.

'What happened here?' Nakeya broke the silence at last. 'What happened to all these people? The populace of an entire city, all dead where they stood. It is fantastic. Unbelievable.'

Sinbad shrugged. 'Some plague, some pestilence,' he suggested. 'Who can say? All that we know is that this city is haunted by Hadana the marid, and somewhere here we will find the Carpet of Suleiman.'

'Will we, though?' asked Ahmed. 'This city is huge, an endless maze. Where can we hope to find what we are looking for?'

'We can only try our best,' said Sir Acelin. 'And once we have buried our dead, we must all set off for Djinnistan. Unless you are afraid to come with us, Ahmed.'

Ahmed snorted. 'I'd be more afraid to stay in this city of the dead!' he said. 'As soon as we find that carpet, I want to be out of here. It gives me the creeps.'

Footsteps rang out, loud and harsh in the stillness. All four whirled round. The street was empty.

Round the corner came a burly figure.

'Sir Barnard!' exclaimed Sir Acelin, stepping forward. 'Is it you?'

Sinbad saw as it drew closer that it was indeed the knight, who had last been seen climbing the wall. 'We thought you were dead,' he called.

Sir Barnard shook his head. He looked dazed, as if not sure where he was. 'No, I live,' he muttered. 'I have been wandering these streets. I heard voices…'

Enthusiastically, Sir Acelin said, 'Indeed, we thought we had seen the last of you. But what in God's name did you see? Sinbad told us he saw a vision of Paradise that almost lured him to his doom.'

Sir Barnard's eyes were bright, almost feverish. They lingered on Nakeya. 'I saw no Paradise. Come with me.'

He walked ahead. The others exchanged puzzled looks. 'Where are you going?' Sir Acelin shouted after him.

Sir Barnard looked back. 'To the palace, of course.'

The others rode after him through the maze of streets. Through two bazaars they went, each one strewn with withered corpses; the silk market, and then the perfumers' market, on the far side of which stood an imposing edifice, green with lapis lazuli, having a great onion dome atop it and several spires. A flight of steps led to a colonnade of green marble pillars, within which a tall set of double doors stood.

They dismounted and tethered the dromedaries to one of the pillars. Sir Barnard led them up the steps and through the doors, which stood slightly ajar.

Within was a vestibule where armoured

men sat upon ivory benches, each one dead and withered. The walls were hung with weapons and armour. Ignoring all this, Sir Barnard led them through into a large hall. Within several pavilions had been pitched, each of which seemed to contain treasures beyond count. But Sir Barnard led them through this hall without a glance at its contents, through a door of teak and up a long, marble floored hallway, then ushered them into another chamber which lay directly beneath the onion dome.

Pillars of green jade stood on every hand; lamps hung from chains, shedding a guttering light despite the years of desolation and desertion. In the middle of the chamber, beneath the apex of the dome, sat a dais, and upon the dais stood two statues, one of ivory, one of ebony, in the form of slaves bearing weapons. And between the two statues, lying unrolled upon the dais, was a magnificent carpet.

Sinbad strode forwards. 'Is it...?' he said, his mouth dry. 'Can it be...?'

12 DEMON LOVER

The carpet was large, big enough to fit all five of them comfortably. It brought to Sinbad's mind the rugs the Turcoman nomads made, and it was woven in arabesques and curlicues in deep reds and blacks and greens, all as fresh and bright as the day they were dyed, having an abstract design of a great bird in its centre. Either end was fringed with tassels.

'Wait, Sinbad!' said Ahmed. He pointed at the two statues. 'I don't like the look of them…'

'They are only statues, Ahmed,' said Sinbad irritably. 'We have nothing to fear from statues. Can't you see it? This must be the Carpet of Suleiman! Now we can fly to Djinnistan…'

He broke off. The doors slammed behind them, and the flames in the lamps flickered. A deep booming laugh echoed round the chamber. Sinbad and the others whirled round.

Sir Barnard's face was wreathed in shadows and his eyes glowed a fiery red. 'Fools you were to walk straight into the heart of my domain,' he said in a voice like the screeching of monstrous birds. 'But the bait was good. Ja'afar knew that it would be.'

'Ja'afar?' Sir Acelin demanded. 'You're in league with that pagan wizard?' He shook his head sadly. 'Sir Barnard, what has become of you?'

'That isn't Sir Barnard,' said Ahmed warningly. 'He knows the city too well for a man who has never been here before.'

'Then who in God's name is it?' Sir Acelin demanded.

Sir Barnard shimmered, and in his place stood a darkly handsome, saturnine young man. 'It's Hadana,' said Nakeya in a soft voice that thrilled with horror—and something else.

The young man laughed with joy. 'When Ja'afar called upon me to aid him,' he told them, 'I thought that it would be merely another job of work. We marids are often obliged to run errands at the behest of such sorcerers. He succeeded in fashioning a talisman, you see, inscribed with my true name.... But no matter! I was bound by the wizard to lure you to your doom, to take the Carpet of Suleiman and conceal it here, and to slay you when you had entered into my trap. But what jubilation I feel to see that with me you bring my long lost love!'

Nakeya took a step towards him. Sinbad looked from the marid to the Abyssinian. 'Nakeya, what are you doing?' he said nervously.

'Get back from him!'

'Sinbad, Sinbad,' said Hadana, his eyes flashing hotly. 'You came here for the Carpet. Well, you can have it!' He laughed. 'I don't want it! I don't want to do Ja'afar's dirty work!'

Sinbad was astounded. He glanced at Sir Acelin, who smiled back.

'Don't trust him,' Ahmed warned. 'He plots something!'

'You say we can have the Carpet,' said Sinbad slowly. 'But did not Ja'afar persuade you to lead us to our doom? I don't believe that truly is Suleiman's Carpet.'

'It is,' said Hadana with a laugh. 'The work of Bilkis and her maids. And you may have it. But it is not a gift. I want something in return. Or rather...' His eyes drifted to Nakeya. 'Or rather, someone.'

Twin clashes of steel rang out through the chamber as Sinbad drew his scimitar and Sir Acelin unsheathed his broadsword. 'Impossible,' said Sinbad firmly, grabbing the girl with his free hand and thrusting her behind him. 'We'll fight you before we let Nakeya into your clutches.'

The dark young man's body began to swell. His eyes became like two bonfires, his flesh grew thick and black. His mouth opened and out came, not words but a jet of flame.

'Give her to me!' the marid roared. 'It is she who I love!'

'Sinbad, let me go!' Nakeya shouted in his

ear. 'He will kill you!'

'He'll have to!' Sinbad said steadfastly. 'Ahmed! Keep her safe!'

He pushed Nakeya into the hands of the little man, who seized her firmly. Hadana rose from the ground, two wings beating on his back, and belched a gout of flame at the little group.

Sir Acelin ran forwards, brandishing his sword, and deflected the flame with his blade. The steel grew white hot, and Sir Acelin swung it round. With a great roaring sound the glowing metal sliced through the marid's right leg, which dropped to the ground and exploded in a thousand fragments, but as it did so, Sir Acelin's own sword shattered.

Sinbad ran forwards as the marid swooped downwards, and attacked in a flurry of blows.

Nakeya was stronger than she looked. Soft and pliant as her flesh was, she possessed a wiry strength and Ahmed found himself hard put to subdue her. Struggling, they fell to the ground.

'Let me go!' she cried, trying to break free. 'I must go to him!'

'You will not!' Ahmed said. 'Sinbad's not going to sacrifice you, not even to get the Carpet.'

She struck him backhanded across the face and he fell back against a jade pillar, striking his head.

'Hadana!' Nakeya cried out, running forward. 'Show yourself not in that form! Return to the form I knew you in first! He who I remember from those nights in the chapel on Mount Abora. The Hadana I love!'

Sinbad and Sir Acelin turned open mouthed to see the girl approaching across the blazing floor. With a booming laugh, Hadana swooped down and suddenly the dark young man stood there, standing uncomfortably on his single remaining leg.

He reached out towards her. 'Come to me!' he crooned. 'Oh, come to me! And our child? What of our child!'

'I gave birth to a horror of horns and fangs and wings that flew away the moment it was born,' Nakeya cried. 'Then I was expulsed from the convent of Mount Abora and was sold as a slave. I hoped you would come after me! But now I have brought it about that I have returned to you.'

'Oh, my love,' said Hadana sadly. 'You were far beyond my grasp. I can thrive only in the wilderness and the waste places of the world, for such is my kismet. I could not follow you into the cities of Mankind. But you love me so much that you have returned to me!'

Ahmed watched dazedly from where he lay. He shook his head to clear it, and got stealthily to his feet. Now Nakeya was giving herself willingly to the marid, the deal would most certainly be off. So it would be up to him, the poor thief, to ensure they got what they had come for!

He crossed to the dais and reached out. And

then it happened, what he had feared. With a grinding, clanking sound, the two statues stirred into life. Black statue and white statue loomed above him, lifting their weapons to strike him.

'Now, look here, you two,' Ahmed said nervously. 'Let's not do anything hasty! I'm sure even automatons are willing to negotiate!'

They both lunged. The clash of their weapons rang out across the chamber.

As the marid extended his arms to embrace her, Nakeya produced the brass vessel from beneath her garments. With a flourish, she opened it. The marid shrieked out in fear at the sight of Suleiman's seal on the leaden stopper.

'No!' Hadana roared. 'The fate I have evaded for so many centuries!'

A wind sprang up from nowhere, a swirling vortex that plucked at the clothes and hair of everyone in the chamber. Hadana's form twisted and distorted, as if he consisted of nothing more than smoke, and the wind tugged at him, dragging him towards the brass vessel. With a last wail, the marid vanished inside, and Nakeya rammed home the stopper.

Silence descended, like that silence that falls upon the desert after a sandstorm has blown itself out. Nakeya staggered suddenly, and Sinbad dropped his scimitar with resounding a clang to catch her.

She nestled against his broad shoulder. 'I thought you had decided to go back to your old lover,' Sinbad joked.

She looked up at him, eyes half closed. 'More than half did I think I loved him,' she murmured. 'Until I saw him again. Then it all came back to me. Ever since then my life has been a living hell. Until now.'

'Hey!' came a small voice. 'Somebody get me out of this!'

They looked round. On the dais, two statues, one black, one white, stood locked together, weapons sunk into each other's torsos. Caught between their tangled limbs, unable to move, but one hand still grasping the weave of Suleiman's Carpet, was Ahmed.

Sinbad laughed and went to help him.

It took the combined strength of Sinbad and Sir Acelin to free Ahmed from the two statues, which had so fortuitously destroyed each other when the little thief ducked to evade their blows. They pushed the statues to one side, rolled up the Carpet, and carried it from the palace.

Later, after they had buried the bodies of the Arab sailors who had flung themselves from the walls, and Ahmed had untethered the dromedaries and let them wander away in search of food, Sinbad and Sir Acelin unrolled the Carpet on the dusty ground. Nakeya sat on the lowest step, holding the brazen vessel between her fingertips and studying it gravely. Ahmed came to join her, carrying the saddlebags which he had removed from the dromedaries before letting them free.

'Why don't you get rid of it?' he asked her, nudging her in the ribs. 'Tell you what, as soon as we reach the sea, you can drop it over the side.'

She shook her head. 'I think I will keep hold of it for a while,' she said. 'It might prove useful on our journey.'

'So you are coming with us?' Sinbad asked, joining them. 'I thought perhaps now you have been set free, according to the terms of the caliph's agreement, you would want to go back to your people.'

She shook her head. 'I have no people now,' she said. 'My place is here. I will fly with you to Djinnistan, and help you rescue the princess.'

'Ah,' said Sinbad awkwardly, glancing back to where Sir Acelin seemed to be speaking sternly to the Carpet. 'That could be a problem. We don't seem to know how to get this thing to fly.'

Ahmed put his head in his hands. 'After all that!'

Nakeya was looking at his right hand. 'Ahmed!' she said suddenly. 'Your ring!'

Ahmed lifted his head and stared at the ornament. 'Another useless trinket,' he said dismissively. 'What of it?'

'That is the Ring of Ja'afar,' said Sinbad. 'With it he commanded djinn and cast magic spells. Give it to me!'

Futilely, Ahmed tugged at it, but it would

not come off. 'I've been trying to get rid of it,' he complained. 'Now it won't shift at all. It won't come off!'

'Then it is you who is destined to wield it,' Nakeya stated. 'Come over here!'

They all gathered on the carpet, bringing their saddlebags filled with their belongings with them. Nakeya told Ahmed to stand in the middle of the arabesque design. He looked at the other three in confusion. 'What now?' he asked.

'Speak to the Carpet,' said Nakeya commandingly. 'Address it.'

Feeling foolish, Ahmed said, 'O Carpet of Suleiman, hear my words.' He broke off. 'What am I supposed to say?'

They all exchanged glances.

'Tell it to fly us to the edge of the world,' said Sinbad with a shrug. 'Take us to Djinnistan!'

'O Carpet of Suleiman!' Ahmed declaimed in resounding tones. He discovered that he was rather beginning to enjoy himself. 'Transport us as fast as you can to the kingdom of the djinn!'

With a lurch, the Carpet rose into the air. Ahmed fell backwards and Sinbad caught a hold of him. Higher and higher the carpet lifted. The four passengers sat down, clinging on as the wind blew cold about them. The City of Brass lay beneath them, as tiny as a child's toy. Desolate palaces and shops, markets and temples, walls and towers all grew smaller and smaller as the Carpet of Suleiman ascended.

The whole desert extended below them, rolling leagues of sand. Sinbad saw the valley where stood the column of the ifrit, glimpsed a flash of light that must mark the statue of the horseman on the hill, saw the endless flatness in the midst of which was the palace of death.

And so they began to fly towards the fabled emerald mountains at the edge of the world.

BOOK TWO: THE MAGIC CARPET

1 THE WIZARD KING

Endless paddy fields and terraces unfolded below them, a carpet far more intricate than the flying one on which the four travellers sat; it rolled beneath them with repeated motifs of farmland and small, intricate, walled towns. A miniscule blue black dot rushed across the landscape at the same speed as them, the shadow of the carpet of Suleiman. They were so high above the countryside that clouds were visible beneath them, tiny white scudding skeins of wool. They crossed a range of hills and a broad river flashed beneath them, its waters yellow with silt, choked with boats and barges, and then they were crossing farmland again.

This far inland, Sinbad was all at sea. He had travelled through China some years before, but it had taken him long days of riding down broad, busy roads that were now threads of grey entangling the fields, hills, and woods. Furthermore he had never ventured as far as the dwellings of the emperor himself. And yet that was their destination: the summer palace of the Son of Heaven, the Chinese emperor Tianzi.

'How does the emperor come to know so much about djinn anyway?' asked Ahmed, shivering and holding his cloak close as the wind tugged playfully at his turban. It was cold up here above the clouds, and they were all suffering , but Sinbad had decided to fly as high as possible. Already they had met with unwelcome attention not only from a hungry roc as they traversed the Indian Ocean, but also from ambitious archers while flying over the wild hills of Nagaland. They would only fly in low when they were nearing their destination.

'It is said that he had many dealings with them in his youth,' Sinbad explained. 'Despite humble birth, he made himself a man of great significance in China with their assistance, and married the emperor's daughter. Long ago he succeeded to the throne and now he rules a tranquil empire.'

It was a peaceful scene, but Sinbad knew that the laws that kept it so were harsh, and the caste of officials that administered them was corrupt.

'He is a sorcerer, Mon Dieu, a wizard king!' said Sir Acelin, holding his cloak as it fluttered in the wind. 'The man who rules this heathen land is naught but a magus, who achieved his rule by wizardry and deceit!'

Sinbad laughed. 'If dealings with djinn

make a man a magician,' he said, 'then we are all of us sorcerers here. Three wizards and one particularly beguiling witch,' he added, giving the last of his companions a gallant smile.

Nakeya greeted his frivolity with a look of disapproval. 'Hadana is the only djinn I have ever known,' she said, resting a hand on the brazen vessel that lay beside her. 'And I was unwilling. That said, it is the duty of every man and woman to circumvent the beguiling snares of Evil. I was very young.'

'What is that place below us?' Ahmed asked suddenly, pointing. The ring on his finger flashed redly in a ray of sunlight.

Before them lay an area of mist-hung cedars and fertile meadows through which ran a river which rose from a cave amidst the woods. Ten miles of parkland was surrounded by walls and towers, martial in aspect, where the tiny figures of armoured, spear bearing guards were visible. Within them sprawled a veritable paradise. Amidst the trees the roofs of pagodas and pavilions and palaces were visible.

'Ahmed, my friend,' said Sinbad. 'Take us down towards that palace at the centre of the park.'

Herds of deer broke from the cover of the trees and raced across the meadows as the carpet's shadow flew amongst them. An overpowering waft of scent rose from the blossoms and blooms that brightened tree and sward. Under

Ahmed's direction the carpet flew down a valley between two wooded hills and over a grassy ridge. Beyond it a palace stood beside the meandering waters of the river.

Its dome was easily as large as that of the caliph's palace in Baghdad, while the building as a whole was constructed of marble and jasper and chalcedony. Carved into the walls were numerous images of beasts and birds and trees and men.

Riding out from the palace was a group of horsemen in lacquered armour bearing pikes, escorting a horse drawn palanquin. The horsemen rode round in circles in the meadow, pointing up at the carpet in bewildered wonder. Sinbad thrust his head over the side as they hovered high above the meadow, and called out in his best Cantonese, 'Good morning, gentlemen. Please tell us where we can find the Son of Heaven!'

Another rider trotted forwards, a man in the buttoned hat and long sleeved robe of a mandarin. His face was sallow, and two long thin moustaches drooped from either side of a censorious mouth. He peered up at the carpet.

'What is this outrage, this abomination!' he cried. 'You come in search of my master, his imperial majesty? What warlocks are you that you fly through the air on a Persian rug?' He gave a sign to two of the horsemen. Sinbad saw that these carried compound bows.

'He thinks we're wizards too, sailor-man,'

said Ahmed, tugging futilely at the ring on his finger as the horse archers put arrows to their bows. 'What would my dear old mother think?'

'Sinbad!' Nakeya gripped his arm. 'They mean to kill us!'

'My name is Sinbad,' the sailor shouted. 'I come to speak with your emperor with regards to a certain matter. Tianzi is renowned in my own country for his knowledge of the djinn. I am seeking their kingdom.'

A cry came from within the curtains of the palanquin. As Sinbad turned to look in that direction, he saw a head appear at the gap in the curtains. It wore a strange hat with a flat horizontal piece from which hung numerous beads.

'Sinbad!' the man called. 'Is it truly you?'

Hampered by voluminous yellow robes, the man climbed down out of the palanquin, and his horsemen galloped to surround him. 'Out of my way, curse you,' he told them. 'I would speak with this far famed man.' He put his hands on his broad hips. 'O famous sailor,' he called up to Sinbad. 'Pray descend to the ground, come and speak with me. Word of your fabulous adventures has reached even as far as China.'

Ahmed directed the carpet to descend and they landed on the meadow with a bump. The air was warm, scented with jasmine and wood of aloes. Birds sang amongst the trees, or flitted from branch to branch. Butterflies fluttered from flower to flower. The harsh faced horsemen gaped at each other in astonishment.

Sinbad stepped from the carpet, stretching before giving the emperor his deepest salaams. The mandarin rushed forwards. 'Kow-tow!' he growled furiously. 'Abase yourself before Tianzi, Son of Heaven, the mighty emperor of all China. All of you! Prostrate yourselves!'

'Lee Chang!' said the emperor chidingly. 'Let us not stand on ceremony here, O chamberlain, in this our summer palace. Besides, here is the famous traveller Sinbad about whose journeys I have heard many a tale. We shall repair to our palace where a small repast shall be served and Sinbad and his companions may relax after their magical journey. You must tell me all about it,' he added in an undertone, gesturing to Sinbad and the others to follow him.

Pausing only to roll up the carpet, which Ahmed and Sir Acelin carried over their shoulders, Sinbad and the others did as he bade. The mandarin and several of the guards dismounted and followed them within.

'Tell me, O Sinbad,' the emperor said as they sat at a great banqueting board, creaking under the weight of numerous dishes filled with exotic food. 'Is it true that your famous journeys have reached as far as my own realm?'

Sinbad put down his chopsticks, took a sip of rice wine, and glanced at the emperor, trying to conceal a certain weariness. Already he had been asked to tell the tale of his fabled seven voyages, to the delight of the emperor and the feigned pleasure of the empress and the gathered courtiers. He felt nervous relating his more recent adventures.

'I did indeed pass through China a year or two ago, O monarch of the age,' he admitted. 'I was on my way to remote lands to the north of your empire, and China lay along the route.'

The emperor nodded wisely, and looked in the direction of the scowling mandarin, who also sat at the banqueting board. 'Then the reports of my spies, which Lee Chang saw fit to dismiss, were true. Sinbad the Sailor was in my land. When I heard word of your presence, I sent men to find you, but wherever they searched, you were always one step ahead of them, and once you passed out into barbarian lands beyond the Great Wall, they lost all track of you. I was disconsolate! But now you have come back, and this time to see me, of all people!'

Sinbad laughed urbanely. 'O king of the age, you are one of the most famous people in the world. My own fame pales in comparison beside that of the emperor of China. You rule the widest of empires, and your adventures as a young man outdid my own for their magic.'

The emperor looked wistful. 'It seems so long ago,' he said with a sigh, and a fond glance at the empress, a handsome Chinese woman in her middle years, clad in fantastical robes of silk. He reached over and patted her hand but she withdrew it disdainfully. 'And it was only magic that could have worked it.'

The empress snorted, and returned to picking at her food.

'I was not born to all this, as you know,' the emperor went on. 'My father was a poor tailor in one of the cities of Chinese Turkestan. When he died, and only his widow remained to raise me, I must admit I ran wild. Of course,' he added, 'I was known by a different name in those days. My father Mustapha named me Aladdin.'

Ahmed glanced up briefly from guzzling bird's nest soup.

'As you so rightly say, my imperial husband,' said the empress impatiently, 'this was all long ago. With the aid of your sorcerous devices and wicked spirits, you won my hand and became Son of Heaven on my dear father's death. Let us forget your miserable upbringing, and the underhand means you used to make yourself emperor, and think only of the present.'

Sinbad coughed. 'With the greatest respect,' he drawled, 'it was your husband's well-known dealings with the djinn that brought us here.

'Let me explain,' he went on as he became conscious of the eyes of all the courtiers upon him, 'that Princess Abassa, the sister of my own liege lord, the Caliph Harun al-Rashid, has been abducted by the wizard Ja'afar, his former vizier. It is believed that she is his prisoner in the kingdom of the djinn.'

'A wicked magician, eh?' said Aladdin nostalgically. 'How I wish I had been there. I have a short way with such folk, you know. And so your caliph prevailed upon the most famous sailor in the world to go in search of her?' He pursed his lips and shook his head. 'Ah, but this is a voyage beyond even your reach, O Sinbad.'

'Please tell us what you know of the djinn and their country of Djinnistan, O monarch of the age,' Sinbad said. 'It is for that land that we are bound, but we know little except that folk say that it is on the edge of the world.'

'I have never been anywhere near that far,' Aladdin told him, 'and I do not believe that even the African magician whom I knew in my youth had ever visited the kingdom of the Djinn. Yet I spoke much with the djinn when I was young and I learnt from them. It is said that Djinnistan lies amongst the emerald mountains at the edge of the world, the Mountains of Kaf. Its chief province is the Country of Delight, and its capital is Schadou Kiam, the City of Jewels. It is sundered into two parts, the Desert of Monsters and the Desert of Demons. And you say that you believe this Ja'afar you speak of has gone to ground there?'

Sinbad nodded. 'So we believe,' he said. 'Did you ever learn from your consorting with djinn how a man might reach Djinnistan? May I remind you how urgent it is that we rescue the princess?'

Aladdin tugged at his long moustaches, incurring a look of disapproval from his wife. 'I recall somewhat of the route,' he said. 'A long way, even further than the Indies where you have had your adventures. If one were to sail south east from the shores of China, one would eventually reach the Islands of Wak-Wak...'

'Wak-Wak?' said Sinbad with a laugh. 'Is it the home of ducks?'

Aladdin shook his head, smiling merrily. 'It is said that the inhabitants of the greatest of the islands spend their early years growing upon a tree, upon which they are heard to cry out wak! wak! whenever the sun rises, until they reach maturity, whereupon they drop from the tree in the form of fully grown women.'

A shadow crossed his face. 'But before the traveller reaches the fabulous Wak-Wak Islands, he stands in danger from the notorious Black Mountain that stands amid the seas. It is made of adamant and exerts a strange force which iron and steel finds irresistible. Many a vessel has been wrecked upon its cliffs.'

'Even in Arabia,' said Sinbad darkly, 'we have heard tell of the Black Mountain. It is for the reason of avoiding its magnetic spell that we avoid using iron when we build our dhows. But tell me more of the Wak-Wak Islands.'

'It is said that some are the homes of birds, some of wild beasts, one is home to the djinn, while magicians lair in the caves of mountains on another of the islands,' said Aladdin, 'as well as the island of women I have already spoken of. Then there is the island of the serpent queen. Should a traveller survive all these perils, they will find themselves crossing an ocean whose waters are green as jade, as is the sky.'

'Why is it such a strange colour?' asked Nakeya inquisitively.

'Why, O beauteous Abyssinian maid,' said Aladdin, 'it is because of the proximity of the emerald mountains that encircle the world. Sail on across those waters and at last a fortunate traveller will reach the mountains of Kaf. Or perhaps it would be better to say an unfortunate traveller. For he who comes ashore in Djinnistan will encounter perils too numerous to mention. And even then you would have all the mountains of Kaf, the Desert of Monsters and the Desert of Demons, in which to seek your errant princess and her wicked abductor.' He smiled at Sinbad. 'I counsel you: abjure this perilous quest, O sailor. Better that you remain at my court, where you will be forever welcome.'

Sinbad looked pensive.

2 THE WAY TO DJINNISTAN

A day later the carpet was soaring through wet, chilling clouds. Far below it, the landscape changed rapidly to one of seascape as the coast gave way to rolling billows rushing across azure waters. Soon the sea rolled from horizon to horizon, and looking back the way they had come Sinbad saw no sign of land.

Even this high above the waves, he could smell the salty tang of the sea. He breathed deeply, filling his lungs. Looking over the side he peered into the still, deep waters. Again the shadow of the carpet was visible, shooting over the ridges and furrows that corrugated the weed grown sea floor. He had seen a ship's shadow racing along in the same way when he had sailed beyond the Sea of China, beyond the Spice Islands. For a moment he saw a strange coral formation that bore an uncanny resemblance to a castle tower, then it was gone. Absently, he remembered what he had seen years ago in the waters off Pohnpei...

He lounged back on the carpet, looking round at his companions. Sir Acelin was praying, Ahmed was looking keenly about him. Nakeya knelt at the side of the carpet, peering backwards, her eyes serious.

She looked up and caught his gaze. 'It is still a long way to the mountains of Kaf,' she cried over the sigh of the wind. 'Perhaps I could entertain you with an air on my dulcimer.'

She crawled unsteadily to the middle of the carpet where their belongings were piled, and began to play mournfully.

Sinbad had turned down Aladdin's fulsome offer without a qualm. It had been well meant, and he believed that the emperor had been sincere. Aladdin had spoken at length concerning the ways of the djinn, and when they had told him that they carried one with them, imprisoned within the brazen vessel Nakeya carried, he became most animated.

'You have Hadana the grandson of Iblis at your beck and call!' he had exclaimed. 'There must be a tale or two behind that feat. But mark my words, he will not fulfil your desires unless you have a means to command him. Have you any other talisman?'

Ahmed had sighed, and showed the emperor his hand. 'This is the Ring of Ja'afar,' he said. 'I stole it at the urging of the caliph Harun al-Rashid, and yet I wish that I had not. I have no interest in dark sorcery and would rather sell it. And yet no man will buy it.'

'I would not sell it for all the gold in the world,' Aladdin had told him sternly. 'I have a ring of its ilk, aye, and a lamp, too. Both were instrumental in my young days.'

He took the ring from Ahmed.

'You can have it,' said the thief, with a grin. 'For a small consideration.'

'Belay there!' said Sinbad. 'With that ring we control the carpet.'

Aladdin shook his head. 'Nor would I not buy it,' he said to Ahmed, who sighed with regret, 'for all the gold in the world and all the perfumes of Arabia. No, it is your destiny to wear that ring. It will control not only the magic carpet, but also the imprisoned djinn. But not indefinitely. Only three times may you summon the djinn and command him. After that, according to the ancient covenant of Suleiman, he will be free to return to his own kind.'

Nakeya looked disconcerted. 'Then with this ring,' she murmured, taking it from the emperor and sliding it firmly on Ahmed's finger, 'we can make use of Hadana's powers?' She bit her lip doubtfully. 'I would be afraid to see him again.'

'He can't cast a spell on you,' Ahmed assured her, 'as long as I wear this ring.'

'I mislike these dealings in dire sorcery,' Sir Acelin had said softly, and Sinbad had hardly been able to fault him.

Now he gazed covertly at the knight, whose lips still moved in prayer. Then at Ahmed, who was lying back comfortably, gazing at Nakeya as she plucked at her strings. The plaintive melody she played vied with the wailing of the wind for mournfulness. Sinbad sighed to himself. They could not rescue the princess soon enough for him. Snatch her from Ja'afar, fly her back to Baghdad, and then he would bid farewell to his companions. Sir Acelin could ride back to the barbarous countries of the west, Ahmed could slink back to his alleyways in the thieves' quarter, Nakeya could enjoy her freedom. And Sinbad would finally return to his townhouse and his patiently waiting wives. Assuming, that was, that the saucy wenches had not found themselves lovers in his absence...

He looked ahead, eyes caught by the dark mass that had swum into sight on the distant, hazy horizon. The carpet lurched suddenly, sending Nakeya tumbling undignifiedly into Ahmed's flank. Her dulcimer bounced across the carpet and plunged over the side. Ahmed leapt to grab a hold of it as it went but was flung from the carpet by another lurch, snatching a stray tassel in his left hand only just in time. Sinbad seized a hold of Nakeya, who was showing signs of following him, but they were both knocked flat by Sir Acelin's mailed form as it crashed into them. The knight went plunging over the side.

Nakeya clung to Sinbad, eyes very big. The carpet was pitching downwards, spiralling through the air. 'What's happening?' she shrieked. 'We're falling into the sea!'

'No, we're not!' Sinbad said urgently. 'Look!'

Nakeya turned and her eyes widened, her lips parted but no sound came out. Sinbad could understand how she felt.

The darkness on the horizon had resolved itself into a towering high mountain, black as jet —or adamant.

'The Black Mountain!' Nakeya said wildly, as the carpet plummeted still further towards the sea. 'Aladdin warned us of it...! Why have we gone this way?'

'This is the way we have to go to get to Djinnistan!' Sinbad said. 'But I thought it was no threat to us. We're not in a ship, and we're flying over it.'

'But something is drawing us towards it.'

'I think I have an idea what it is,' said Sinbad grimly, crawling to the edge of the carpet where Ahmed's hand was just visible, clinging on. Peering over the edge, he saw the white faced thief hanging desperately from the tassels by one hand, while beneath him, his heavy weight causing him to swing back and forth in the cold sea air like a pendulum, gripping tightly onto the thief's legs, was the mailed form of Sir Acelin.

Ahmed looked upwards. 'Sinbad!' he yelled over the howling wind. 'You've got to help us!'

The carpet shot through the air like a stone flung by a ballista, whizzing towards the Black Mountain. As if by magic, Sinbad's scimitar leapt from its sheath and went whirling away into the sky. He groaned.

'My sword! And Sir Acelin's armour! The iron in them is being drawn towards the adamant by its magnetism!'

Nakeya gasped. 'We've got to get them back up here!' she cried.

'We've got to get Sir Acelin out of his armour,' Sinbad countered. 'A good thing we have so few other iron belongings. Luckily that vessel where you keep the djinn is of brass, the stopper of lead.'

Nakeya bit her lip. 'Do you think...?' she murmured. 'Do you think Hadana would help us?'

The Black Mountain was whirling ever closer. 'This is no time for meddling with dark forces,' Sinbad said reprovingly. He began climbing down, using the complaining Ahmed as if he was a ladder.

'I'd have thought it was the best time!' Nakeya cried. 'Ahmed, give me your ring.'

Ahmed's reply was muffled by Sinbad's chest, which was in front of his face, but it didn't sound complimentary.

Clinging on to Ahmed's legs, Sinbad came alongside Sir Acelin. The knight peered up at him, blinking in the harsh light of the sun which flashed on the visor of his helmet.

'Doff that helm, sir knight,' Sinbad said, but the roar of the wind was so loud that Sir Acelin could only shake his head dumbly to indicate his incomprehension. Impatiently, Sinbad reached out for the chinstrap of the knight's helmet. Panicked, Sir Acelin seized his wrist in a gauntleted hand and tried to fend him off. Sinbad fought back, and just succeeded in forcing the rawhide strap over Sir Acelin's chin. The helmet whipped away into the blue yonder, snatched by the invisible force of the adamantine mountain.

Sir Acelin's pale face gazed painedly into Sinbad's own. 'Off with it!' Sinbad bellowed angrily. 'All of it! All of your armour, you cursed infidel!'

Sir Acelin seemed to catch something of this, and comprehension dawned on his face. He took one look at the rapidly nearing Black Mountain, at the helmet still spinning straight towards it. They heard the clang as the helmet struck it, distant as it was. But the black cliff was drawing ever closer.

Sir Acelin unbelted his scabbard and dropped his sword, which instantly whirled away, then began struggling out of his mail coat. Sinbad did his best to help him but it was almost impossible. Single handed, Sir Acelin wormed his way out of his mail, but as he did so, his grip on Ahmed's legs weakened, and abruptly he fell, leaving Sinbad clinging on to it.

Sinbad gasped as he saw Sir Acelin falling towards the water. Still the carpet shot helplessly towards the Black Mountain. Sinbad watched numbly, overweighed by the mail coat he held in his hand.

'Sinbad!'

Nakeya's voice broke into his thoughts. 'Sinbad, let go of the mail coat! Or we'll be dashed against the cliff!'

Sinbad shook his head, coming to himself. His hand was cold, seemingly frozen to the mail. With an immense effort he let go, and the mail coat plummeted, then was whipped away to smash into the black cliff with a ringing sound.

With Ahmed's help he clambered back onto the carpet, the thief alongside him. With a stilted stuttering salaam, Ahmed set down the dulcimer in Nakeya's lap.

'My thanks!' she said.

Sir Acelin was still plummeting towards the spreading waters beneath the black cliff, but the carpet floating placidly in mid-air.

'Ahmed!' Sinbad shouted. 'Your ring! Speak to the carpet—tell it to fly down and pick up Sir Acelin.'

Ahmed gave the order and the carpet swooped downwards, hurtling towards the water, then shot straight up under Sir Acelin's plummeting form. It shook with an almighty thump as the falling knight landed atop it. The impact was almost enough to pitch the others over the side, and a second time Ahmed snatched a hold of one of the tassels to avoid falling into the water. So close they were to the surface of the rolling sea that his shoes were soaked as he was dragged along.

'Up!' he shouted, and the carpet began to rise. Sinbad flung out a hand and gripped onto Ahmed's wrist, helping him climb back onto the carpet. As they circled round the vast black shape of the adamantine mountain, Nakeya knelt beside Sir Acelin's semi-conscious form, dabbing at his brow with a wet rag. Sinbad and Ahmed squatted beside them.

The Black Mountain receded into the distance as the carpet flew on. They had successfully passed the first challenge, but almost at the cost of their lives. Now their knight companion was weaponless and unarmoured, and seemingly incapacitated.

Sir Acelin's eyes flicked open. 'Mon Dieu!' he murmured. 'Am I in heaven?' He focused on Nakeya. 'Surely it is the Saracen paradise, for this is the most beautiful houri my eyes have ever beheld!'

She flushed at his words, her skin growing darker. 'The fall has surely addled his wits,' she murmured dismissively, and lifted up her dulcimer. Inspected it for signs of damage, and took up her plaintive air once more.

They flew onwards in a silence broken only by the wind and the strains of Nakeya's dulcimer. As the sun began to set, Ahmed commanded the carpet to hover over the sea while they took turns to sleep. Sir Acelin took first watch, waking Sinbad somewhere around midnight, but the knight did not roll himself in his cloak at once. Instead he sat beside Sinbad as the sailor gazed out at the rolling black waters, spangled with glittering reflections of the stars. It was a sultry night, and now the wind had dropped and the carpet was stationary Sinbad revelled in the warmth of the air on his skin.

'By Mountjoy and St Denis, I am as naked as a babe without my armour,' said Sir Acelin, who had forgiven the sailor his angry words. 'I have lost much on this voyage. Loyal companions, and now my armour, which was a legacy from my father.' He turned to look at Sinbad, and the sailor saw the gleam of his eyes as he studied him. 'My liege lord bade me to protect you on your journey home. And when I heard of the princess' abduction I knew that I could not simply turn and ride back to my home country. But it has taken me further and into weirder and wilder lands than ever I dreamt of.' He paused, then added, 'I suppose that these seas are familiar to one so well-travelled as you, O Sinbad.'

'I've sailed the seven seas,' Sinbad said, 'yet we are in strange waters now. Even my journeys have never taken me this far. Not one of the fleetest of ships of the Arabs has sailed as far as Djinnistan, and we must be a long way past even the furthest east I have travelled.' He shrugged. 'Much of my adventurous life has taken me to uncharted seas. For all I know I have been this way before. But the Black Mountain is something I had never seen, although I have heard the tales, of course.'

'I am a knight,' Sir Acelin said bitterly. 'I have seen battle and strife. Never before have I felt fear for my life, since I have always believed that if I die fighting for justice I will go to Our Lord. But when I thought I would drown in the waters of the sea, I was afraid. Do you hear me, Sinbad? It was then that I felt fear's cold hand for the first time.'

Sinbad clapped him on the back. 'Every man feels fear sooner or later,' he told him with a grim smile. 'It's no victory to be brave if you feel no fear. What makes a man courageous is to feel fear and face it, fight it and conquer it. It's time you slept. Tomorrow will look different.'

In the morning, Nakeya, who had taken the last watch, awoke them all. Nothing was left of the provisions they had brought with them from China, which had fallen into the sea, but Ahmed produced a hastily cobbled together rod and fished from the side of the carpet as it hovered directly above the calm waters. Cooking his catch proved difficult, and they were forced to eat the fish raw. Such was the custom in the isles of Al-Yaban, off the coast of China, as Sinbad told them in reminiscent mood.

Bellies full, they flew on as the sun rose high above them. The dark shadow of the carpet flitted across the spreading waters, and the blue sky gleamed brightly. Thinking he detected a hint of green in the cerulean vault, Sinbad peered eastwards in the hopes that the emerald peaks of the mountains of Kaf might hove into view. He was disappointed on that count, but he spied something else.

'Ahoy!' he cried, in his excitement shouting out as if he was aboard his dhow and had a full crew to command. They followed his gaze.

On the horizon loomed the grey tumbledown bluffs of an island. And as the carpet flew closer, the discordant squawking of birds reached their ears.

3 THE ISLAND OF BIRDS

'This must be the first of the islands Aladdin told us about,' said Nakeya.

'You're right,' said Sinbad, raising his voice as the shrieking of the creatures reached a deafening pitch. 'The first of seven islands, the emperor told us. We must fly over them before we reach the green sea beyond which lie the mountains of Kaf.'

'Can we not go any higher?' Ahmed said after a moment, as a waft of stinking guano from the island reached their nostrils. Nakeya made a moue of disgust and pinched her nose.

Sinbad turned to Ahmed. 'You're the one with the magic ring,' he reminded him curtly.

'Carpet of Suleiman—arise!' Ahmed called out, and soon they were flying high above the island.

It was a craggy, barren looking place, with only rough turf and stunted trees covering its rocky eminences. On all sides were high cliffs and bluffs where sea birds congregated in their shrieking thousands, albatross and boobies, crakes, frigatebirds and kittiwakes and herons and petrels puffins and guillemots and shearwaters, and many more. Some had nests built on ledges, so many of them that the bluffs were veritable cities of birds.

Other birds circled in the air above them, and the carpet was forced to fly even higher to avoid these flocks. The trees inland were bowed under by more birds, and even more were visible nesting on the turf itself, some winged, some flightless: cassowaries and emus, bustards and buttonquails, drongos and hoopoes and trogons, shrikes and doves, birds of paradise, sunbirds, and fairy bluebirds amongst many more.

'Sacre bleu! This place is foul,' said Sir Acelin, and Sinbad did not think that the knight was speaking ironically. 'I can think of nowhere further in spirit from Aladdin's paradise in China. The hand of man has never tamed this land, it is the home of birds alone. But it affords us an opportunity.'

'An opportunity?' Ahmed said sardonically. 'The only opportunity I can think of is to fly out of here as soon as possible.'

'But we have had no food since our contretemps with the Black Mountain,' Sir Acelin reminded them all. 'And furthermore, no fuel. What food we have eaten recently has been raw, and I do not believe it was good for our bellies. I myself have been troubled with the bellyache.

But here we have fuel and food in abundance.'

'You can't mean those birds,' Nakeya protested. 'There are so many of them!'

But he nodded. 'That—or their eggs,' he said. 'There are many of them indeed, surely sufficient for our needs, and also there is wood. Let us land near the trees and light a fire, and see what birds we can catch.'

Ahmed looked to Sinbad. The sailor nodded thoughtfully. 'It's a good plan,' he said. 'Take us down. I could do with a change from raw fish.'

With a sigh, Ahmed gave his commands to the carpet, and soon they were descending.

The stink of guano grew stronger, and Sinbad wondered if he would be able to stomach anything he ate on the island, assuming they caught any birds or found any eggs. But by the time the carpet landed with a gentle bump on the grass sward amid shrieking flocks of birds and a gentle wind, he discovered that either the miasma of foul odours had been blown out to sea by the wind or else he was growing accustomed to it.

He rose and stretched, covering a yawn with one hand. The birds that had flown up on all sides shrieking during their descent had now settled back on their perches. Now despite a hubbub of bird calls, it was much quieter, and he stepped off the carpet and onto the grass with a sense of relief to be on firm ground again.

A grove of stunted trees stood nearby, boles

twisted and bowed by the sea winds. In the distance, Sinbad glimpsed the blue grey wastes of the ocean rolling as far as the shimmering horizon. The sky above was filled with circling birds, and from the distant cliffs came a constant clamour.

'Nakeya, Ahmed, see what firewood you can find beneath those trees,' he told them. 'Sir Acelin, you and I will forage for food.'

He picked up a fallen branch and hefted it in his hand. It was no substitute for the scimitar he had lost to the adamantine mountain, but it was heavy enough to make a good cudgel. Any birds that tried to peck at him would regret their importunacy. And perhaps, he mused, he could use it as a throwing stick of the kind he had seen wielded by the islanders in the remote southern country of Luca Antara.

When they returned half an hour later, carrying a brace of boobies while nursing a few pecks and scratches, they found Ahmed had constructed a windbreak using the magic carpet and several wooden stakes. In its lee a fire was burning smokily. Beneath the impromptu canopy Nakeya was plucking dulcetly at the strings of her dulcimer, eyes dreamily fixed on the enigmatic horizon, while Ahmed was covertly studying her serious face. The thief sprang to his feet suddenly as the Arab and the Frank trudged up to join them, and Nakeya looked up in turn, a broad smile transforming her grave features.

'Success!' Ahmed crowed, dancing up to inspect their catch. 'Personally I saw nothing wrong with fish, but each to their own. The fire's ready.'

He frowned at the slender rivulet of blood that ran down Sir Acelin's face. 'That looks very nasty,' he commented with a chuckle, as they sat down by the fire and began plucking the first of the boobies. 'The birds didn't yield their tribute without a fight, then?'

Sinbad gave him a rueful look. 'They mobbed us,' he admitted. 'We went down to the cliffs to forage for eggs, but with no success. Frigatebirds ganged up to drive us away. On the way back, tails between our legs after our ignominious defeat, we found a placid flock of boobies amongst the trees, and catching them proved a much easier business.'

As Nakeya tended to the knight's fresh battle wounds, he gutted the first booby, and spitted it over the fire. Soon they were sharing cooked bird flesh between them, eating with their fingers in lieu of the costly table utensils that Aladdin had given them on their departure. The flesh stank and it was of the texture of rotting leather, and it tasted of rotting fish, but in their hunger they managed to swallow it all without vomiting.

Ahmed pulled a face. 'Anything's better than this foul fowl flesh.'

Sinbad regaled them with the famous tale

of his encounters with the roc, that bird so huge it could snatch up goats or even entire elephants, carry them off to its nest and tear it apart to feed its young.

'But the floor of the deep, steep valley where dwelt the one who carried me off was littered with diamonds, and there were men, foreign merchants, who harvested the jewels by flinging in hunks of meat in which diamonds would stick, and when the rocs carried the meat to their nests, these brave fellows would drive the birds off and take back the meat loaded with diamonds. When they flung in one carcase, I strapped myself to it and was carried upwards to a nest by a roc. Rescued from the next by these merchants, I finally made my triumphal return to Baghdad with a fortune in diamonds.'

Ahmed spat into the fire. 'And even that wasn't enough to put you off travelling,' he muttered to himself. 'There's no hope for some people.'

Sinbad rose to his feet, smiling blandly. 'Time we were on our way,' he told his companions.

They had smoked the meat of the remaining boobies in the hopes that it would both preserve them and improve the flavour. He packed it into a satchel while Ahmed and Sir Acelin took down the carpet and spread it out on the turf. The circling birds set up a renewed squawking as Ahmed said;

'Carpet of Suleiman—rise!' and the carpet began to lift.

But as they were cresting the rise of bluffs in the centre of the isle, a more frenzied squawking met their ears. They rose high enough to see the sweep of the islands down to the further shore, and the sea beyond. Rapidly crossing the choppy waters in the direction of the shrieking birds was what looked to Sinbad's eyes to be nothing so much as a waterspout, but when it reached the shore it looked instead to be a whirlwind of green vapour. And yet there was barely a breath of wind over that hot and foul-smelling island.

'What is it?' asked Sir Acelin.

'It's coming closer,' said Ahmed uneasily. 'I don't like the look of it.'

Sinbad felt an awful sense of recognition. He had seen something like it before. But before he could open his mouth to speak, Nakeya said:

'Look!'

Screeching birds flying up all around it, the whirlwind was now tearing across the island towards them. And now huge features were visible amongst that swirl of air. A great grinning jowled evil green face, a grossly fat body, great trunk like arms and legs.

'A flying djinn!' yelled Ahmed, raising the hand on which he wore the ring. 'O Carpet of Suleiman—take us away from here!'

The carpet banked suddenly and turned about, flying out to sea. The djinn made a course correction. They could now hear the roar of the wind, and a great booming laugh that went on and on.

'Hahahahahahahahahaha!' it roared. 'Hahahahahahahahahaha! Hahahahahahahahahaha!'

'This is the djinn I saw in Baghdad,' yelled Sinbad, 'or at least his kissing cousin.'

'The one who bore off the princess?' shouted Sir Acelin. His hand went vainly to his side where his sword had once hung. 'Then it must mean that we are close to Djinnistan!'

'But what can we do now?' Nakeya shrieked. 'We're in no position to fight, and it's coming after us.'

They were above the water now, and the isle of birds behind them was a chaos of shrieking avians as the djinn tore after them. Now the djinn was above the water, which churned and threshed in its wake, great turbulent waves as if a storm had struck it. Ahmed urged the carpet to fly faster, but anyone could see that the djinn was gaining on them. Its laughter rose to a deafening pitch.

'We go against all the laws of chivalry,' Sir Acelin cried. 'We must turn and fight!'

'With what?' Ahmed demanded. 'We're weaponless, and I doubt swords would make a mark on that thing even if we had any!'

Sinbad looked troubled. 'This creature is a thing of magic,' he said. 'In which case, it must be fought by magic.' He turned to Nakeya. 'We must call Hadana to aid us.'

Nakeya gasped. 'But he will only come to us three times, then he will never help us again.'

'Yes, girl,' said Sinbad roughly. 'There is no other way. Where is your vessel?'

Unwillingly, she produced it. Sinbad turned to Ahmed. 'With your ring we can control Hadana. As soon as the marid appears, tell him, in the name Bismillah Alruhmin Alrahim, to save us from our foe.'

'You can't just say that,' Nakeya warned them. 'You must be careful about your wording. Tell Hadana to attack the djinn that pursues us!'

Her last words were almost blown away by the wind. Turning Sinbad saw the grinning green face of the djinn taking up the entire sky. 'Do it!' he shouted at Nakeya. 'Open the vessel!'

Teeth gritted, Nakeya hauled out the lead stopper. A loud popping sound was audible even over the roaring sound of the encroaching djinn, whose green misty fingers were reaching for the carpet.

For a moment there was nothing. Then, with a hissing sound, a dark cloud poured from out of the brazen vessel, rapidly growing in size until a saturnine youth stood in sombre garb before them on the carpet. He turned to Nakeya and smiled sweetly.

'O my love!' Hadana boomed. 'You have freed me from my prison! Now I shall carry you off to my palace in the sands of Africa, my dear one, where we shall dwell in bliss for all time!'

'Ahmed!' Sinbad yelled. Even as Ahmed lifted up his ringed hand and spoke the magical phrase, the carpet shuddered in the wind of the djinn, and Sinbad was flung over the side. He seized hold of a passing tassel and clung on frantically.

'Bismillah Alruhmin Alrahim!' Ahmed cried. 'Hadana, attack the djinn!'

'What, now?' the marid roared.

'Yes,' Ahmed shrilled. 'Now!'

'O very well, by Iblis! To hear is to obey, O Son of Adam!'

Scowling petulantly, Hadana leapt into the air, bat wings bursting from beneath his black cloak, ferocious talons appearing from his fingertips.

'Zoba'ah Abu Hasan!' he boomed. 'I know thee, cur! Slave of sorcerers! Cursed interrupter of trysts! Prepare to meet thy match!'

As the marid flung himself at the pursuing djinn, the carpet shook and shuddered in the great wind of his passing. And as Hadana and Zoba'ah Abu Hasan's tussling figures tumbled away into the great blue vault of the sky, growing smaller and smaller until they were little more than dots, barely distinguishable from the surrounding sky, Sinbad's grip on the tassel weakened, and with a cry he fell down towards the spreading sea.

'Sinbad!' Sir Acelin shouted, scrambling forward with hand outstretched to seize his wrist. But Sinbad was gone. And in his vain attempts to rescue the plummeting figure, Sir Acelin overbalanced and he too fell into the abyss.

Nakeya ran to the side, but Ahmed gripped her by her shoulders as she prepared to dive. He shook her.

'They're both gone!' he shouted, gesturing at the turbulent waters far below. There was no sign of Sinbad or Sir Acelin. 'No sense in throwing yourself after them.'

Nakeya broke free of his grip. 'You despicable coward!' she cried. 'Take us down after them!'

Ahmed shook his head. 'No one could have survived that fall,' he said brutally. 'They must both have drowned.'

'I won't believe it,' Nakeya said. 'Take us down. We must rescue them.'

Ahmed shook his head. 'The sea is deep, we will never find them. Something I learnt growing up in the thieves' quarter was when to cut my losses. Better we forget Sinbad and the knight and look to our own safety.'

4 THE ISLAND OF BEASTS

Without any warning, a vortex of air appeared swirling above the carpet of Suleiman. Ahmed cowered back, Nakeya cried out in horror. Then it spun itself into a funnel shape, hovering directly above Nakeya's brazen vessel which she still clutched, and rapidly vanished inside.

'Hadana,' said Ahmed. 'He must have defeated the other djinn, or at least driven him off. Put the stopper back in!'

'He is what we need.' Nakeya's hand hovered over the hole. 'Hadana could help us find the others...'

Ahmed seized her hand. 'We have only two more chances to summon him. Don't waste them. If Sinbad and Sir Acelin are going to turn up, they will do.'

He took the stopper from her hand and thrust it firmly into the hole. Then he raised his ringed hand. 'Carpet of Suleiman! Take us to yonder island!'

Shortly afterwards they were hovering over another island. This was not infested by birds of all species, but looked lush and inviting, rolling, forested hills making up the most part of it, while a river rushed down from a central peak. They landed on the beach.

'Why did you bring us here?' Nakeya asked. 'I would have thought you would want to fly back to your own city, and take up your squalid life of thieving again.'

Ahmed looked pained. 'I want to find the others as much as you do,' he said.

'That wasn't what you said earlier,' Nakeya reminded him. 'When you refused to search for them.'

'I was upset,' he said. 'Besides, it would be futile searching the water from the carpet. Before we got close enough to locate them, the carpet would be drenched, and not all the magic in the world would keep it aloft. Better that we make ourselves some kind of raft and paddle back to look for them.'

Nakeya bit her lip as if she doubted his words. 'Very well,' she said, looking up at the treeline that came down as far as the edge of the beach. 'But how do we do that?'

Ahmed stepped off the carpet onto the white sand. 'It'll be easy,' he said, holding out a hand to help her down. 'You've heard Sinbad's stories, haven't you? He always builds a raft when he's shipwrecked.'

Nakeya allowed him to help her down, and hand in hand they walked up the beach, gazing at the trees that towered inland. All was still. Not a breath of wind stirred the sultry air. All they heard was the soft crunch of their feet in the brilliant white sand.

A roar rang out from the trees. Frightened Ahmed clung to Nakeya as a shrieking wail ensued, followed by the threshing sound of some beast fighting for its life. Then a sullen, brooding silence descended over the trees and they heard no more.

Disdainfully Nakeya pushed Ahmed away. 'You really are a coward,' she said accusingly. 'Get your hands off me!'

'This island is inhabited by worse horrors than the last,' said Ahmed, disregarding the insult. 'We should go back to the carpet.'

'Oh no,' said Nakeya firmly. 'We're going to build a raft and then we're going to search for Sinbad and Sir Acelin. I know Sinbad can swim, and I hope that Sir Acelin can too. Maybe they're trying to keep afloat even now. So there's all the more urgency in getting that raft built.'

Fearless, she strode up the beach. Ahmed stared after her in horror. He looked about. Sea and sand and forest was all he saw, that and the overarching, pitiless sky. Ahmed thought fondly of the winding alleys of the thieves' quarter, where a man might have his purse cut and his throat slit before taking two steps. How he wished he was back in those more congenial climes!

The Abyssinian girl had reached the trees. Ahmed sighed. 'Wait for me!' he yelled, and ran after her.

He found her staring up at a tall tree. 'What do we do?' she asked him. 'Cut it down?'

Ahmed shook his head. 'We've got no way to do that,' he said. 'No axe, no saw. What we need to do,' he added, eyeing the awesome gloom beneath the trees, 'is to find enough fallen wood to bind together into a raft. Then we can set out across the water in the direction of the Island of Birds.'

They began walking. Ahmed, in his heart of hearts, knew that he knew nothing about building rafts, but he was not prepared to let Nakeya know that. The haughty Abyssinian had already made it clear she had little time for him.

'I suppose,' said Nakeya, after they had walked up the wooded slope for several minutes, 'this must be what Aladdin called the Island of Beasts. And that roar we heard was one of the beasts in question.'

'I suppose you're right,' said Ahmed fearfully, looking about them. It was dark on all sides except back the way they had come. He caught a glimpse of the shore and the rolling surf beyond. 'What's that?' he cried, pointing.

A canoe was visible, out to sea. Long enough to contain a score of rowers, who were all bend-ing their backs as they passed, as far as Ahmed could discern, but it was too far off to make out much. Several more followed.

'This island is inhabited after all,' he said, 'and by men as well as beasts.'

'You don't know they were men,' said Nakeya darkly. 'And you don't know they dwell on this island. They're sailing past. For all we know they come from some other island. If you remember what Aladdin said…'

'Aladdin, Aladdin, Aladdin,' Ahmed mocked her. 'Never mind what the emperor said. Don't you see? These natives have canoes. We should stop them and ask them to help us search for Sinbad. Come on.'

He led Nakeya at a run through the trees, back the way they had come. The crashing if their passing, as they stepped on fallen twigs and forced their way through undergrowth, made a terrible clamour that broke the expectant hush. As he ran, Ahmed saw that they had climbed higher than he had realised. The beach was a long way down the slope. That was when he heard, over the din of their own descent, stealthy sounds from the undergrowth.

'Wait!' he said, putting up a hand for quiet. Unable to stop herself, Nakeya cannoned into him and they both fell sprawling to the mulch.

Nakeya got up into a crouch, peering over Ahmed's head. Dusting himself down, Ahmed rose.

'Stay still!' Nakeya hissed. She was looking over his shoulder. Ahmed froze.

'What in Allah's name is it?' he whispered.

'Slowly—very slowly—turn around,' she urged him.

Ahmed did as she bade, turning inch by inch until he was looking in the opposite direction. The blood seemed to stop flowing in his veins when he saw it. Crouching on the tree branch above them, moving slowly, stealthily, lambent eyes intent on them, long tail twitching back and forth as it prepared itself to spring, a great cat of some kind, its tawny hide spotted with black.

The big cat gathered itself together, ready to leapt at the two motionless trespassers in its domain. Then suddenly there was a roar from elsewhere in the forest and the scampering of tiny hoofs. And they came leaping past them, under them, over, them, almost bowling them over in their rush: dozens of delicate deer like creatures, running as fast as they can from the huge lion crashing after them. Ahmed and Nakeya cowered as it leapt upon one deer and brought it down, snapped its neck with a single blow of its paw, tearing at its side with long incisors even as the deer was still in its death throes.

With a snarl, the cat on the tree branch turned and slunk away into the gloom.

Still the lion tore at the deer's carcase, the fur around his mouth black with blood. Nakeya looked at Ahmed. He gestured with a sideways nod of his in the direction of the beach. Slowly they got to their feet and began making their way down the slope.

The lion lifted his bloody jaws, shook his mane, and gave a deafening roar. They spun round and froze. The wild beast was gazing at them, its eyes full of a strange wisdom beyond that of the greatest Sufis and mystics. Then, insouciantly, the lion shook his mane again and buried his face hungrily in the gory hole in the deer's flank.

'Come on,' said Nakeya, seizing Ahmed's hand in a surprisingly strong grip, and they hurried away down the wooded slope.

They came out into bright sunlight, their feet crunching again in the sand. The sea rolled away to the horizon, where distant dots circled and wheeled in a column that marked the site of their previous landfall. Of canoes the dancing waters were entirely bare.

Ahmed flung himself down on the sand, and after patiently watching the water a while, Nakeya sat down beside him.

'By now, surely our friends are drowned,' she said in a desolate voice.

Ahmed opened one eye. 'Are you suggesting we give up the search?' he asked.

'Search!' Nakeya said. 'We've made little headway with any search. Instead all we've done is find that we are on an island inhabited by savage beasts who dedicate all their time to hunting and eating each other—and us! We aren't safe here.'

Ahmed got up and examined the sand.

'No sign of pawprints,' he reported after a while. 'Those creatures must stay in their forests. We're safe from them. But...'

'But?' Nakeya echoed inquisitively, shading her eyes as she looked up from where she sat.

Ahmed's eyes were guarded. 'People have passed by since last we were here,' he said slowly. 'I found footprints, and signs that something had been cast up out of the sea, and the mark of where canoes were dragged ashore. And Nakeya...'

'What is it?' she said urgently.

'I can't seem to find the carpet.'

She sprang up, staring at him.

'Are you sure?' she cried. 'Have you looked?'

'Of course I've looked,' he said impatiently. 'There's no sign of it!'

Nakeya hunted up and down the sand while Ahmed watched in brooding silence. At last she turned to face him. 'They must have taken it.'

'The men we saw?' Ahmed asked.

'If they were indeed men,' said Nakeya ominously. 'Some of them came ashore here for some reason and while we were gone they found the carpet. We should have left one of us on guard here.'

'Never mind that,' said Ahmed. 'We've got to

find them.'

'The footsteps lead this way,' said Nakeya, pointing towards a wooded headland that jutted out into the bay.

'Footprints,' said Ahmed. 'Not footsteps. You hear footsteps, you see footprints.'

She stared at him as if he was mad. 'They go this way, whatever you choose to call them.'

'You're right,' Ahmed conceded. 'And that's the way we must go.'

'Are you sure?' Nakeya asked. 'We don't know who they are or what they're capable of. And we're unarmed.' She looked doleful. 'We don't even have my dulcimer.'

'We must be thankful for small mercies,' said Ahmed piously as he began trudging up the beach. She scowled at his retreating back but followed him.

Rounding the headland they saw a pillar of smoke rising into the sky from a long way down the wide beach that opened up beyond it. Shading his eyes, Ahmed saw that a group of figures was camped in the lee of the forest that swathed the slopes above them. Near the camp was the mouth of the river that ran down from somewhere beneath the rugged peak. A single canoe was visible on the sand nearby.

'Can you see the carpet?' asked Nakeya.

'I can't even make them out, really,' said Ahmed. Light flashed on something held by one of the far off figures. 'But they're armed.'

'And we're not,' Nakeya murmured. 'Well, we must go and speak with them.'

'They could be cannibals,' said Ahmed.

'I don't think so,' said Nakeya. She rose and began to walk through the trees that grew closest to the beach. Ahmed followed her, walking as quietly as he could, but all his skills as a thief were frustrated by the forest. Sticks snapped under his tread, vines caught his ankles, undergrowth rustled portentously. From time to time they heard roaring from deeper into the interior, the uproar of hunter and hunted, a grisly song of death and devourment.

They heard a crashing noise from up above, followed by another and another. Ahmed looked up to see the brown shapes of moneys whizzing past as they leapt from branch to branch. One monkey chased another, shrieking angrily. Another jumped with a crash through the leaves and landed on the branch beside a third, who was dozing, but awoke with a wail and shot up the tree bole.

Something larger and darker crashed through the trees. Suddenly all the scurrying monkeys vanished into the treetops. The larger creature was swinging through the trees towards Ahmed and Nakeya. What it was they could not make out, since it was obscured by a green tracery of leaves that thrashed as it proceeded, but it gave an impression of being big and savage.

'Come on,' said Ahmed urgently, and together they hurried away into the undergrowth.

By the time they reached a spot overlooking the camp, the sun was setting, staining the western ocean a lurid blood red, foreshadowing great slaughter, and shadows were lengthening on the edge of the forest. The roars and howls and shrieks of beasts deeper within the forest were distinctly audible, and Ahmed jumped with fright at every one. After a while, he became convinced that something was following them through the tree canopy, but Nakeya laughed at him.

Lying on the edge of a bluff, they looked down, seeing the river winding past, where two figures were filling waterskins, and the camp itself where the people from the canoe were sitting around a smoking fire, eating and drinking. In the trees nearby patrolled guards, spears in hand. Some of the people were talking, two of them dominating the discussion. One seemed to want to go deeper into the wood, the other seemed to think taking to the water again was a better option.

'There!' said Nakeya.

Ahmed followed her pointing finger and saw, rolled up on the sand by the fire, the unregarded bundle of the carpet. Beside it were the rest of their possessions, including the brazen vessel that contained the marid Hadana.

He frowned. There was something odd

about these people that he couldn't quite put his finger on. Then he realised it.

'They're all women,' he muttered in surprise. 'Women, with spears and wearing armour.'

'If you'd paid more attention to Aladdin,' Nakeya said waspishly, 'you'd remember that he told us about an island of women.'

'But this isn't it, surely,' Ahmed protested as another reverberant roar echoed from deep in the trees. 'This can only be the island of beasts.'

'But it is to be presumed that these visitors have come from the island of women,' said Nakeya patiently.

Ahmed opened his mouth to say something cutting, but he broke off. Nakeya glanced at him. He looked meaningfully over his shoulder.

A woman warrior was standing astride him, holding a spear to his back. Its wickedly sharp point was pricking directly between his shoulder blades.

5 THE ISLAND OF DJINN

Two more warrior women emerged from the gathering gloom, seizing Ahmed and Nakeya. Protesting, the latter were bundled into the camp. More women sprang up, spears in hand as the patrol entered the firelight, the kicking, struggling forms held over their shoulders. Their hair was long and black and coarse, their skins dark brown, not as dark as Nakeya's, but darker than any Indian's, while their eyes were almond and their faces had a cast to them reminiscent of the people of Aladdin's empire. They all wore lamellar armour.

One tall woman who wore a winged helmet sprang up from her place by the fire. She prowled up to the three warriors with their captives, and gestured for them to be flung to the ground.

Ahmed landed painfully beside Nakeya. He peered up at the woman in the winged helmet. She seemed to be a leader of some sort. 'What do you want with us?' he asked.

Surprisingly, the woman replied in guttural,

thickly accented Arabic. 'We have been looking for you. We knew there were more interlopers.'

'More?' asked Nakeya. 'What do you mean?'

Another woman joined them, this one wearing a helmet like the leader but this one wingless. 'I tell you, Mawmas, we should kill them here and follow the rest back to Wak-Wak. We have one prisoner. Any more would only mean more mouths to feed.'

'And I tell you, Fyraju,' said the woman in the winged helmet, 'that I am in command here. I told you we should search the forest for the interlopers, and now they have been found. Now they will be taken back to the queen to be questioned as to how they came into our islands. Only then will they be slain.'

'May I ask a question?' Ahmed said, smiling his most charming smile. 'Before you kill us out of hand, here or elsewhere, let me tell you that we are looking for two of our companions who were lost at sea. Did I hear you aright? You found others like us?'

'One other,' the woman named Mawmas corrected him. 'We were with a larger cohort of women, patrolling the islands as is our wont. Reaching this shore we saw a body washed up on the shore. Investigating, we saw that it was a man, half drowned but still living. He was taken to our chief island of Wak-Wak for interrogation and execution by our queen, Noor al-Hudha, while my women were left behind to search the beach for signs of other intruders. We found your belongings but no sign of you other than footprints leading into the forest of beasts…'

'This man you found,' Nakeya said. 'Can you describe him to me?' She looked meaningly at Ahmed. 'It could be Sinbad.'

Ahmed nodded excitedly. 'Or Sir Acelin.' He turned to Mawmas. 'What did he look like? Was he an Arab like me? Or a long nosed Frank from far off infidel lands?'

Mawmas frowned. 'I did not see him but from a distance,' she said dismissively. 'He was an interloper—as are you. It is the law of our queen that all men who trespass on our islands must die.'

Ahmed swallowed audibly. 'That must cause problems,' he said with a laugh. 'I mean, where do little warrior maidens come from if you kill all men?'

'You ask many questions,' said Fyraju. 'I say this, Mawmas, we should kill the man here and now. The woman can be spared but she will have questions to answer from Queen Noor al-Hudha.'

A crashing came from the nearby trees, and a huge ape leapt down and stood before them on all fours, eyes wide, fascinated by the light of the fire. Women sprang up, spears at the ready, and rushed forwards shouting. Mawmas shouted orders urgently, gesturing with her sword.

Nakeya rolled over to Ahmed. 'You were right—we were being followed! Now's our chance!'

She indicated the carpet, which lay beside the camp fire. Women warriors were racing towards the great ape, who had seized two of their comrades and was hugging them brutally to his hairy chest. Two loud snaps rang out and the women's corpses dropped to the ground. The great ape faced the other women, leering and drooling.

Ahmed nodded, and together they ran towards the carpet. A figure stepped into the firelight, spear levelled. A helmet glinted on her head.

'Leaving us?' said Fyraju with a sneer. 'I think not. All men who trespass in our land must die!'

She lunged at Ahmed, who leapt to one side, while Nakeya tried to grapple with the woman but Fyraju knocked her sprawling to the ground. Ahmed turned to see Fyraju coming after him, spear at the ready. Sand crunched beneath his feet as he dodged another lunge, but he stumbled and fell backwards. The warrior woman stood astride him, spear lifted high...

And she fell backwards, as something crashed into the back of her head. Ahmed saw that it was the rolled up carpet, and Nakeya was holding it, having used it as a kind of flail to knock Fyraju from her feet.

Ahmed got up unsteadily and together they unrolled the carpet. Nakeya held the brazen vessel under one arm.

'Get aboard,' she urged.

'That's far enough,' said a guttural woman's voice.

Ahmed turned to see the warrior women had returned, two of them bearing the carcase of the great ape on a litter of spears. Several of them showed signs of being mauled or bitten, but they were triumphant, it seemed. They moved to surround the two fugitives. The woman named Mawmas went to Fyraju's side and helped the woman rise.

'You thought you'd escape while we were fighting the wild beast?' Mawmas barked. 'Now we have you surrounded. Fyraju, it seems you were right. We already have one captive to question. These two must die!'

The warrior women lifted their spears like javelins to cast at the two interlopers. Nakeya shouted to her companion:

'Your ring! Ahmed, your ring!'

As the women cast their spears Ahmed shouted his command to the carpet and it shot into the air. One spear sank into its weave, others flew around them. But soon they were a hundred feet above the camp, and the warrior women were splotches of frustrated darkness, barely visible in the firelit gloom.

Ahmed seized the spear that had pierced the middle of the carpet and wrenched it out, then flung it overboard. It whistled away into the darkness. There was a cry from far below.

Ahmed beamed. 'A lucky shot,' he said. 'They'll think twice before they trouble any shipwrecked mariners.'

In the starlight, Nakeya's expression was unreadable. Shivering, she crouched over the brazen vessel, idly running her fingers down its sides as if caressing a lover. 'Sinbad is a prisoner of their queen. This Noor al-Hudha.'

Ahmed moved over to sit beside her. 'Cold?' he said, and put an arm round her shoulders. She pushed him away.

'Not so cold that I want you pawing me, coward,' she told him. 'We must go to the chief island.'

The night wind moaned around the carpet of Suleiman. Cold starlight was all they had to see by. The moon had yet to rise. Ahmed was forced to hug himself against the cold, since Nakeya had given him such a frigid reception.

'Where is that?' he asked. 'Do you know?'

Nakeya gave a shrug. 'Those women we escaped from said that it is where Sinbad was taken. We must go there. They mean to execute him, didn't you hear?'

'We'll get nowhere in this darkness,' said Ahmed. 'We don't know where we're going and even if we did we wouldn't be able to see it. The other women who carried him off will have to paddle their canoes all the way. I shouldn't think they will be paddling at night. They must have weighed anchor somewhere.'

As he spoke, the moon rose over the dark skyline, and in its silvery sheen they noticed another island in the middle distance, a dark hummock amidst the star strewn waters. Ahmed strained his eyes but from this far away and in this darkness he could see no sign of any canoes.

'Take us down,' he commanded the carpet, and they began a spiralling descent. Soon they were flying past the shore, but all was darkness. The wind roared, but as they flew along the coast, Nakeya said she thought she heard voices.

'Listen,' she insisted, and Ahmed did his best. Then he heard it: a voice wailing a name, but the growl of the wind almost entirely obscured it.

The wind dropped but the voice went on. 'Ahmed...! Ahmed...! Ahmed...!'

'Is it Sinbad?' Ahmed said wonderingly.

'It sounds like him,' Nakeya said, as the wind blew louder and the voice grew fainter. 'Somewhere down on the island below us. But how did he know I was here?'

'He's a very clever fellow,' Ahmed said. 'Needs to be, with all the hair's-breadth escapades he lands himself in... But what do you mean, how did he know you were here? It was me he was calling.'

Nakeya turned to survey him superciliously. Her white teeth gleamed in the moonlight as she grimaced. 'What are you talking about?'

she said irritably. 'You must hear him calling my name. Listen: "Nakeya... Nakeya... Nakeya..."'

Ahmed listened, but although he still heard Sinbad's voice, the words were hard to make out now the wind had risen again. He could not rightly say whether Sinbad was calling Nakeya's name or his own.

'That doesn't matter,' he said. 'If Sinbad is down there, however he knows that we're here, he must need help. He has escaped those warrior women, I should think, but has now been benight.'

He commanded the carpet to descend, and a quarter of an hour later they were standing on a cold, moonlit beach, the carpet beside them, gazing up at a line of black cliffs. Still the wind moaned, still that muffled voice called.

'We must go inland,' said Nakeya. 'We must find Sinbad.'

'We'll break our necks, climbing those cliffs in the darkness,' said Ahmed. 'We must wait until morning.'

Nakeya sat down beside him. Still the voice wailed on in the wind. It was cold, and neither of them could sleep. Eyes wide, faces haggard, they awaited the dawn.

At last the sun rose in the east, sending blue black shadows crawling across the sand. Stiff and aching, Ahmed got to his feet. Nakeya had fallen asleep sitting beside him and he shook her by the shoulder. Her eyes sprang open and she looked about her wildly.

'The voice,' she said. 'It's stopped.'

Ahmed listened. The wind had dropped, the voice had ceased. It must have happened long before dawn's earliest light, but he had been so numb he had not noticed. He rooted around on the carpet but there was no sign of the dried bird meat. Perhaps it was just as well, but he was very hungry.

The cliffs loomed above them, but in the morning light it was possible to see a path leading up a narrow valley or ravine that led inland. The wind moaned and sobbed around strange rocky outcroppings that resembled giants from some pre-Adamite aeon, petrified by the passing of the ages. In places, the wind sent up dust devils, pillars of dust reaching high into the sky. They swirled around the two travellers, and Ahmed coughed in the dust.

Nakeya put her hands to either side of her mouth and shouted, 'Sinbad! Sinbad? Sinbad, where are you?'

Echoes rang back from the towering outcrops. Nakeya trotted ahead, Ahmed following behind looking circumspectly around him at the barren landscape. The ravine narrowed. He looked back but saw no sign of Nakeya.

She reappeared from a gap in the rock at the head of the ravine, grinning.

'Have you found him?' Ahmed said, running towards her.

'Look!' Nakeya said, leading him through the gap.

The ravine opened out into a lush green valley where palm trees grew and nightingales sang. In the middle of fertile fields stood a vast palace of white marble, lofting to the azure sky numberless domes and minarets that gleamed in the morning sunlight.

'Ahmed...! Ahmed...! Ahmed...!' drifted a distant voice.

'I'm coming, Sinbad!' cried Nakeya. She ran towards the palace.

'Wait, Nakeya!' Ahmed panted, running after her. 'He wasn't calling you... Listen, I don't think that was Sinbad...'

She flung an impatient glance over her shoulder and disappeared through the open gates of the palace.

'Sinbad!' she cried as she vanished from sight. 'Oh, it's you! It's you! It's...'

Her voice broke off. Heart pounding, Ahmed ran after her.

Fountains played in the middle of a broad courtyard, their prismatic spray like a rainbow as they flung their sweetness into the spicy, perfumed air. The courtyard was surrounded by white walled buildings whose inviting archways hinted of coolness within. A grove of lemon trees and orange stood in the middle of the courtyard, home to sweetly singing birds.

Ahmed plucked an orange and bit into it

hungrily. As juice ran down his chin he studied his surroundings.

Of Nakeya there was no sign.

Ahmed paced forwards, wishing he had some kind of weapon. Despite its beauty this place had an eerie, uncanny, brooding quality. Where was Nakeya? Where was Sinbad?

Then he saw a turbaned figure standing deep within the grove, its back to him.

'Sinbad?' He scowled. 'Sinbad, is that you? Where is Nakeya?'

He ran forwards, pushing his way through the trees. It was hot and humid in there, and the tart scent of citrus was almost overwhelming. Sinbad was visible ahead of him, always too far off to make out for certain. Ahmed reached the centre of the grove, where a deep stone pond seeped water onto the moss-grown ground. He sat down on the cracked flagstones, fanning at his face.

'Sinbad?' he called feebly. 'Nakeya? Anyone?'

He was alone. And he felt it. A deep sense of loneliness overwhelmed, as if he was lost amid the sands of the Rub' al Khali. The sense of depression weighed down on his spirits like a physical weight. It was futile, everything he was doing. He felt a sudden urge to cast himself into the water, drown himself, extinguish his life.

He put his hand to his brow, and as he did so, the Ring of Ja'afar shot out a blinding ray of light. In an instant the stone bowl was gone, the lemon grove was gone, the white palace winked out as if it had never been.

He stood in a barren wilderness, surrounded by rocky outcrops and dust devils. Nakeya lay before him, and above her hovered a whirlwind. Eyes blazed within it, staring hungrily at her. It resolved itself into the form of a vast, grinning, green skinned man, pinning her to the ground with a clawed hand.

6 THE EMPIRE OF WOMEN

At the same instant, the rocky outcrops revolved, transforming as they did so into menacing figures, with vast eyes and tusk filled mouths. They loomed over Ahmed.

'Your ring!' Nakeya cried. 'Your ring!'

Ahmed stared at the silver ring on his finger in bewilderment. What was it? What was he supposed to do with it? Fear filled his mind.

A shadow fell over him. It was a djinn, reaching for him with huge taloned hands. Impulsively he flung his hand out as if to drive it away, and was surprised when this seemingly barren effort bore fruit. The djinn and all its companions halted in their tracks, great flaming eyes fixed on the ring.

Ahmed grinned. Holding his hand before him, ring outwards, he advanced on them, striding confidently across the rocky soil. To his astonishment, djinn fell back on either hand until he reached the one who held Nakeya. She gazed piteously up at him.

'Say the words!' she cried. 'The words!'

Ahmed gaped at her. 'Bismillah Alruhmin Alrahim!' he cried.

The djinn who held Nakeya took an involuntary step backwards, releasing the girl. Fast as summer lightning, Ahmed reached out and seized her wrist with his left hand, hauling her to her feet while keeping the ring held high.

A djinn made a feint for the ring. Ahmed whirled round, dragging Nakeya with him, and thrust it at his foe, who took to the air in fury and hovering over their heads, shrieking and wailing. This was taken as a sign by the others to do the same, and the sky filled with wrathful djinn like a flock of frustrated vultures when a predator drives them from its prey. Ahmed lifted his ring hand high, and the djinn swooped and fluttered on every hand, unable to reach them.

'Back to the carpet!' Nakeya cried. 'Sinbad isn't here, it's a land of the djinn. If we stay here they will sooner or later find some way of overcoming the magic of the ring.'

Ahmed had already realised this. Still holding Nakeya's wrist, he turned and ran with her at his side, back down the ravine up which they had trudged, and down onto the beach where the water lapped hungrily at the sand and their carpet lay where they had left it.

A djinn hovered over the carpet, an awesome figure of smokeless fire, that seemed drawn by a terrible fascination to the brazen vessel that sat primly in the middle. Ahmed leapt onto the carpet, ring held upwards, and the djinn drew back, hissing like a seething cauldron before vanishing into the air above.

They both stood on the carpet, Nakeya clinging to Ahmed for support. 'O Carpet of Suleiman!' Ahmed cried. 'Take us away from this place.'

'Take us to Wak-Wak!' Nakeya added.

The carpet began to rise, then shot away, rounding the island where still the angry djinn circled and swooped above a lifeless landscape where stood no mighty palace, no fertile field. Only stretches of rock and sand with occasional withered vegetation lay beneath the sinister figures, barren and bare of life.

The Carpet of Suleiman flew above the rolling waters of the sea, its two surviving passengers sitting wearily in its midst. By noon, Nakeya was calmer.

'Where is Wak-Wak?' Ahmed asked her. 'Isn't that the name of all these islands?'

Nakeya leaned against him, clutching his arm. He could smell the scent of her hair and it smelled good. 'Did you not hear what those warrior women said? There is a chief island called Wak-Wak. These other islets belong to its queen.'

She disengaged herself from his arm, moved a little away from him on the carpet. 'You really should listen more to what people say,' she told him reprovingly. 'You could learn much. Become a wise man.' She looked out into the haze. There was no sign of any island, and they had been flying all day. 'When we reach the chief Wak-Wak isle, we must find where Sinbad is kept imprisoned, and free him. Then we will be able to fly onwards to Djinnistan.'

'First of all,' said Ahmed, 'we need food. I've wisdom enough to know that. The last thing I ate was an illusion, and I am starving. Aren't you?'

'When I was a nun on Mount Abora I learnt to go without,' she said, 'Gluttony is a sin, you must know.'

'I hardly think it gluttonous to want something to eat,' he said impatiently. He nodded at the brazen vessel. 'Call up Hadana and tell him we want a three course banquet like the one we had in China.'

She gave him a cold stare. 'Only twice more can we call him to do our bidding,' she reminded him. 'Let us not squander what we have.'

Ahmed growled to himself. There had been a time when he had known what it was to go hungry, but then he had learnt the art of thieving and had never gone hungry again. In Baghdad, food was always available, if you knew where to look. Some of those stall keepers in the bazaar were woefully careless about their own wares...

There were no bazaars here, but just as Ahmed was considering trying to catch more fish, an island swam up out of the noon haze directly ahead of them.

A chain of mountains ran down the middle of the island, which was much larger than any of the previous ones, and the lowlands were green and fertile, with trees growing down to the shore. Further inland they saw herds of elephants roaming amongst the trees. On a headland stood a large fruit bearing tree. Closer to the shore was a grove of oranges, and Ahmed directed the carpet to land amongst them, where he succeeded in sated his hunger on real fruit.

Nakeya joined him, and despite her claims to austerity and asceticism she ate as voraciously as he did, gazing about herself curiously. In the distance, the tall tree on the headland was visible over the tops of other trees.

'This must be the island,' she declared, 'because it is here that the carpet has taken us. But I saw no sign of any inhabitants.'

'Maybe those charming ladies we met on the isle of the beasts have their houses on another part of the island,' Ahmed speculated as he built up a fire on the sand beside the carpet. 'It is too dark now to explore, but in the morning we can scout out the whole place if need be, learn where this queen lives and where she is keeping Sinbad.'

Absently he wondered what had become of Sir Acelin. Drowned, presumably. The Frank had possessed none of Sinbad's sailor luck. After all, who did?

'Of course,' said Nakeya, lying herself down on the carpet in the warmth of the flames. 'We must find Sinbad and rescue him.'

Ahmed wanted to ask how she hoped to do that with only the two of them against an island of warrior women, and them unarmed. Perhaps it was for this that she was keeping Hadana's next summoning. He lay down beside her, insinuating himself closer. With a soft grunt, she wriggled away on her shoulder blades.

Women were so changeable. That noontime she had actually seemed quite fond of him. Now she was being unfriendly again. Ahmed rolled over but as he was about to fall asleep he heard a strange noise.

'Wak! Wak! Wak!'

A chorus of voices drifted down from inland. It was like nothing he had ever heard before. The sunset transformed the rich green trees into grey ghostly half shapes. The noise faded away as the light receded. Soon only a few voices were still crying 'Wak! Wak! Wak!' and 'Wak! Wak! Wak! Wak! Wak!' but then even they were silent.

Ahmed sat up and poked at the embers of the fire with a fallen branch. He turned and saw Nakeya watching him in silence, propping her head on her hand.

'Did you hear that?' he demanded. 'It sounded like a thousand voices, all of them saying the same thing.'

'Oh! Do you listen to nothing?' she said with a snort, and rolled over again.

Bewildered, he sat gazing at her dark shape as the firelight flickered. After a while, with a heartfelt sigh, he lay himself down again and sought sleep vainly for several hours. When he slept, he dreamed that he was back in Baghdad, but no longer was he a thief, but instead the grand vizier. It was a nightmare.

He woke as dawn's light was streaming over the rugged mountains. There was no sign of Nakeya, and the fire was cold. Kneeling beside it, he tried to work out where the weird voices had come from the night before. Hearing a sound, he turned and saw Nakeya coming back up the beach, struggling back into her robe, her hair dripping with sea water. She had been bathing in the sea, Ahmed realised, and her glossy skin was still wet in patches, but it soon dried in the morning sun.

'We shall scour the island for any sign of Sinbad,' said Nakeya firmly. 'If we remain aboard the carpet, you should be safe.'

'I should be safe?' asked Ahmed, as the carpet rose into the air in accordance with his instructions.

'Of course,' said Nakeya. 'You have the most to fear in this, the empire of women.'

Ahmed grunted and the carpet soared inland. Again he wondered how the Wak-Wak people could exist if the women killed all men. Moments later he was to learn the explanation.

As they drew closer to the tree on the headland, Ahmed saw that the fruit that hung from it varied greatly in shape and size, presumably based on ripeness. Some of it was dark and spherical, dangling down from the boles by a thin tracery of tendrils. Others seemed to have grown limbs or branches that dangled down from the main fruit. Still more were even more developed, even larger. His eyes narrowed, then widened in pleasurable surprise. They looked almost like...

'Women,' said Nakeya as the carpet took them even closer to the tree.

It was true. Hanging from the branches were long, elegant, slender yet curvaceous fruits, brown skinned and with long black hair by which they dangled. As Ahmed watched open mouthed, one ripe fruit dropped from the tree and landed with a thud somewhere on the forest floor below.

Peering over the edge of the carpet, Ahmed saw the girl who he had mistaken for a fruit of the tree, standing coltishly on the green sward, staring about her more like a wild animal than a fallen fruit. Other women were visible, clad in lamellar armour and carrying spears, and they were rounding up more fallen fruit women and as far as Ahmed could see before the carpet swooped away over the trees, leading them towards a group of huts deeper in the forest.

'Aladdin told us all about this,' Nakeya added. 'You never listen.'

Ahmed remembered what the emperor of

China had said. He had thought the man was repeating fables, travellers' tales. After all, Aladdin had never been in these waters. Not even Sinbad had been here before. Wherever he was...

They flew on, over forests and clearings where they saw elephants with women mahouts on their backs, carrying fallen logs down towards a settlement by the coast. Occasional farms broke up the monotony of leaf cover. Then the trees grew scarcer as the land rose and became rocky, and they flew up over the mountains where morning mist still hung about their peaks. Down below the rock was bare and stony, with green spots of vegetation visible only in a few rare places. Nothing seemed to live up there, but then Ahmed saw a line of caves in the side of a cliff, and thought he saw dwellers moving about, looking up at them.

But the carpet swept onwards and soon Ahmed was unsure if he had seen it or if it had been some kind of mirage brought on by a diet of fruit. Nakeya had seen nothing.

They soared over a ridge and saw the far side of the island opening up before them. Wooded hills rolled down towards the green waters of the sea. Farms and walled villages were to be seen in places. The hills gave way to farmland. Ahmed kept the carpet high up for fear they would be seen by the women who tilled the land below.

They drew nearer to the sea. Surf crashed

against high cliffs. There was something weird, eerie, about the entire scene. Ahmed had already noted that the sea had a greenish cast to it, and now he pointed it out to Nakeya.

She sat up and stared out to sea, hand shading her big wide white eyes. 'Perhaps we are not so far from the emerald mountains,' she murmured to herself.

'What's that down there?'

Ahmed indicated a sprawl of houses that lay between two cliffs, leading down to the shore. Wooden wharves and jetties projected into the water, and a flotilla of canoes were moored beside them. A long, crowded street wound up between flat roofed houses towards a white walled palace higher up the slope. Up it was striding a procession of women, some riding on elephants, others on foot, driving before them a man.

'It must be Sinbad,' breathed Nakeya as they watched from high overhead. 'We must rescue him.'

By the time they had drawn closer the procession had reached the top of the street wehre it gave way to steps. The steps led to the palace. Outside the palace a woman sat upon a throne, watching the approach of the women warriors. Nearby stood a bare chested woman, holding a scimitar almost as big as she was.

The man at the head of the procession tripped and fell, and the women guards beat him with their spear shaft as he lay there. Bleeding, he got to his feet and staggered on up the steps.

'He goes to his death,' said Nakeya ominously.

Now the man stood before the throne. A guard forced him to his knees before the woman who must be the queen, Noor al-Hudha. They dragged his head back so he was looking straight at her. The shadow of the carpet fell upon them, and the queen looked up in surprise. As she did so, Ahmed recognised the man who they held prisoner. But it wasn't Sinbad.

It was Sir Acelin.

7 THE PEOPLE OF THE SEA

When Sinbad fell, he hit the turbulent waters with a deafening smack that knocked the breath from him, then went under, helplessly, losing sight in the murky green depths of the storm wracked sky where two djinn battled for supremacy and the magic carpet flew hectically through the thunderous air.

The din faded as he sank, a deafening silence swallowed him up as his helpless body plummeted downwards through the waters, trailing a line of bubbles. Multicoloured fish swam past, showing scant interest in this visitor from the overworld as he descended like a meteor through the water.

At last, gently, he touched the bottom, sending gobbets of slime drifting leisurely upwards. He had been able to swim as long as he could walk, and he had had much practise during his years as a somewhat hapless mariner. Many had been the time when his ship had foundered, and he had been thrown into the waves only to be cast up on the shore of some hostile island, usually inhabited by cannibals and monsters. But not this time.

This time it had been him who had gone to the bottom. The roaring in his mind grew, and he began to see spots at the edges of his vision. Vainly he struggled, his movements hampered by the pressure of the water. The sea around him grew darker. A herd of fish came swimming round a coral outcrop. That couldn't be right. Fish didn't swim in herds. Shoals was the word. Yes, shoals. And yet, somehow, as he breathed his last breath, "herd" seemed to be right.

He blacked out.

Sinbad awoke to feel what seemed to be hands caressing his bare flesh. For a while, it was pleasant; the hands, slender and deft, stroked every inch of his skin as if they were working in some kind of oil or lotion. Then panicked visions of giant fish nuzzling at his body flashed silently through his numb mind and he began to struggle. The hands grew firmer, pressing him back, caressing and coaxing him. Sensation ebbed until at last he felt himself hanging suspended in nothing, nowhere. His eyes flickered open.

He was looking up at the roof of a cave. As he sat up, the cave seemed to spin round and round. A girl sat on a weed festooned boulder, her arms wrapped around her legs, her chin resting on her knees, two or three vivid hued fish darting protectively around her.

A pearlescent sheen lay upon everything. Outside the cave were weed festooned rocks and shoals of brightly coloured fish. The cave itself was underwater. And yet somehow he was breathing.

The scene shimmered before him as he stared at the girl. She was stark naked, and her pale pearlescent skin had the same nacreous sheen as the cave walls. Her long, lustrous hair waved lazily in the water currents like seaweed. She looked quizzically at him, lifting an eyebrow as thin as a Ramadan moon. He opened his mouth to speak and bubbles drifted out. More bubbles escaped his mouth as he fell backwards onto the ledge of stone where he lay amidst soft green moss, on the verge of consciousness.

'You must eat.'

The voice glided coaxingly inside his brain, teasing out the folds and crannies of his grey matter just as those fish hands had caressed his every inch. Had that happened?

Where was he?

He opened his eyes. Water surrounded him. Above him rose the cave roof, but now he was in its mouth, looking out through the green depths. Fish swam past, mouths downturned, seeming to view him with disdain.

He was propped against a table-like rock upon which sat several large oyster shells. One contained the meat of the oyster. Two others were packed to the brim with seaweed of different kinds. The girl floated at his side.

She gazed solicitously at him, then executed a graceful backwards somersault and swam sleekly back into the cave, revealing to Sinbad's incredulity that she had a small, dainty tail. Shortly after, she returned carrying a larger shell that contained what looked like fish steaks.

'Shark meat,' she explained, bubbles cascading from her mouth as she spoke. She indicated the shells in front of him. 'Oyster. Sea grape. Sea lettuce.'

Sinbad tried not to stare at her, but at his gaze she turned away a little, scarlet mantling her pale cheeks.

'I thought you were a dream,' he murmured. He looked down at himself to see that he too was naked. 'Where are my clothes?' Panicked bubbles escaped his mouth in a long chain that vanished into the murk overhead.

'I took them from you,' the girl said. 'You were drowning. If I had not anointed your limbs with this unguent,' and she picked up a smaller shell that contained a few smears of some kind of yellow paste, 'you would not have been able to survive down here. Your clothes... drifted away on the current.'

Sinbad took the shell from her slender fingers but lost his grip on it and it floated away. With a swift kick of her legs the girl darted after it and brought it back.

'What is that?' he asked. 'And who are you?'

'It is a preparation of the liver fat of the Dandan fish,' said the girl. 'And my name is Khadijah.'

'Khadijah?' Sinbad was amazed. It was such a normal, everyday name for so exotic and peculiar a maiden. He introduced himself. 'You say your name is Khadijah? You are a Muslim? I have... never heard of this fish,' he added.

'Many of us down here are Muslims,' said the girl. 'Others are Christians, Hebrews, idolaters. Some are even fire worshippers, but these days they only thrive around certain volcanic trenches which they consider sacred. The Dandan fish is the largest fish in all the seas, bar the Bahamut itself.'

Sinbad investigated the oyster. It seemed identical to the ones he had eaten on the land, and he swallowed it down with a gulp. A great improvement on bird meat. He helped himself to sea grapes, which proved to be ropes of tiny green bubbles, resembling grapes but tasting salty and fresh. The bubbles burst in his mouth as he ate them.

'I have never heard of this fish,' he repeated, 'and I am accounted a great sailor among my own people.'

Khadijah looked indignant. 'Sailors know nothing of the water on which they sail,' she told him. 'But I will assure you that many of your kind have met the Dandan. It sometimes devours men who fall overboard, if it finds them, but it seldom profits by such dealings. When we find its carcase, we cut out the liver and pound it until it becomes this grease with which we anoint our bodies.'

'Without which you would drown?' Sinbad asked, trying a shark steak. It was entirely raw. There must be no fire down here, of course, except in those miraculous areas where the undersea fire worshippers dwelt. But he was becoming accustomed to eating fish Al-Yabani-style.

'It is good to speak with you,' she said. 'I dwell all alone, with only my fish to keep me company.' She waved a hand in the direction of the shoals that darted back and forth or grazed the sea bed outside the cave. 'I meet people only when I go to the mosque in Madinat Almuhit.'

Sinbad noticed a large grouper who seemed to be taking a proprietorial view of the shoal. 'You're a shepherdess!' he exclaimed.

She frowned. 'I do not know. What is this "shepherdess"?'

Laughing until bubbles fizzed in the water above his head, Sinbad told her a little of the world ashore, and she reciprocated with tales of the ocean floor. Soon she was asking him what had brought him to her country.

Sinbad grew sombre. 'I have been sent on an important mission by the ruler of my homeland,' he told her. 'I am bound for Djinnistan.'

'I have heard of these people, the djinn,' said Khadijah. 'They ruled the land ere the coming of the Sons of Adam. One of their kind was that

Iblis who led a rebellion against Allah. In the mosque in Madinat Almuhit I heard the story as a little girl. Perhaps the Imam Albahr will be able to tell you how you can reach your destination.'

Sinbad nodded. 'I must go there at once, in that case,' he said, then paused. 'You did not see any others of my kind in the water? We were attacked by a djinn and I was knocked into the sea. I think my companions might have followed me.'

'No one reached these depths,' said Khadijah. 'Perhaps they were cast ashore by the waves.'

Sinbad sighed. 'I cannot hope to find them now,' he told himself. 'I must complete my mission for the caliph.' He appealed to her. 'I do not know where this mosque is. Can you take me there?'

She looked at him as if he had proposed something improper. 'I have shared the hospitality for which my people are justly famous,' she said. 'But I cannot abandon my shoal. I was set here to watch over my fish by my grandfather, who rules over these maritime pastures.'

'Can you at least point the way?' Sinbad asked. 'Does the city lie to the north, south, east or west?'

Locks of her hair waved around her face as she pondered the matter. She gazed thoughtfully at Sinbad, then coloured and looked away.

'I will take you there,' she purred. 'It is a two day's journey.'

Sinbad lay a hand on her slender, pale arm. 'I

cannot ask you to risk your grandfather's wrath for me,' he said earnestly. 'You have done so much for me already. I only ask you to give me an idea of where to go.'

She shook her head, and her hair whirled back and forth. 'I helped you as I would help any lost traveller. But I will help you to reach Madinat Almuhit because there are many dangers on the journey, and besides...'

Again she looked away.

'What of your fish?' Sinbad asked.

'Wait here,' she instructed, then with many a kick of her shapely legs she swam out into the shoal. Reaching the grouper, she halted in front of it, and for a while all Sinbad could see was the line of bubbles drifting upwards from Khadijah's mouth. A similar line appeared from the grouper's jaws.

Khadijah gave a flick with her feet, turned about, and swam back to Sinbad. She beamed at him.

'He has agreed to guard the fish while I am away,' she said importantly.

'The fish?' asked Sinbad, looking over at the proud old grouper. It began bustling around the placidly grazing fish as if sharks and octopuses were circling out in the green murk.

Khadijah looked surprised. 'Of course!' she said with a giggle. 'I was only now talking to him. Did you not see?'

She took a long staff made of narwhal horn

from her cave and together they began to swim into the murk. Forests of weed waved on either side like trees in a high wind, but there was no wind, it was only the current.

After a while, Sinbad found it difficult to believe that he was walking underwater. His mind kept trying to tell him that this was a normal place, a rocky plain where plants grew and birds—no, fish!—darted amongst their fronds. The fact that he was swimming through the water somehow failed to dispel the illusion. The fact that the sun was only visible as a watery gleam high overhead, filtering down through the green murk did nothing to discourage a conviction that he was traversing the overworld. He wondered if he had somehow struck his head on a rock and was dreaming all this.

Sinbad had never dreamed of the colours he saw at the bottom of the seas, amongst the ooze of dead fish. Green anemones grew amidst pink coral, orange and white clownfish darted in shoals, blue jellyfish drifted past. From time to time, the waters grew darker, the shoals of fish scurried away into rocks, and larger, more sinister shapes circled overhead. First it was sharks, then a manta ray. Another time an octopus jetted out from a cave amongst barnacle-rough boulders, skin dark as ink, only to blush bright scarlet with distress as Khadijah struck at it reprovingly with her narwhal staff.

When the light vanished from the waters

above, they made camp amongst the slimy rocks and slept, continuing in the morning. They swam round tall cliffs, so high their tops vanished out of sight in the undersea gloaming, and Sinbad guessed they marked the position of one of the Wak-Wak islands. A forest of giant kelp where crabs and lobsters lurked gave way to a broad plain where bright emerald fields of sea lettuce waved in the current. Naked men with tails like Khadijah tended these fields, and the shoals of fish that fed there. She greeted some of them when they swam over.

They crossed a ridge. Down in the valley below them stood a city.

Easily as big as Baghdad, it seemed to be constructed of great reefs of coral, grown for the purpose. Dwellings and counting houses and clearing houses and shops and palaces all rose from the muck at the bottom of the sea, and the water was thick with traffic, swimming men and women, and others riding past on huge sea horses, or sitting in great scallop shell chariots drawn by huge eels.

Near the centre of the busy place, which Khadijah confirmed was the city of Madinat Almuhit, was a great coral outcrop carved into a dome, and outside it towered minarets of coral.

'That is the mosque,' declared Khadijah, and she swam towards it.

The mosque was bigger even than the great mosque of Al-Mansur in Baghdad. People were drifting towards it in small groups, and Sinbad guessed that the time had come for prayers, although he had no idea of how the muezzin could make the call to prayer in these conditions. He wondered how exactly the people of the sea had been converted to Islam.

They swam closer. The mosque was unlit within, and its entrance was hung with weed, like the entrance to an undersea grotto rather than a place of worship. Khadijah swam in front, leading Sinbad towards the great entrance and the darkness beyond. A ray of light filtered in through a hole in the dome. People were praying on the sand beneath them.

A group of men swam up on either side of the entrance it. They were armed with tridents and they surrounded Khadijah and Sinbad. Then an elderly man swam out of the mosque. He was white bearded, and his body was withered.

'By the beard of the Prophet, a Son of Adam!' the old man exclaimed. 'Just what we needed. My thanks, girl, for luring him here.'

8
UNDERWATER JIHAD

Sinbad shot Khadijah a betrayed look. But to his surprise, the girl showed every indication of being as shocked as he was.

'I did not lure him here, O imam!' she said hotly. 'I brought him here because he seeks aid in reaching the country of Djinnistan! Sinbad, for Allah's sake, believe me!'

The Imam Albahr shook his hoary head. 'No matter, girl,' he said. 'This comes most opportune. Word has reached us that a Dandan fish has been sighted on the border between our country and that of the idolaters.' He looked impatiently at Khadijah. 'Well? Is it not obvious, girl?' he added in hectoring tones. 'We need this son of Adam to catch the fish.'

'Why do you need to catch the Dandan? And why do you need me?' Sinbad demanded, swimming forwards. The guards, all stalwart fellows with magnificent physiques, and strong, powerful tails, closed in around him. One pricked his throat with the tines of his trident.

'Bring him with me,' said the imam without answering either of Sinbad's questions.

The men seized Sinbad by the arms, swimming with him in the Imam Albahr's wake, and they entered a coral edifice adjacent to the mosque. After a pause Khadijah swam after them, and drifted at the back of the large chamber into which the imam swam. A youth sat upon a throne of sea shells, biting at his nails.

'Peace be upon you, Amir Alma!' cried the imam. 'We have obtained a Son of Adam, O auspicious ruler!'

The youth looked up in surprise. With a kick, he swam up from his throne and came to inspect the prisoner, peering impersonally into Sinbad's face. 'A living man! I had not expected such. In my father's time we gave only drowned men to the Dandan. I was told that the fish was afraid of living men.'

'Now wait a minute,' protested Sinbad. 'I thought you were good Muslims in this kingdom. Do you plan to sacrifice me to this monster fish?'

The youth looked offended. 'By no means!' he said. 'It is the idolaters who offer human sacrifices to the Dandan, not we.'

'Then what in Allah's name do you plan to do with me?' Sinbad wanted to know.

'Take him to the cage,' said the imam to the

guards in an undertone, 'and we will make ready for the hunt.'

'I shall take a troop of my finest cavalry with me,' the youth was saying. 'There is a chance the idolaters will attempt to steal a march on us, since the fish has been seen close to their own waters. If necessary, we must fight them for it. It will be a glorious battle.'

'It will be a holy war, O auspicious ruler,' the imam assured him.

The guards took Sinbad by the arms and swam away with him. He struggled fiercely, but one of the men struck him under the chin and he sank back in a daze.

Sinbad recovered his wits when a muffled clang dinned on his throbbing ears. Looking muzzily about himself, he saw that he was floating inside a spherical cage of rusty, weed garlanded iron, attached by a long chain to a flat rock outside the mosque. It was just large enough to contain him, though not happily, and he saw that there was a hatchway in it which had just been locked by one of the guards. The guards swam away heedlessly into the city as Sinbad shouted out to them, large bubbles streaming up from his mouth and out of the cage into the freedom of the waters above.

He watched them go dolefully. The guards, like the bubbles, vanished into the green murk, leaving Sinbad alone. Overhead the light was receding, and the waters around Sinbad were beginning to grow cold. It seemed he was being left here overnight. And in the morning? What then? Something to do with this monster fish, whose liver fat he wore as an unguent on his skin. And so did the others. Had Sinbad been chosen as bait for the Dandan?

But Alma had said that a living man, a living son of Adam, would frighten the fish away. From what Sinbad had heard of these huge creatures, that was difficult to believe. He could not believe anything as comparatively small as himself could frighten such a fish.

As the shadows grew inkier, he heard stealthy splashing sounds from the water nearby. Turning as best he could in the cage, he peered into the gloom. Was someone out there? Were they coming for him? Some scavenger or robber of the city, come to see what pickings they could get from the prisoner? Some carnivorous fish?

He glimpsed a pale gleam amongst the waving weed. Then something darted out into the open and swam like an otter straight towards his cage, seizing a hold and clinging on with hands and feet. Sinbad found himself gazing in astonishment into the face of his erstwhile companion.

'Khadijah!' he cried, and huge bubbles floated up from his mouth.

She motioned him to silence, and began to

inspect the lock. In a quieter voice, Sinbad said. 'What happened to you? And what do they mean to do with me?'

She looked up from the lock. 'I am trying to concentrate,' she told him crossly. 'This lock is very complicated and rather old. I do not know if I can open it.' She went on as her clever, slender fingers probed the mechanism, 'When the Imam's guards took you into the Amir's palace, I followed behind them. No one noticed a girl. So I heard what the Imam said. He plans to give you to the Dandan fish.'

'So I understand,' said Sinbad. 'But how? And why? And what is this about the fish being afraid of men like me?'

'You know that my people need the unguent made from the Dandan's liver fat to survive underwater,' she said, still peering distractedly at the lock. 'Whenever one is seen in our waters, the Amir tries to catch it so that its liver can be used to provide more unguent. There is always a need for more since the unguent's efficacy lasts only so long. The fish is afraid of Sons of Adam because to them your flesh is the vilest poison. And because we cannot hope to prevail against the Dandan if we go up against it, we use the bodies of drowned sailors, if we can get them, to poison the fish. Drowned men are sufficiently mangled by their time under the sea for the Dandan to be fooled into thinking they are eating some sea beast, and so they die of the poison.'

'But I'm not dead,' said Sinbad a little pathetically. 'Do you mean they hope to kill me, and use my body to poison the fish?'

Abruptly she ceased her investigation of the lock. 'This is hopeless,' she said. 'I do not think I will be able to free you.' She looked up. 'I do not know what it is they plan to do,' she added. 'I know no more about Dandan fishing than most people of my kind. It is only the Amir and his courtiers who hunt the Dandan. It is a royal fish and not meant for the likes of my kin.'

'You'd better get away,' Sinbad said sadly. 'Thank you for trying to help me, but I have caused you enough trouble as it is. You must return to your sea pastures and your shoal.' He slipped a hand through the bars to pat her affectionately on the shoulder. She took his fingers in her own hand and kissed them.

Tears brimmed in her eyes, mingling with the surrounding salt water. 'I don't want to leave you,' she gulped. 'I have never known anyone like you.'

'Go,' he said firmly. 'And—thank you!'

Disengaging her fingers from his own, she nodded bravely. 'Go with Allah,' she murmured.

She swam backwards a little, regarding him, then executed a swift backflip and swam sleekly into the gloom. Sinbad gazed after her receding figure a long time after it was gone.

In the morning the crash of the cage door awoke him. Opening his eyes, he saw sunlight streaming through the upper waters, and surrounding him was a troop of trident bearing warriors. Further away, on the edge of the weed forest, a group of men and women sat upon giant sea horses. Sinbad recognised both the Amir and the Imam amongst them. Some had leashed barracudas swimming alongside them, or carried spears or tridents in their hands.

Sinbad fumed as he had his arms bound behind his back, and a leash attached. He was led out of the cage and the guards swam with him to the group who Sinbad guessed were the courtiers Khadijah had mentioned.

To his surprise, Amir Alma rode up to him and said, 'I wish to invite you to join us in our hunt.'

'Invite me?' Large bubbles drifted from Sinbad's mouth. He indicated the cage. 'You have a strange way of going about it.'

Amir Alma glanced over at the Imam, who was watching disapprovingly. 'My apologies, noble traveller,' the Amir said. 'Some of my ministers were... overzealous. You must understand that your presence on our hunt is vital to its success. I would not want, however, to force you to join us. Unlike certain others.' Again he looked at the Imam, who said nothing. 'Please say you will join us,' Amir Alma added. 'I will reward you munificently.'

'All I want,' said Sinbad, 'is to return to the surface.'

'That can be arranged,' said the Amir. 'But first I would request the honour of your presence on the hunt.'

Sinbad nodded unwillingly. The Amir would be able to force him if he didn't agree. He accepted the situation philosophically.

After a brief speech by Amir Alma, the courtiers and guards set out in a hubbub of merry chatter and strident blowing of conch shells, Sinbad in their midst, the Imam and the Amir at their head. Sinbad gathered that Alma had newly succeeded to his late father's throne, and his courtiers showed scant respect for him. The Imam himself treated him as if he was little more than a precocious child. Perhaps Alma hoped that by succeeding in this hunt, he would earn his subjects' admiration.

Madinat Almuhit stood in the middle of the kingdom, a long way from Khadijah's shoals but also far from the borders with the country of the idolaters where the Dandan had been reported. They progressed across the sea floor, over endless brown, waving forests of giant kelp and across silvery stretches of sand and broken shells, past undersea mountains and across deep trenches that glowed with a fiery light from deep below. They came to several cities of coral. None were comparable to Madinat Almuhit, but the citizens welcomed the hunting party with lavish hospitality.

Several days passed, marked by the ebb and

flow of the gleam overhead, and Sinbad saw much of the undersea kingdom. In many ways it resembled the dry land realms, although they had customs and manners that Sinbad had seldom encountered even in the most barbarous of overworld countries. He had visited enough savage lands not to be shocked by the sea folk's nudity; besides, he was naked himself. He learnt that buying and selling did not exist amongst them, and he wondered what happened to Khadijah's fish. Did her own family eat them? Gold and jewels had no value amongst these people, and there were no bazaars in the many cities.

Later he learnt that if a man wished to marry a woman he must bring her family a dowry of fish, thousands of them. So that was where their wealth lay! It made a kind of sense. And now the Amir was hunting after that fish which had the most value to the people of the sea, and which was also the most dangerous. Yet Sinbad still did not know what his own role was to be.

One day they came out of a jungle of giant kelp to see a city in the plain beyond. It was in ruins. From the reactions of his captors Sinbad saw that this was a recent development; they had not been anticipating this.

Swimming forwards, with the guards fanning out to guard the courtiers, they entered the city. Savage fish fought over the floating corpses of slaughtered sea people, and the coral buildings had been ransacked. It was a grisly scene. When at last the guards found a few survivors cowering in some of the houses, the very old or very young, the story they told was one of horror.

'The idolaters,' the word went round. 'A raid across the border.'

The city was close to the idolaters' kingdom, and this had been a surprise attack, a raid during which the idolaters had carried off many men and women as slaves. Amir Alma listened to the tale in growing anger, and clenched an impulsive fist.

'We must attack at once!' he said, but the Imam counselled against it.

'We are but few,' he reminded the young Amir. 'Soon, when the time is right, we will enter the idolaters' domain under arms and teach them to fear us. But until we have the Dandan fish we cannot return to Madinat Almuhit and raise an army.'

'You are right, of course,' admitted Alma unwillingly. He gritted his teeth. 'Have they any news of our quarry?'

The Dandan had been reported among the plains of the north only two days earlier, they learnt. 'Then that is where we shall go,' declared Alma. The expedition set forth shortly afterwards, leaving the survivors with vital supplies and promises that vengeance would be enacted upon their oppressors.

Through the waters the expedition swam.

The idolaters' attack made their hunt all the more urgent, and the courtiers, whose participation until then had been light hearted and merry, was now grim and serious. Conch horns were blown in warlike manner now, rather than out of high spirits. Shoals of brightly coloured fish fled before them as the hunting party advanced through the giant kelp forests and came out into the plains of silvery sand. They were eager to find the Dandan, and they cared little for anything else.

Perhaps it was this very eagerness that was their undoing. For even as they sighted the sandy plains and began to issue forth from the kelp forest, dark figures on sharks shot up from behind a ridge.

The attack passed as if it were a dream, so silent were the attackers. Blades of sharpened shell sliced through water and flesh alike, and the sea flushed crimson with blood. The guards did sterling work against their enigmatic attackers, but soon they were forced to fall back.

More and more of the dark figures, appeared out of the kelp forest at their back, some on shark back, others swimming. The Amir's small force was swiftly surrounded. Some of the courtiers broke and swam for a gap in their enemies ranks, but they were slaughtered to a man, and the waters ran with their blood. The courtiers' hunting fish swam back and forth in a frenzy, some unable to contain themselves and attacking still living men.

A desperate charge by the Amir and his surviving guards broke open a gap in the attackers, who Sinbad guessed to be the idolaters, and some of the latter turned tail and fled—literally; Sinbad saw that they had tails like Alma's own people. But before he could exploit the advantage the Amir's valour had created, Sinbad himself was seized by two idolaters who bound him and bore him away through the blood marbled waters.

9 THE DANDAN

As he was carried along a ravine between two towering island cliffs, Sinbad gained a clearer impression of his ferocious captors.

The darkness of their skin was achieved by the application of some kind of war paint. Sinbad guessed that it was combined with an unguent similar to the one worn by the Muslim sea folk. After all, both sides needed the peculiar properties of the Dandan liver fat to survive down in this undersea realm. It was clear that the idolaters were members of the same race, even if religion divided them. Not for the first time Sinbad wondered how people, seemingly akin to his own folk although they did not claim a common ancestor, had come to live in the sea.

Evidently it was not their natural element: the fact that they required such elaborate preparations to live day to day under these conditions was a clear indication of this. He had asked Khadijah what she knew of her race's earlier history, but she could tell him nothing except that she had heard a tradition that they had gone ashore in long ago Pre-Adamite times. But by now, they were so accustomed to their underwater existence that were they to spend any significant time ashore they would die just as surely as a fish would.

Sinbad might have found it in his heart to pity the people of the sea, caught as they were between two existences, both of them potentially hostile to their lives, had they shown him more consideration. With the obvious exception of Khadijah, they had treated him as little more than a prize, although Sinbad was still unsure as to what role he would play in their hunt for the Dandan.

There was no pursuit by Amir Alma's forces. Sinbad had to admit to himself the likelihood that the Muslim sea folk had all been slaughtered. When the troop of idolaters reached a submarine cleft in the side of the ravine, they halted. After expelling several large and angry crustaceans, they made camp within its shelter, corralling their sharks nearby. Sinbad addressed one of the guards while the others began to eat a supper of various seaweeds foraged from among the rocks. Fish were caught, but most of these were thrown to the sharks.

'What do you mean to do with me?' Sinbad asked, struggling to find a less uncomfortable position. He had been bound to a barnacle encrusted rock, and with his hands tied behind him he was in a certain degree of agony.

The idolater bared his teeth at the captive,

and brandished his narwhal tusk spear.

'Do you speak Arabic?' Sinbad asked. The idolater replied threateningly in a heathen tongue the sailor did not recognise. It reminded him a little of the language of the black pigmies of the Andaman Islands, but not enough for the exact meaning to be clear. All Sinbad could glean from the tirade was that the guard was in no mood for polite conversation.

'Maybe one of your comrades would be willing to talk to me,' Sinbad said, trying to sit up.

Angrily, the idolater shouted something to the others. After a series of irate negotiations, another, larger idolater swam across to them. His face was brutal, his eyes glittered malignantly, he wore nothing but a necklace of shark teeth. Elaborate cicatrices had been cut into his cheeks. When he spoke, Sinbad saw that his teeth had been filed into points.

In the Arabic used by the Muslim sea people, the idolater said, 'What is it you want?'

'That's exactly what I want to know from you,' Sinbad replied. 'Why have you carried me off? Why did you attack Amir Alma's people?'

'The Amir's people had crossed our border,' said the idolater. 'We ambushed them because they were intruders into our country.'

'We're in your country?' asked Sinbad. 'Amir Alma didn't seem to think so.'

'The border was agreed upon by treaty after the last war,' said the idolater. 'Oh, and we know why Amir Alma violated it. Our spies brought us word of his expedition, and they told us about you.'

'Oh really?' said Sinbad with an amused laugh. 'I didn't know the fame of Sinbad the Sailor had reached this far under the ocean. None of your enemies seemed to have heard of me.'

The idolater gave a scowl. 'I have never heard of any Tinbad the Tailor,' he said. 'All that we know is that you are said to be a Son of Adam, from the surface. We need the Dandan fish as much as Amir Alma's people do.'

'So you want me to aid you in hunting the one that has been seen in these waters?' Sinbad asked. 'I'd be happy to. I have no loyalties to Amir Alma. But do you think you could untie my hands? It's very uncomfortable.'

'Help?' The idolater grinned like one of the sharks his people rode. 'We don't want your help, Son of Adam. We're going to take you to the temple outside our chief city. Then we will lure the Dandan there, and it will come, as its fellows have come since time immemorial, to feast.'

'You feed these fish?' Sinbad asked.

'We worship them as gods,' said the idolater simply. 'Do they not bring us life, down here in the water? We teach them to come to our temple for food. A slave or two is offered up every month. They come, sometimes more than one, when the blood fills the water and the smell is borne far and wide. And they feast.'

'How does it benefit you to feed your own kind to the Dandan? ' Sinbad asked. 'At least Amir Alma's people hunt them.'

'We teach them to come to our temple for food. And then, whenever we find a Son of Adam in our waters, we sacrifice him, and the Dandan comes and devours him. And that is his last meal. He dies there, poisoned, and we can cut him open and take his liver.'

Sinbad studied the brutal faced man. 'This is how you treat your god?' he said. 'You trick him and poison him?'

The idolater shrugged. 'I know nothing of theology,' he said. 'I am but a simple warrior. It seemed to me that the tradition contains many fabulous tales and fabrications whose intention is to put a gloss on the lamentable necessities of a life that is both futile and unpleasant. But the priests tell us that this is what our people have done since time immemorial. It is our custom, and this time you have been chosen.'

He executed a curt backflip and swam away.

Sinbad made no attempt to escape. If the opportunity arose, he would seize it in both hands, but for the moment those self-same hands were tied. Any attempt to escape under these conditions and with a spear carrying guard keeping vigilance over him would be futile.

He wondered if this was what Amir Alma had also been planning, although he could not believe that a Muslim would consider perpetrating an act of human sacrifice, even in the hunt for this Dandan. And what of Amir Alma and his men? Had all been slain by the idolaters? And if not, would they come after him?

If he fell into their hands again, would he be any better off? Ever since he had sunk into this submerged land he had been at the mercy of powerful forces. Only Khadijah had treated him with kindness. He hoped she was back with her shoal, that her absence had not been noted by her family before she returned. He wished only the best for her. As for himself, and his own future, it was looking very bleak.

The green light outside drained away, and soon inky night was upon them, as if expelled by a fleeing octopus. Sinbad dozed as best he could in his uncomfortable position. He must have fallen asleep, because at some time in the dark of night he was awoken by noise and confusion from within the cleft. It seemed that some submarine monster had crept into the shelter of the cave and surprised the sleeping idolaters. Sinbad could taste blood in the water, although in the utter blackness he saw nothing of what was happening. He struggled against his bonds. Could this be a chance to escape?

The shouting died away. As bubbles floated out from the cleft into a glimmering shaft of watery moonlight, Sinbad saw that they were followed by another floating shape, a gigantic lobster, its green shell hacked and scored with sword cuts and spear thrusts and shark bites. Its blood tainted the moonlit waters a ghastly black that spread until all was dark down in the cleft. Something rose up from the sea floor and swallowed it in one gulp.

As the moonlight poured down into the cleft once again, glimmering upon the scarred faces of frightened idolaters, Sinbad wondered what it had been, this vast creature that had terrified them so.

The following morning, the green light of day had filled the cleft, banishing darkness for now and revealing an eerie faery wonderland of sea sculpted rock and exquisite marine vegetation. Grudgingly, the guard untied Sinbad from the rock, leaving his arms bound, and carried him outside as the whole troop issued forth. A few inky swirls of blood drifted in the water but otherwise the sea was its usual murky green self.

By mid-morning, the temple had been sighted. It was a tall, pyramidal building of black basalt that stood high on an undersea ridge, beneath which sprawled a large town of cave like dwellings. As the troop of men swam across the water above the settlement, more idolaters swam out from their houses to see them pass, raising a cheer at the triumphant return of their valiant warriors.

Word of their coming had preceded them; a reception committee awaited them on the steps of a large staircase that led up the side of the pyramid. At its top was a flat expanse of basalt, broken only by a stone altar of crude design and a roughhewn statue of a sitting man, its lines blurred by long centuries of water erosion.

The sides of the basalt pyramid were carved with strange, mind twisting designs of sharks and octopuses enmeshed in fishy combat, and a long avenue of eroded statues led from its foot to the nearby town. Sinbad wondered at the purpose of steps in this world where everyone swam. He recalled ancient legends of long forgotten empires inundated by rising sea levels.

Sinbad was taken before the reception committee. Most of the priests were withered old men, with younger acolytes attending to their needs. The priests carried staffs of whalebone, and wore elaborate necklaces and masked headdresses of shells, while the acolytes bore curved daggers of night black obsidian. They welcomed the coming of the warriors with their captive, and it became clear that preparations had already been made.

Sinbad, handed over to the idolatrous priests by the garrulous, brutal faced leader of the warriors, found himself taken to the altar and tied to it by ropes of woven seaweed. He tried to struggle but it was futile, he had squandered his last chance, and now he was doomed to death in the jaws of the Dandan. Knowing that he would be poisonous to his devourer was scant consolation.

A masked priest produced a knife of shell, and brought it slashing down. Sinbad winced at the pain and struggled in his bonds as blood drifted from the gash in his flank. Another priest seized his arm and slashed it. The initial pain of the cuts was exacerbated by the sting of salt water. Another priest slashed his chest. Sinbad swore and cursed and struggled but to no avail. The whole pack of them cut at him with small, painful nicks, not enough to do real damage, but each one releasing blood into the surrounding water until he was surrounded by a dull, diluted scarlet cloud.

The high priest swam forward, accompanied by an acolyte who held a wickerwork basket. At the high priest's order he opened it. Fish guts and hacked up fragments drifted out into the water, adding to the miasma of gore that haloed Sinbad's bound form. When this was complete, the high priest gave a sign and the priests and acolytes swam for safety inside the temple.

Sinbad lay helpless amid the noisome cloud of blood and guts. Through it he could make out the town far below him. It was deserted, or rather its inhabitants had also sought shelter in their dwellings.

A shadow fell upon him. He looked upwards and his eyes began to focus on a sleek figure descending towards him. He struggled against the bonds as it grew larger and larger... Then went still as recognition, wonderful, incredulous recognition, dawned.

Swimming down through the haze of blood, Khadijah landed in a crouch beside him, sawing at the seaweed ropes with a sharp piece of broken shell. Sinbad's heart swelled with admiration for this intrepid girl.

'How in the Prophet's name did you get here?' he asked.

'I've been following you for days,' she told him, her slim muscles working beneath her lustrous skin as she sawed frantically. 'Ever since Amir Alma took you away.'

'You didn't go back to your shoal?' he asked. What had possessed her? 'Your grandfather will be angry with you.'

She grimaced at him, then continued sawing. 'I followed the Amir's hunting party as far as the border, hoping always for a chance to free you. I lived on shellfish harvested from the rocks, slept cold and alone outside the camp, waited with growing despondency for an opportunity to reach you and set you free. Then the idolaters attacked and slew many of the Amir's men and worst of all, you were carried off by the enemy.'

'And now you come to rescue me at the last moment. But what of Amir Alma's hunting party? Was the Amir killed?'

'Amir Alma escaped,' she said, as the last of the bonds parted under her frenzied ministrations. 'He went back for...'

Sinbad wondered why she had broken off at that point. Gore and fish parts obscured his vision and he wafted his hand through the water.

Something vast was drifting into sight. Sinbad glimpsed a pair huge fish jaws, huge, staring eyes, a fat squamous body, fins as huge as a ship's sails, a great tail that propelled the enormous fish forwards until it was directly above the pyramid. He watched helplessly as his blood drifted up through the waters, and the lumbering fish began to descend.

'It's the Dandan,' Khadijah shrieked. 'It's come for you.'

10 INTO THE BLUE

As the carpet shot towards her, the queen of the Wak-Wak fell backwards in an undignified sprawl across the throne. The executioner lifted up her great scimitar and swung at the carpet, but it whipped past her, bowling her over. Ahmed reached out from the edge of the carpet and snatched up the kneeling Sir Acelin from the guard woman who held him in nerveless hands. The carpet banked and flew upwards. Ahmed clung onto Sir Acelin's shoulder, but even unarmoured the Frank was heavy.

'Help!' Ahmed shouted, darting an urgent look at Nakeya. She moved to grab him in turn but suddenly he was gone. The carpet rocketed upwards. Nakeya looked in every direction. Finally she looked back to see the rapidly receding Wak-Wak city. It was so small now that the warrior women resembled scurrying ants.

Ahmed struggled to his feet, Sir Acelin at his side. High up in the sky, the carpet was already a tiny dot. He shook his head.

'Nakeya,' he said bitterly.

A spearhead pricked him. He looked back down to see that he and the knight were surrounded by a ring of spears, clutched in the slender hands of women warriors. Each one was young and exquisitely beautiful. Just the kind of company Ahmed liked, as a rule, but he had no fancy for spears to the throat.

He touched the spearhead gently with the flat of his hand, gesturing to its owner to remove it from the immediate vicinity of his gullet.

'Ow!' he said, staring at the blood that ran down his palm. These spears were razor sharp!

The warrior woman reversed her spear and struck him with the haft. Ahmed lurched, clutching at his ringing skull. Sir Acelin seized him and held him up.

'Do not antagonise them,' the knight said.

Ahmed turned to stare at them. 'Antagonise them? Don't you realise we've antagonised them by existing? They don't need men, these ladies. They're not even real people! They're nothing but walking, talking fruit!'

'So I understand,' said Sir Acelin. 'So I learnt on my long, painful journey here. They were about to execute me when...'

'Silence!' cried one of the guards. 'Bring these men before the queen!'

Queen Noor al-Hudha sat on her throne, intent in conversation with a woman in the long, brocaded robes of an astrologer. She looked up as the thief and the knight were both hauled before her. 'The rite will begin again,' she said, 'in half an hour. This time two men will die for violating our territory.'

'Now wait a moment,' said Ahmed with a nervous laugh. 'Please, let's be reasonable. There's really no need for all this.' He gave what he wrongly believed to be his most charming smile. 'I'm sure we can talk things through, come to some mutually beneficial solution to our problems.'

'Silence, you leering jackanapes!' cried Noor al-Hudha. 'When the sun reaches its zenith, it will be the most auspicious moment. Is that not right?' She looked to her companion for confirmation.

The astrologer nodded. 'When the sun reaches its height,' she intoned, 'death will come to those who would violate our territory.'

'No, no, no,' said Ahmed. 'You've got it all wrong! I've no wish to violate anyone's territory! Although I'm sure, under different circumstances, after a few glasses of a decent vintage, with suitable musical accompaniment and a good meal inside us, we could become... well, properly acquainted. But!' he added, raising his hands in protestation, 'I certainly don't want to force the issue!'

A guard struck him in the mouth and he sank back onto his haunches.

'A brief reprieve,' the little thief muttered, as salt blood trickled down his chin. He squinted up at the sun. 'So tell me, Sir Acelin. What is the plan?'

'Halt!' Nakeya cried, waving her arms wildly. 'Stop! Cease! Desist! Turnabout!'

All her efforts to control the carpet were futile. It flew on heedless of her words. What was she doing wrong? The wind whistled past so fast and so loud, chilling her to the bone so she could barely think.

Ahmed had always been the one who issued the commands. Now he was gone, fallen into the clutches of the Wak-Wak who killed all men. Nakeya was desperately trying to turn round and go back to rescue both Ahmed and Sir Acelin, but she was finding it impossible without...

Without Ahmed's ring! Without the Ring of Ja'afar, that was. The magic ring that Ahmed had stolen from the sleeping sorcerer when this whole business had begun. Nakeya remembered very little of the grand vizier's palace revolution; the slaves had been confined to barracks at first, and then Ja'afar had announced a new age of austerity in which musician slaves and dancing girls were hardly encouraged. And before she had known what was happening, Ja'afar was gone and the true caliph reinstated.

She remembered how Ja'afar had returned: flying into Baghdad with that djinn to carry off the caliph's beloved sister. The whole experience must have been much like this, being on an out of control flying carpet, whirling like a storm tossed leaf across the wide blue yonder. Except Ja'afar would have been in control of his djinn...

Djinn!

The thought broke through Nakeya's frozen mind, and with it rushed a flood of other notions. She had her own magical aid! Looking down at the brazen vessel at her side, she reached impulsively for the leaden stopper, with its inscription showing Solomon's Seal. But wait! She remembered what Aladdin had said: "Mark my words, he will not fulfil your desires unless you have a means to command him." If she released Hadana a second time, how would she bind the marid to her own will without Ahmed and the Ring of Ja'afar?

Hadana was not loyal. He was a slave, and he would obey only insofar as he could be compelled to do so. And yet he represented her only chance. Otherwise she might well reach Djinnistan and the emerald mountains of Kaf alone. Or maybe it would carry her off into the furthest reaches of the sky, to heights where only Alexander the Great was said to have flown.

She released the leaden stopper. For a moment, nothing happened. Then a dark cloud began to swirl from the vessel, billowing out behind the carpet as they flew onwards into the realm of clouds.

The saturnine figure of Hadana swelled into being, smokier and more insubstantial than his last manifestation. A look of alarm was on his face.

'O my love!' he cried out. 'Again you summon me to do your bidding. It is a pleasure to behold your sweet visage again after an eternity of imprisonment within that brazen vessel. I have longed to see you once more, to beg you to soften your heart towards me... But where are we going with such frightful rapidity?'

'Hadana!' Nakeya cried. 'I am aboard the magic carpet, but I do not know how to master it. I do not have the talisman Ahmed used to command it and now it goes wherever it wishes.'

'If you lack the Ring, O my love,' said Hadana cunningly, 'how can you hope to command me?'

Nakeya bit her lip. It was hard enough to think, clinging to an out of control carpet, without being posed such conundrums.

'There is no fooling you, I see,' she told him flatly. 'I am doomed, I see now, as are my companions, who are fated to die a terrible death at the hands of the women of Wak-Wak. I... had thought that you might do my bidding regardless.'

Hadana laughed loudly. 'Think you so, my love?' With a gesture, he stilled the carpet and it hovered in silence high above the clouds.

Nakeya smiled sadly at him. 'Indeed we

were lovers once,' she said, as the wind moaned disconsolately to itself. 'And perhaps we could have been lovers again, in after times, when all is peace. But not now. Not now that I am doomed to a terrible, unnamed death. And only because you would not do as I ask. There was a time, I still remember it, when you would obey my least command—out of love!'

A tear welled up in the marid's eye. 'Aye,' he said. 'Out of love. But where is that love now?'

'I have long been a slave…' Nakeya said.

'I too am a slave,' moaned Hadana. 'Do you not yearn for freedom?

'Freedom is what we all desire, O my love,' said Nakeya. 'One day will we both be free, free to be together. But not if I am dead. And I will die, unless you obey my commands. Not out of sorcerous coercion, but out of love.'

'O my sweet!' boomed the marid. 'Command me! Command me, and one day both of us will be free, free to love again!'

'Take me back to Wak-Wak,' Nakeya urged him, 'so that I can rescue my companions from Queen Noor al-Hudha. Then Ahmed will be able to command the carpet again, with the Ring of Ja'afar.'

'But then I will perforce be sent back into that brazen vessel,' wailed the marid, 'to another eternity of waiting. Waiting for you!'

Nakeya bit her lip.

'The sun is at its zenith!

At the astrologer's words, Ahmed and Sir Acelin were hustled across the stone flags to the execution block where the bare chested executioner stood leaning on her massive sword.

'Now!' Ahmed cried. As he kicked out at his captors, Sir Acelin broke free and ran straight towards the executioner. Sweat gleamed on her oiled torso as she swung the scimitar at him, but he dodged the attack and ducked in low, grasping her round the waist and bearing her to the ground with a thud and a clang.

Ahmed spun round and leapt down, fists lifted, as Noor al-Hudha cried out in anger from her throne and women warriors rushed forwards, spears at the ready. He dodged, ducked and wove as they tried to spit him on the wickedly sharp spearheads. Laughing, he spun round again—or tried to. Somehow he couldn't move.

Looking down he saw that a spear had passed through one leg of his baggy trousers, pinning him to the ground. The women laughed as they came to surround him. He tugged at his trousers. With a ripping sound he broke free, but only in time for two of the women to seize him.

'Let Ahmed go!'

Sir Acelin stood over the prone figure of the executioner, negligently holding the massive scimitar in one hand, pointing the blade directly at the women warriors. They gave ground as he advanced, but one of the women holding Ahmed's struggling figure placed a jewelled dagger to his throat.

Queen Noor al-Hudha laughed. 'Drop that blade, O son of Adam,' she said commandingly. 'Let fall that blade or your companion dies.'

Sir Acelin sketched a courtly bow, all the time keeping his stolen scimitar levelled at the women warriors. 'Your majesty,' he said urbanely, 'you mean to kill both of us as it is. The sun is at its zenith, and we male interlopers must die. Is that not how it goes? What if I forsake my vows of chivalry and offer violence to your own august personage?'

The queen gave another laugh, this time bitter and humourless. 'You will be slain like the dog you are if you lay a finger on me, son of Adam! Do you not see that you are surrounded?'

'Surrounded,' Sir Acelin acknowledged, 'and like to die. But this overlarge headsman's blade is quite big enough to reach you with little effort on my part. So if Ahmed dies, or you try to kill me, I will slice your most beautiful head from your shapely shoulders.'

A bow twanged, and the scimitar leapt out of Sir Acelin's hand, an arrow jutting from the hilt. He saw one of the women warriors lowering a bow. The blade clanged to the ground beside the throne, and the executioner bounded over to seize it. She returned to her feet with the sword in her hands, and advanced towards Sir Acelin.

Behind him was only the abyss. He was at the edge of the cliff, at the bottom of which lay the spreading waters of the ocean. In recent days he had survived one unexpected plunge, but he doubted he would do so twice. Nevertheless, he turned, about to leap over the edge.

'Sir Acelin!' Ahmed shouted. The knight glanced over at him. The thief was gazing in wonder at the sky above. A shadow fell upon Sir Acelin's teetering form, and he turned again. But this time he stumbled and fell over the edge.

The air whizzed past as he plummeted.

Unexpectedly he hit something soft and undulating, yet at such a speed as to knock the breath from him. Recovering, he saw that he was lying on the carpet again, Nakeya kneeling in the middle as it flew, and beside her sat Hadana the marid. They shot back up the cliff and then the top of it opened out before them.

Ahmed was still struggling as the women carried him across to the block where the executioner stood, scimitar in hand. She lifted it high in the air, and it flashed in the noon sunlight as the carpet shot down, and Hadana the marid seized Ahmed from amongst his captors and hauled him up onto the carpet.

Arrows swooped through the air all around them as women archers tried to bring down their flying forms. But soon they were out of range, vanishing rapidly into the blue green haze that hung over the eastern ocean.

11 QUEEN OF THE SERPENTS

The Dandan wriggled downwards, and the water bubbled. Its jaws opened wide, and its tail swung faster. Sinbad shoved Khadijah away, and she went tumbling away through the water, out across the idolaters' town.

To his horror, the giant fish changed course and veered after her.

Gazing over her shoulder at the enormous fish, Khadija turned smoothly in the water and kicked fiercely. But still the Dandan pursued her, bearing down on her. Despite its bulk, it swam rapidly, fins plying the waters like the oars of a galley, thrusting through the water like a ship in pursuit of a single fish.

More figures were descending through the murk in the Dandan's wake, sea men mounted on sea horses. Sinbad tore his attention away for a moment to see that they were led by a familiar figure—Amir Alma. The Amir clutched the reins of his sea horse in one hand, brandished a trident in the other. Seeing Sinbad, he called out to him.

'The fish! The fish! Cry out, O Son of Adam! Cry out!'

Sinbad didn't understand. The Dandan's jaws were gaping now as it closed in on the desperately swimming girl. He began swimming after it. Weaponless and naked, he could not hope to prevail, but he felt compelled to make some attempt. After all, it was his fault the fish had gone after Khadijah.

Amir Alma and his courtiers—there were far fewer than when last Sinbad saw them—pursued him. Amir Alma reached Sinbad's side.

'You must kill the fish!' he urged him. 'Only you have what it takes.'

Sinbad gave him an angry look. 'It's not going to eat me now it's got Khadijah's scent,' he protested.

Amir Alma shook his head. 'The very shout of a son of Adam is sufficient.'

'What did you say?' Sinbad demanded. Then he saw the Dandan's jaws close around Khadijah's desperately swimming form. 'No!' he shouted.

A storm of bubble broke from his mouth and went spiralling upwards through the green murk. To Sinbad's surprise, the Dandan's fins stilled and drooped, and the fish itself went limp in the water. Its jaws, brimming with fangs, hung slackly open, and a moment later, two bare, slender arms poked themselves from between those serrated teeth, followed by Khadijah's bewildered face. She pulled herself out of the dead fish's mouth and swam towards Sinbad.

Sinbad embraced her, then turned to Amir Alma. 'What happened?' he demanded. 'The fish seems to have suffered some kind of seizure. What brought it on?'

Khadijah clung to Sinbad as he did his best to sponge off the slime that coated her slim white form with a piece of seaweed. After Alma had despatched his men with flensing knives to butcher the sinking carcase of the fish, he joined Sinbad and Khadijah.

'Your voice,' Amir Alma said simply. 'Your voice itself slew the monster fish. This was always the plan, although things did not go as I had wished.'

Finding this hard to follow Sinbad looked around. 'Where is the Imam Albahr?' he asked.

Mournfully Alma shook his head. 'Death, the Destroyer of Delights and the Sunderer of Companies snatched many of my companions from me. It has been an ill-fated hunting expedition, this. But now my people have what they sought.'

Smaller fish were gathering like vultures in the water above the sinking carcass. By now it had hit the bottom, but Amir Alma's men cut open its side and began removing the vast gory lump that was its liver. The smaller fish were tearing pieces off the carcass, squabbling with each other as they did so. Alma's men swam up carrying the liver, and began to cut it up into smaller chunks, the water growing inky with blood as they did so. The liver was so large it was bigger than the mainsail of Sinbad's dhow.

'Sinbad,' said Khadijah. 'You slew the Dandan fish.'

'I did?' said Sinbad in surprise. 'How did I do that?'

'With your voice,' said Amir Alma, 'The voice of a son of Adam, which kills the fish just as surely as devouring your carcass would have done. The Dandan cannot survive the sound.'

'And you say this was the plan all along?' Sinbad said. 'That was why you took me with you? But why did you not say?'

'We could not know if you would do as we bade you,' Alma said. 'I argued with the Imam that we should negotiate with you but he was ever mistrustful of strangers. Besides, if you refused, we could have killed you and fed you to the fish.'

'That would have made you no better than the idolaters,' said Khadijah spiritedly.

'Speaking of which…' Sinbad began.

Filtering from the temple was the high priest and his fellow priests and acolytes. They were glaring in anger at the butchered carcass, and the gory lumps of liver Alma's courtiers were stowing in their saddlebags. One put a conch shell to his lips and blew a note that throbbed through the waters. Far off in the town, dark figures began pouring forth, spears in their hands.

'Better a dead dog than a live lion,' said Sinbad. 'I strongly advise you and your men to leave with what you have, before you lose it to the idolaters.'

They were not safe until they had reached a fortified city some way across the border. The idolaters' attacks on the return journey had diminished the already reduced numbers and it was a reduced yet triumphant hunting party that entered the city. But once they were safe, and the Dandan liver had been turned over to the alchemists for the production of the vital unguent, Amir Alma summoned Sinbad and Khadijah to his palace in Madinat Almuhit.

'You have been of inestimable aid, O Sinbad,' said Amir Alma. 'How can I ever repay you? You will be given palaces of your own, and the finest fish will be yours to eat. You shall be, by royal appointment, chief hunter of the Dandan.' His eyes took in Khadijah, who remained close to Sinbad. 'And this maiden of whom you have grown so fond! Should you want to take her to wife, she is yours.'

'And what would you say about that, Khadijah?' Sinbad asked quietly.

Khadijah looked demurely away. 'I would happily be your wife if you wished to stay in this realm,' she said, 'but you have already told me that you have your own life to live. I would die were I to follow you onto dry land. And yours is a roving disposition. You would not remain here for long.'

Amir Alma looked piqued. 'You mean to depart?' he demanded of Sinbad.

'With your permission, O king of the age,' said Sinbad. 'You must understand, I came here on a quest for my own liege lord.' He explained his situation to the Amir.

'I see I cannot detain you,' Alma said, nodding, 'although I and my realm, and one of my subjects in particular, will mourn your departure. But you say you do not know where this carpet of Suleiman is to be found? Your companions' whereabouts are unknown to you? How do you propose to reach Djinnistan?'

'Ah, well,' said Sinbad awkwardly. 'I'm sure I will find a way. I must try, at least.' He paused. 'Khadijah told me that the Imam Albahr might know a way. But he is dead.'

'Follow me,' said the Amir mysteriously, beckoning.

Amir Alma sat down beside the window of his palace. Joining him, Sinbad saw that it provided an unrivalled view of Madinat Almuhit, and the sea pastures beyond. In the distance, high crags rose into the upper waters, but their peak was out of sight.

'The mountains of my country are islands in your sea, Sinbad,' said the young Amir. 'Some of those islands you have visited already on your voyage. Others will be new to even you, who are so renowned a traveller in your own country. It is said—but Allah is wiser—that on the mountain, or verily the island that lies above my kingdom, there dwells the queen of the serpents. She knows where grows a herb on the heights of the mountain, which has this property: if a man anoint his feet with a salve produced from the self-same herb he can walk across any body of water.'

Sinbad was speechless. Khadijah hugged him close. 'Do you see what this means? You could walk from here to Djinnistan. You don't need this magic carpet of which you speak.'

'But I wish I knew what had happened to my friends,' Sinbad said softly. Then he shot her a look. 'Are you so happy to get rid of me?'

Khadijah shook her head. 'No,' she said. 'I do not think I will ever forget you. But we are people of different elements; you of the land, me of the sea. And so you must leave me, and I will go, weeping, back to my life with my fish.'

Sinbad looked stricken. 'Your grandfather!' he said. 'He will be angry with you now. You have been away much more than a few days.'

Amir Alma laughed. 'Word has been sent to that fellow,' he said, 'who is one of my most ardent subjects. He has been eating his heart out, believing that Khadijah had been lured away by some dissolute passing rogue. Now he knows the truth, he is only too grateful that he will see his beloved granddaughter returned to his side.'

Sinbad rose. 'I must go, then,' he announced. 'I must see how this serpent queen of whom you speak can help me.'

'But do not go yet,' the young Amir protested. 'Before you depart a banquet will be held at which you will eat of the best fish my kingdom has to offer! There will be music and dancing and poetry! Say you will stay, for a day more at least?'

Sinbad did indeed stay for another day, and leave-taking was heart-breaking. But at last he bade a farewell to the people of Madinat Almuhit and started climbing up the undersea cliffs alone. With him he carried a garment woven of the finest seaweeds of Alma's kingdom, which he would don when at last he rose from the waters to find himself standing in shallow waters off a rocky strand.

Inland, the peak of a mountain was visible above the tops of trees that waved gently in the wind, reminding Sinbad of the forests of giant kelp in that undersea realm he had so recently quit. He shook his head, chastising himself. He had that topsy-turvy. It was the kelp that had reminded him of the forests of dry land. The sun beamed down from a cobalt sky, and it seemed strange that he was not viewing its watery light through a green murk of weed.

Without tarbush or turban or trousers, he waded up through the surf and finally climbed up onto a rock where he sat in the sun, letting it dry his limbs. When it had done so, he scraped off what remained of the unguent, struggled into the simple robe of woven weed, and began to make his way from rock to rock until he reached the jungle.

A strange musky scent hung in the air. Animal life was evident on all sides, and it seemed strange to see birds wheeling overhead but no fish; to see spiders scuttling along tree boles but no crabs. He heard a croaking of crickets, a susurrus of insects, a hissing of snakes.

A large green snake drooped down from a branch above him, its large intelligent eyes regarding him with an expression that spoke of age-old wisdom. A forked tongue flicked in and out, tasting the air.

'And are you the queen of the serpents?' asked Sinbad, feeling foolish.

The snake did not answer, but slithered down onto the ground and glided away along the jungle path. At a turning, it looked back at Sinbad. To his surprise, and he had thought few wonders could surprise him these days, he found himself following it.

The jungle fell back to reveal a lake in which many serpentine forms swam. On the far side of the lake rose the craggy foothills of the mountain at the centre of the small island. The snake he had followed was curled up on the banks of the lake, and beside it was a much larger snake. It reared up to reveal that instead of having a serpent's head it had the face of a woman.

'Sinbad,' the snake woman hissed. 'Peace be upon you, O far famed traveller. I am Yamlikha, queen of the serpents.'

At that the snakes in the lake sent up a hissing chorus. Sinbad, feeling as if he was in a dream, went up to the snake queen and made his salaams.

'And upon you be peace, O Yamlikha, queen of the serpents,' said Sinbad. 'I was told by the king of the sea that you could help me. I must go to Djinnistan in the Mountains of Kaf, and the Carpet of Suleiman that was my transport thither has been lost.'

'The Carpet was seen a day ago above the islands of Wak-Wak, many leagues from here,' said the queen of the serpents.

Sinbad studied her face. Despite her serpentine torso she had the look of a woman of mature years, proud and undaunted, with a broad brow and deep, dark eyes ringed with kohl. From between two coral red lips flicked a forked tongue and she spoke sibilantly. 'I am told that a herb grows upon your island,' Sinbad said, 'that produces a salve with the magical property of rendering the man who anoints his feet with it able to cross any body of water.'

'Indeed there is such a herb,' said the queen of the serpents. 'You mean to use this salve to travel to the mountains of Kaf?'

'I know of no other way to reach the kingdom of the Djinn,' said Sinbad. 'If you can tell me of another, please point me in its way.'

'Travellers have come to my island in times long gone,' said the queen, 'and all sought the herb. Only one visitor was man enough to take it from where it grows atop the highest peak. And you? Are you man enough to ascend the peak, O Sinbad?'

'As a lad,' Sinbad explained, 'I would climb to the highest yardarm of my ship to spy out the way ahead. At first I was afraid that I would fall to the deck far below, but soon I knew that there was nothing to fear but that I would lose my life. And life is a bridge. One should cross it, not build a house upon it.'

'You are wise,' said the queen of the serpents approvingly. 'As wise as the wisest serpent. The man I speak of imprisoned me and forced me to aid him, but you, O Sinbad, I will help willingly. Since you have proved yourself so wise, my chamberlain will go with you to show you the way.'

The green snake hissed, and Sinbad made his farewells to the queen. Sinbad followed the green snake and together they went round the lake of serpents. Reaching the crags, the snake began to glide up the sheer side. Sinbad searched the rock for hand and footholds and began to climb...

12 THE SEA OF JADE

Sweat trickled down Sinbad's brow as he reached for another crumbling handhold in the fragile rock of the cliff face. Mercilessly the sun beat down from the gleaming sky, and Sinbad resembled a fly on a house wall as he crawled with painful slowness up the mountainside. All the time the green serpent glided upwards relentlessly from rock to rock, pausing only to look back at Sinbad with seeming scorn in its inhuman eyes.

The sun was scorching hot, sweat ran down the sailor's skin to sizzle and dry up in its rays. His seaweed coat had been reduced to rags. His tongue felt like a fragment of desert dry wood as he climbed on and on. But he would not give up. Although from time to time his numb hands failed to grasp the next handhold and he would lose his grip, he rescued himself each time with a wild lunge at a passing ledge and caught a hold again. His remorseless progress reminded him of an automaton a magician had set about a monotonous, repetitive task and then abandoned, forgotten, forsaken, to continue its duties mechanically until the day of doom.

At last his bleeding hand reached up, seizing for something to cling onto, and settled on… nothing. Baffled, Sinbad looked up, blinking away the rivulet of sweat that ran into his weary eyes, and saw that he had reached the top. Grass grew up there and as he hang there gazing upwards he caught a sweet scent of herbage.

The green snake was waiting for him, forked tongue darting out to taste the air. With a groan, Sinbad hauled himself up onto the grassy sward with both arms, bringing up his aching legs one after another, and pitched forwards to sprawl undignifiedly on his face. For a long while he did not move but lay there groaning softly.

He was woken from a half daze by a cold touch to his temples. Opening his eyes he saw that the snake had pressed its blunt, scaly head against his skin. It gazed hypnotically into his eyes and its tongue flickered out.

'Very well, O very well, wise serpent,' Sinbad grumbled, getting to his knees and looked about him.

He saw a broad meadow, dotted with flowers, that swept away towards the highest peak. A gentle breeze stirred the grasses. Sinbad got up into a crouch. So much grass, so many flowers. So many herbs, growing amidst the foliage. He recognised a tuft of basil by the leaves and the scent. Lemon balm grew nearby, exuding a scent like lemon mixed with mint. Mint itself thrived amongst the grass, and comfrey was another herb Sinbad recognised, but there were many plants that were unfamiliar to an Arab's pharmacopeia.

Sinbad turned to look inquiringly at the green snake only to see that it had curled itself round a plant that he did not recognise. The herb was tall and wiry, with pale green leaves, and exuded a zesty scent. Doubtfully, Sinbad knelt beside it and cupped the leaves in his hand. The snake hissed approvingly as he squeezed it and received a smear of green juice.

Soon Sinbad found a large clump of the herb. Busily, he began to pick its leaves, tucking them away in the folds of his ragged tunic. When he thought he had collected enough, he got to his feet and saw that the green snake was already sliding back towards the cliff edge.

The serpent queen smiled dignifiedly, radiating approval at his return. 'Bruise the leaves to express the juice,' she directed him. 'Keep some of it in this belt pouch I will give you, and anoint your feet with the rest.'

Sinbad did as he was bade. 'And this will be enough to keep me afloat?' he asked doubtfully. 'As far as the mountains of Kaf?'

The serpent queen inclined her head, smiling again. Her tongue darted. 'Yes, O Sinbad.

With this, Bulukiya and his companion Affan walked as far as Djinnistan where they discovered the tomb of Suleiman. Trust my word as you wish, or put it to the test.'

'My thanks, O queen,' said Sinbad. 'I go now to make use of this miraculous herb. In what quarter does Djinnistan lie?'

The queen indicated the south west, and Sinbad thanked her and made his farewells. An hour later he stood on the rocky shore, his bare feet smeared with the juice of the herb. Hesitantly, he dipped his right foot into the salty water.

To his surprise and delight, he found that it floated as buoyantly as his own dhow. Tentatively he added the left foot and found himself standing foursquare on the surface of the water. He stood motionless for a long time before he could summon up the courage to try walking. Then he brought his right foot up and it splashed down a short way away. It was like learning to walk again, he thought, as he brought up his left foot. Growing in confidence he begam to stride out across the rolling waters.

Sea birds cried in dismay as they wheeled above him. Beneath him the water was pure and clear, and he could see the bottom. He saw nothing of Khadijah's nation down there, only endless sands and weed grown rocks and shoals of fish with no one to tend to them.

He walked onwards, afraid to stop, convinced that if his momentum ceased for a second he would fall and sink into the depths to drown. Now he regretted his folly in stripping his limbs of the Dandan unguent when he had risen from the sea waters by the serpent queen's isle. Looking back he saw no sign of any land. He was out in the open sea.

He walked on, halting from time to time to rest, snatching fish from the water when he was hungry. The water gleamed with a sheen of emerald green. The sea, the sky overhead, everything on every hand, even the sunlight, was green. Halting and putting a hand up to shade his eyes Sinbad gazed ahead of him. For a moment he thought he glimpsed, on the haze of the far distant horizon, a long line of mountain peaks. They too gleamed with a shade of green.

But surely they were too small to be the sky-high mountains of Kaf. Or was their tiny size an indication that he was still many, many miles from Djinnistan and its mountains? Or—he rubbed at his eyes and looked again—they had vanished into the haze. Had they been no more than a mirage, or some sorcerous illusion?

He focused his mind on putting one foot in front of another.

For the occupants of Suleiman's Carpet, the mountains were an unambiguous presence. They could be seen marching across the horizon as the sun set on the far side of the jade green waters of the ocean; huge emerald mountains they were, peak after peak receding into the haze. Ahmed marvelled at the unearthly blaze of bright green light.

'I never thought I would be able to say this,' he told his companions, 'but we're almost there.'

Nakeya nodded. 'Those must be the mountains of Kaf,' she said. 'Amongst its valleys we will find Djinnistan. How will we recognise it?'

'From Aladdin's account,' said Sir Acelin. 'How did he describe it?'

Nakeya quoted from memory. '"Its chief province is the Country of Delight, and its capital is Schadou Kiam, the City of Jewels. It is sundered into two parts, the Desert of Monsters and the Desert of Demons".'

Ahmed rubbed his chin. It had been a long journey since they had escaped the empire of women, crossing many seas and islands. Now as the sea of jade gave way to the emerald mountains, he was afraid that they could no longer put off facing up to the inevitable: they didn't know what they were doing, and they didn't have the chance of a cat in Jahannam. 'So we're looking for two deserts,' he said briskly. 'And a city of jewels. The latter will be hard to find amidst all this emerald gleam.'

'We have yet to reach the mountains,' Nakeya pointed out. 'What is more, we do not know if Sinbad is alive or dead, on dry land or at the bottom of the sea. It was Sinbad who was our leader. He was the one who had the plan. What will we do without him?'

Sir Acelin laid a comforting hand on her arm. 'Mon Dieu, Sinbad was a remarkable man in many ways,' he told her, his use of the past tense making it clear he doubted that the sailor had survived. 'But we know what we have to do. We must rescue the princess from the wicked magician.'

'You make it sound very easy,' said Nakeya bitterly. 'But consider. We will be weaponless, friendless, only three of us in a hostile land inhabited by the djinn, by the ifrits and the marids. Perhaps worse creatures too. We must find Ja'afar, who is known to be an ally of the djinn, and to take from him the princess barehanded. Only one of us is a warrior, knight, and you lost your sword and armour long ago.'

Sir Acelin looked away, and the wind played idly with his curly hair as he stared unseeingly into the haze. Ahmed took her other hand. 'Listen to me, Nakeya,' he said. 'We're not so lacking in abilities. We even have a friend among the djinn.' He rapped on Nakeya's brazen vessel. 'Hadana is still under an obligation to do our bidding another time. And I've still got the magician's ring.' He raised his hand, and the ring glittered on his finger in the rays of the setting sun. 'Sir Acelin can fight well enough with his bare hands, can't you, my friend?'

The knight looked back. 'Even with full armour, mounted on a destrier, with a fresh lance in my gauntleted hand, I would question my ability to prevail against the forces that face us. But that will not deter me. I shall fight magicians or demons or any other oppressors who stand between me and the princess.'

Ahmed laughed. 'See, Nakeya?' he said merrily. 'With your djinn and my ring and the knight's foolhardy spirit, what do we have to fear?'

They flew onwards.

Ja'afar raised his hands in a mystical gesture. The lamps glimmered sporadically in the gloom of this chamber of conjuration deep beneath the mountain. The fresh blood in which the pentacle had been written on the floor had yet to congeal, the Hebrew letters that had been written within the angles of the symbol glistened in the fitful light. He began to recite the magic words.

The rock shuddered, and with a bang and a booming laugh Zoba'ah Abu Hasan appeared in a cloud of oily green smoke.

'Why dost thou summon me yet again, O magician?' Zoba'ah Abu Hasan roared. 'Have I not done thy bidding more than once?'

Ja'afar held up his talisman, a coin shaped object he wore around his neck on a chain. 'By this trinket art thou bound to do my will as long as it remains in my possession,' he said. 'Thou art slave to the laws put upon thy kind by Suleiman the Magician, sultan of the Hebrews, long ages ago. My plans gather apace, and soon we will be returning in force to Baghdad...'

'I know all of thy plans, O wizard,' said the djinn resignedly. 'Much more of them than I wish to know. Why dost thou trouble me at this hour? Thou hast power over me to bend me to thy will, but I do not relish thy conversation. Have I not done thy bidding? I helped thou snatch the princess, I cast thy enemy into the sea...'

'Ahah,' said Ja'afar, 'Then thou didst not see Sinbad die.'

'No son of Adam could survive drowning,' said the djinn.

'So you maintain,' said Ja'afar, 'but Sinbad is renowned through all of Baghdad's bazaars for his miraculous escapes. I want thee to search the seas for any sign of Sinbad, alive or dead. And if thou findst him still living, bring him to me!'

'To thou?' asked the djinn. 'Thou wantst him alive? I thought thou desired his death!'

'If he still lives, I can find a use for him,' said Ja'afar. 'Now begone, in the name of Iblis!'

'To hear is to obey, O master!' said the djinn. With another deafening detonation, he vanished from the chamber.

Bitterly Ja'afar regarded the talisman. Puissant as it was, it gave him only so much power over djinn like Zoba'ah. He had owned a most powerful ring once, inscribed with Suleiman's

Seal, that had given him great power, but he had lost it, when it had been exchanged for a cursed ring that had blown him halfway across the world to this country of the djinn.

If he had not had the talisman about his person, he would never have been able to gain power over those djinn who now worked for him. One day, somehow, he would regain the ring. And one day he would be avenged upon Harun al-Rashid and the rest of them. He would have power again. Power over the world! And then his enemies, large and small, would suffer. If he lived, Sinbad would suffer. And that was not all. He had uses for that far famed sailor...

With a snarl, Ja'afar turned and strode from the chamber.

BOOK THREE: DJINNISTAN

1 SINBAD COMES ASHORE

Weary, Sinbad crawled through the surf. Before him stretched a wide beach of crushed emerald rock. Towering above him were rugged cliffs of the same aquamarine material. An eerie blue green hue shimmered in the hot, still air. Dripping, he got to his feet. Nothing moved on that weird strand, not a hint of life was there other than Sinbad, who stood naked but for his ragged seaweed tunic.

Groaning to himself, he sat down on a rock, gazing back across the rolling jade waters of the sea, grateful for a chance to rest his tired body. He had *walked* across that sea, for league upon league across the waters, kept buoyant by the magical salve. He'd had to stay upright for all those leagues. And now he was weary. All around him the pebbles of the emerald beach winked in the eerie light. The rock under him was warm in the sun. He lay back against it. His head fell back.

And he slept.

When next he awoke, it was growing cool. The sun was setting over the far off waters, its rays gleaming strangely in the eerie blue-green light. Rested and refreshed, if a little chill, Sinbad rose to his feet, stretching and yawning. All around him the beach was deserted. Long shadows were growing, pointing meaningfully towards the cliffs. Beyond them, out of sight from Sinbad's position, were the foothills of the Mountains of Kaf, amidst which stood the kingdom of Djinnistan.

Looking upwards, he saw a tiny dot soaring across the evening sky. Was it a bird? He remembered the roc. Whatever it was did not seem to have seen him, and it was flying inland, but he thought he had best get under cover, find somewhere to stay for the night. Sleeping out in the open had been foolish, if unavoidable. Who knew what creatures lived here? Djinn, for certain. Was this mysterious flier a djinn? Or something worse?

He crossed the beach until he stood in the lee of the cliffs, where he began hunting round for a way to climb them. Soon after, he found a gully down which trickled a brackish stream, and he drank from it until its saltiness caused him to stop, retching. Now he began to follow its banks inland.

He found himself on a plateau of emeralds that glowed eerily in the half light. It ascended into a line of foothills, and a vast range of peaks marched across the horizon. Each hill and mountain gleamed with the blue green of emeralds, the last rays of the dying sun flashing from the impossibly sharp peaks. Perhaps somewhere up there he would find a cave in which he could shelter. He might be able to get some notion of the lie of the land. Perhaps even learn the location of the city of the djinn.

Half an hour later he was walking along a high mountain path. Shades of night were falling, and he had seen no sign of any cave. A wind plucked at his tunic and his bedraggled locks. He halted, head cocked.

What had he heard? He stood listening vainly until it came again. the sound of mighty feet, tramping down the mountain path. Sinbad turned to go back, but even as he did so, a file of armoured figures turned the corner, each one twice Sinbad's height if not taller. Each wore scale armour of brass. Each looked manlike but was not a man.

Each one had some characteristics that were animalistic. One had the tusks of a warthog, another had the head of a lion. Djinn. They could be nothing else. All were clutching scimitars and spears, and on seeing Sinbad they issued a hunting cry.

Sinbad turned, and ran back along the mountain path.

Turning a corner, he skidded and his bare feet slithered on the gleaming emerald. His arms flailed and he tried to snatch a hold of something, anything, to arrest his fall, but he was too late. He went rolling down the slope, out of control, finally winding up on a rocky ledge with a crash that knocked the breath out of him.

For a moment he lay there in silence. It was almost pitch black now, and he could hear the armoured djinn shouting to each other from further up the mountain. His whole body ached, and his head swam. His legs were a mass of cuts and bruises. The wind mercilessly blew around him. He would have to seek shelter, or he might die of the cold. Grimly, painfully, still half delirious from the battering he had received, he got to his hands and knees and crawled along the ledge.

The voices grew louder. His djinn pursuers had found the spot where he had fallen. They would be coming down the slope in search of him; he had certainly left enough of a trail. Grimly, he crawled on.

He saw the yawning mouth of a crevice in the rock face. Tentatively he investigated. It was too dark to see how deep it was. He was about to crawl away when he heard a thud of great feet from further down the ledge. One of the djinn had jumped down in search of him. Sinbad turned and scrambled blindly into the gap.

It was a dry, rocky, shadow hung cleft. He turned to look out at the mountain slope, gleaming now in the light of the risen moon. A figure stamped past, and Sinbad shrank back into the shadows. A little further, and he found a slope leading downwards. So it was a cave, not just a crevice!

Raised voices floated in from outside. The moonlight cut off fitfully as more figures passed back and forth. Sinbad drew back into the shadows, inching his way down the slope into the utter blackness.

Encountering a cold slab of some metal, he halted, feeling along it with his hands. Looking back over his shoulder, he saw the cave entrance above him, like a dim, shimmering star in the all-encompassing blackness. Figures were moving out there, casting their shadows on the moonlit cave mouth. He sank down into a crouch.

He must remain here until they had gone. They were djinn, he was sure of it. Soldiers of their sultan, he surmised. Did this mean that they were looking for him? That they knew of his presence in Djinnistan? Or was this simply a patrol of some kind? Sinbad knew nothing of this country. All he was aware of was that Ja'afar was here, somewhere, and he held the Caliph's sister prisoner.

The sound of djinn on the mountainside still reached his ears, but he ignored it for the moment, reached out with his hand and felt at the slab. It was curiously regular, the work of men—or of djinn. Shifting along, he learnt that the side of the slab stretched for several cubits before turning at right angles. Carved mouldings adorned it. Sinbad's questing fingers picked out shapes of men and horses, long processions of them, and with them were other shapes, winged men. Angels or demons, Sinbad could not tell in this darkness. Then his fingers traced out a geometric shape, a series of angles. Of triangles. No, he was wrong; it was a five pointed star.

Rising unsteadily to his feet, Sinbad reached out to feel his way along the top of the slab. Touching something soft and withered, he staggered back, stifling a cry, and felt rock shift beneath his feet. There was a clatter of it, and suddenly the air was filled with falling stones. Sweating in fear, Sinbad crouched down, hands over his head, as the fragments rained down. One of them struck his raised arm and he almost fell flat.

The rain of rocks ended as abruptly as it had begun. Sinbad lifted his head to see dust dancing in the moonbeams that had now penetrated the deeper gloom, now that the moon had ascended higher in the night sky outside. He gasped.

The silvery rays glanced off the rubble strewn top of the slab. Now he saw what he had previously only felt. The slab itself glistened with gold. The carved mouldings proved to be jewels. Lying atop the slab, clad in robes of green silk woven with gold, was a body.

A perfectly preserved body, an old man

wearing a crown, with a long white beard that reached down almost as far as the toes of his curly slippers. Two hands were clasped upon a bony chest, closed upon the hilt of a glittering scimitar. The eyes were closed and yet it seemed to Sinbad as if they were staring at him, this desecrator. A large chunk of shattered emerald lay across the body's legs, and other fragments that had fallen from the roof lay scattered about.

Sinbad gazed down at the venerable face of this ancient sultan. This was no djinn, he knew as much; this was a Son of Adam. But who was it, lying in this forsaken cave in the kingdom of the djinn? He crouched down and examined the jewels that studded the golden slab. He found the five pointed star that he had traced out whilst in the darkness. The pentagram. The Seal of Suleiman. He rose again and a second time stared down at the lifeless, ancient face. Was this, then, Suleiman? He who had ruled men and djinn, long ago, and banished the evil djinn to these mountains at the edge of the world?

Sinbad sat down, leaning against the slab. It was an awesome thought. But perhaps it meant that he was safe here. The djinn would not dare enter the tomb of Suleiman. That name struck a chord, and suddenly he remembered that the serpent queen had made mention of such a tomb. Sinbad laughed to himself. He had found it! He alone.

He fell to wondering what had happened to

his comrades after he had fallen from the flying carpet. Had they all been killed by the djinn? Or had they flown on? Were they here even now? Would he meet them in this strange land? He paused to listen. He could hear no noise of the djinn who had been searching for him outside. The search must have moved off. Well, that was good. He decided to wait until dawn, and then continue his journey.

The dawn came after a fretful night. It had been an eerie resting place, curled up by the body of the greatest sultan the world had ever known, the greatest prophet bar one. Sinbad had dozed fitfully but he had been unable to sleep. Now he rose again, seeing the cave well-lit by the light that poured in through the cave entrance. He gave Suleiman one last respectful nod, then after a moment's indecision prised the sword from those withered hands and began climbing up the slope toward the cave mouth.

Shortly afterwards he was peering out of the cave mouth, looking cautiously over the lip of it as he still clung on to the rocks. He was dazzled by the sunlit vista of emerald crags that confronted him. All was still and silent.

He could see no sign of the djinn. He climbed up a little higher until he was sitting in the cave mouth, scimitar across his knees. From here he could see nothing of the ledge, only the valley that spread out beneath him. The sands of a desert rolled to the horizon, flanked by more emerald mountains. And far off, shimmering in the haze, stood the spires and domes and minarets of a vast and fantastic city. This must be it, he told himself. The city of the djinn. Somehow he was sure that there, if anywhere, was where he would find word of Ja'afar and his captive.

Freshened by a new resolve, he strode out of the cave, intending to find some way down the mountainside and into that desert. The moment he did so, he heard a loud stamping sound, and looking one way then the other he saw armoured djinn bearing down on him. Their scimitars flashed in the dawn light.

2 SULTAN OF THE DJINN

The wind that whipped about the flying carpet was gritty and painful. The three occupants lay flat on their faces, clinging on to the gorgeous weave as the storm persisted.

They were flying over the desert. All night they had flown, the three of them sleeping in turns as the carpet took them high above the land. In the distance, barely visible through the stinging clouds of dust, stood the city that they had seen earlier. On every hand, the mountains of Kaf glimmered greenly through the grit, but Ahmed wanted only to find somewhere they could land.

'What city is that?' Sir Acelin cried over the howl of the wind. 'Do we know that we will be met by a warm welcome? What if it is inhabited by our foes?'

Nakeya lifted her face to scowl at him. 'We need to learn where Ja'afar is keeping Princess Abassa. Nowhere else in this wilderness looks likely to provide us with answers.' She turned to

Ahmed. 'I have sand in my hair and grit in my clothes... Bring us down, Ahmed. At least for a while.'

Ahmed shook his head obstinately. 'We're almost there,' he said. 'I think that city is this Schadou Kiam—the City of Jewels. Can't you see how it flashes in the sunlight?'

Nakeya shook her head bitterly. 'I see nothing but these clouds of flying sand. Take us down!'

Sir Acelin gripped her arm. 'Look yonder!' he cried. 'What is that?'

Nakeya shook his arm off, but followed his pointing finger. Ahmed raised his head. Through the swirling storm of grit, a flying shape, like a whirlwind and yet also somehow like a man, sailing over the mountains north of them.

'A djinn,' he cried. 'Well, no surprise. This is Djinnistan, after all.'

'It looks... familiar,' said Sir Acelin musingly.

They watched in silence as the carpet flew on towards the city and the flying djinn vanished over the mountains. 'It resembled the djinn that attacked us at sea,' said Nakeya, and she bit her lip. 'The one who attacked us when we lost Sinbad.'

Ahmed did not want to be reminded of their loss. Without Sinbad, the mission was close to foundering. And what would they do when they finally found Ja'afar? How would they rescue

Princess Abassa?

The leagues of desert passed by and beneath them sprawled the meadows and groves of the Country of Delight, where peacocks called and fountains played. In its midst the great City of Jewels, Schadou Kiam. Commanding the carpet to go into a spiral descent, Ahmed saw that the place was well named. Spires and domes glittered with the light of thousands of rubies and diamonds, opals and beryls and sapphires and pearls. Jewelled palaces lined streets of jade, long boulevards of glittering gems opened out into squares and market places. Like Baghdad, Schadou Kiam was built in a circle, with a river running through the middle, and broad thoroughfares divided it up into quarters. Outside the city stood a spur of the emerald mountains, and on its highest point was a single tower.

They flew down towards the city of the djinn. As they drew closer, Ahmed noted signs that all was not well in Schadou Kiam. In places the garnet encrusted walls were broken down, and some of the palaces in that quarter of the city were in ruin. 'There has been war here, recently,' Sir Acelin commented. 'I know the signs.'

Ahmed glanced at him. The knight's face was drawn and grey. He was a warrior. Why should the prospect of a war of the djinn perturb him so? It troubled Ahmed, of course, but he was a thief, not a hero. He glanced at Nakeya, who rested her hand on the brazen vessel. She gave him a disapproving look, and he returned it with an impish smile.

'Let's hope the war is over,' he said.

They saw figures staring up at them. Armoured warriors stood by the city gates, their accoutrements glittering in the sun. Men they seemed at first glance, but they stood at least eight feet high and had the heads of beasts.

'Djinn,' said Nakeya in a low voice.

Ahmed shot her a look. 'Apparently,' he said. 'Are we going to waste time stating the obvious?' He called down to the guards. 'Good morning!'

A djinn with the head of a bison brandished his spear. 'Who are you?' he called up in a growling voice that echoed from the stones themselves. 'Who are you who comes to Djinnistan by magic? You are no djinn. Are you sorcerers?'

Ahmed exchanged doubtful glances with his companions. He glanced at the ring on his finger, the ring of Ja'afar with which he commanded the flying carpet, and the brazen vessel Nakeya clutched, inside which was imprisoned the marid Hadana. Only Sir Acelin lacked any magical accoutrements, and even he was sitting on a flying carpet.

'No,' he called down. 'We're perfectly normal mortals. We're here on a quest of sorts.'

'A quest?' boomed the djinn guard. 'State your business or be gone from the City of Jewels. The only Sons of Adam to visit Djinnistan are sorcerers.'

Impatiently Sir Acelin pushed Ahmed to one side. 'We would not speak of our business to mere guards,' the knight said haughtily. 'We wish to speak to your ruler! Now make haste, or he will have something to say to you when he learns what a surly reception you give to guests from over the seas.'

'Malik Gatshan is in his palace,' said the djinn guard resentfully. 'Land your magical craft and I will take you into the presence.'

Ahmed spoke the words of command, and the carpet landed with a thump before the towering jewelled gates of the city. The three travellers rolled up the carpet, and Ahmed and Sir Acelin carried it on their shoulders as, leaving the other guards on duty, the guard escorted them through the bustling streets of the city. Nakeya went with them, carrying her dulcimer and her brazen vessel.

The city thronged with djinn, many of them as gigantic as their guide, some with skin of green or pink or yellow, some with bestial characteristics, some angelic, all going about the normal business of a city. In the bazaar, djinn merchants sold jewels to djinn shoppers, who were seen to devour the gems like ripe fruit. They passed a mosque, where devout djinn called the faithful to prayer, and a djinn school where young djinn chanted the lesson in response to a tall, stern faced schoolmaster. Elsewhere they witnessed a hue and cry as djinn watchmen pursued a djinn thief down the winding streets.

But at last they were brought to the vastest of the many gigantic palaces in the city, where they were escorted into a great audience chamber beneath an onion dome in pea green, where they stood waiting upon a pavement of multicoloured jewels for the sultan's pleasure.

Guards lined the walls and stood, holding trumpets, on either side of a high arch between which stood a pair of filigree gates. With a triumphal flourish, the gates swung open and in swept a most magnificent looking djinn, an aged fellow with a vast white beard, a face of bright red in which flashed fiery eyes, with a huge turban upon his snowy brows and a long blue robe that hung down to his ankles. He stepped up onto the dais and took his seat upon the throne.

'Welcome to my kingdom of Djinnistan, O Sons and Daughters of Adam and Eve,' he said in a reedy, aged voice. 'I am Malik Gatshan, sultan of all the djinn. Seldom do we receive visitors from the lands of men. It is a long way for your kind to travel, and only a very few have journeyed here since the days of Sultan Suleiman.'

Ahmed shifted a little, and scratched at the gemstone pavement with one foot. He indicated the carpet that he and Sir Acelin had set down beside them. 'We have a bit of an advantage, O sultan, over the rest of our kind. We have the Carpet of that particular gentleman.'

Malik Gatshan nodded. 'Then you are sorcerers. I thought as much. Most of our visitors from the world of men have been sorcerers. We are not fond of sorcerers, being devout djinn, and having little truck with such folk with their talismans and their amulets, forever invoking we djinn to do their will. They are seldom edifying, the tasks they set us. If it were not for the edicts Suleiman gave us long ago, we would ignore such folk and their wearisome petitions.'

Ahmed coughed. 'We are not sorcerers,' he said. 'But sorcery has certainly helped get us this far. We, ah, found the carpet in the City of Brass.'

'Found?' Malik Gatshan's brows drew down. 'Surely you do not mean that you are thieves! In my realm, thieves fare less well than sorcerers, they have their hands cut off. They find pursuing their larcenous trade most difficult after that. My people have a deep, abiding hatred for thieves and liars.'

Ahmed laughed nervously. 'Of course we aren't thieves, no, nor liars either,' he said with less than scrupulous honesty. 'As a matter of fact, we are emissaries from the Caliph of Baghdad, the renowned Harun al-Rashid.'

Malik Gatshan nestled his chin in his great paws. 'I have not heard of him. What is this insignificant backwater you called Baghdad?'

Ahmed was so outraged he had trouble speaking. Sir Acelin brushed past him. 'Your majesty,' he said, 'Harun al-Rashid rules over the paynim whom we call Saracens. He sent us on a quest to rescue…'

'Paynim, you call him?' the sultan of the djinn inquired. 'You do not mean that this far-off potentate is…' He lowered his voice, 'an unbeliever? There is no god but God and Mohammed is his Prophet,' he added in piously.

'Ah, no,' said Sir Acelin. 'That is to say, yes. In a manner of speaking. The Caliph does not follow my faith. But neither, it seems, do you, your majesty.'

The sultan drew himself up. 'Then it is you yourself who is an unbeliever? All of you are unbelievers? My people hate unbelievers as much as they hate thieves, liars, and sorcerers!'

'No!' Ahmed regained control of his tongue. 'No, O sultan! That's to say, I'm not an unbeliever. I was brought up in Baghdad, city of peace, and they're pretty much all Muslim there. My friends come from other lands, and other faiths. But we were sent by the Caliph of Baghdad on a quest that has brought us to your own kingdom.'

'And you say this Caliph is not an unbeliever?' Malik Gatshan inquired.

'Not at all, O sultan,' said Ahmed. 'He's a good Muslim!'

'In which case,' said the sultan, 'it behoves me to make myself of use to the emissaries of a brother monarch, if he truly is a good Muslim. Tell me what brings you to my land.'

'We have come here in search of the Caliph's sister,' said Ahmed. 'The princess Abassa, who was abducted from Baghdad by the sorcerer Ja'afar with the aid of a djinn.'

'And what was the name of this djinn?' the sultan asked. 'It saddens me that one of my subjects was implicated in such a crime. In league with a sorcerer, no less.'

Ahmed scratched his head. 'Zoba'ah Abu Hasan, I believe,' he said.

'Zoba'ah Abu Hasan?' asked the sultan. 'Lord of the Wind? Why, he is well known to me, a dignitary of the city. He has only recently left the city on business of his own. Or rather that of the sorcerer who is his master. You accuse him?'

'Sorcerer?' Ahmed said. 'I thought you said you hated sorcerers?'

'Perhaps you should discuss that with the sorcerer in question, thief,' came a voice from the entrance.

3 AD-DIMIRYAT

Hands bound behind him with cord that felt as if it had been forged from iron, Sinbad was marched down the mountain path, armoured djinn before and behind him. The tramping of his captors' big boots echoed from the dizzying mountain walls that reared on either side of him, as the aquamarine haze shimmered and danced mesmerically.

But Sinbad paid it no heed. He had his head down, his gazed fixed on his feet as he stumbled down the rocky path. Once he had fallen, and being bound he had been unable to get to his feet. That hadn't stopped his captors kicking and beating him until somehow he regained his footing. Now he was most eager to remain on his feet.

Who they were he did not know. Before he could ask them he had been disarmed, seized and bound. All he gathered was that they believed him to be an ally of their enemies. His protestations of innocence had been cut off. No Son of Adam but a sorcerer, he had been told, was capable of making the journey.

The defile widened and began to flatten out. Down below, a little valley lay strewn with huge emeralds, each one the size of a Baghdad town-house. Sinbad felt a painful jab of nostalgia for his own house, and wished fervently he was back there. If he had been any kind of sorcerer, he could have broken out of his bonds and been there in a twinkling. But he was only a sailor, and Baghdad was far, far away.

Rounding one of the huge emerald boulders they approached a campsite where several fires glowed, and tents had been pitched. More of the djinn warriors sat round the fires, several of them with recently bandaged wounds. A sentry came forwards to challenge the newcomers, who gave a formulaic response and were allowed into the camp.

Sinbad was dragged before a large tent, a pavilion in fact, of crimson silk. Standing in the entrance was another djinn warrior, this one with the head of an elephant. He leaned on a spear whose damascened blade was chased with silver, looking enquiringly at the bound captive.

'We found him sticking his cursed snout into the Tomb of Suleiman!' growled the leader of the guards, a youth with blue skin and a long black topknot. He brandished Suleiman's sword. 'Another sorcerer, I'll warrant. He stole this! Working for Malik Gatshan, like the other.'

'Unbind him,' the elephantine djinn commanded briskly, 'and depart. If I cannot deal with a single Son of Adam, I will never be able to overthrow the sultan. But leave the sword.'

Sinbad felt his bonds loosen. Pins and needles shot through his hands and arms and he worked them to ease it. As the guards hastened away to their tents, Sinbad sat cross legged before the djinn. The djinn returned his gaze, then placed the sword on a low tabouret.

'I am Ad-Dimiryat,' he announced. 'I am leader here. I wish that you would answer some questions. Who you are, what your business is in the Mountains of Kaf, and so forth. Should you prove obdurate, I have djinn who are highly skilled in loosening tongue. But I am a kindly djinn and would prefer not to resort to such methods. Now tell me your name.'

Sinbad rubbed wryly at his wrists, and his bruised ribs. Certainly his captors had been proficient enough in inflicting pain. Ad-Dimiryat was the name of the djinn leader who had allied himself with Suleiman. 'I am called Sinbad,' he said, 'A sailor by trade.'

'A sailor?' asked Ad-Dimiryat sardonically. 'Where is your ship? You would not have me believe that you sailed all this way from the world of men!' His trunk quested about as he peered at Sinbad out of small, piggy eyes that nevertheless held the wisdom of the ages.

'My ship?' Sinbad asked. 'I left her off the shore of Abyssinia, but that was a long time ago. Since then I have sailed not across the waters of the ocean but through the sea of clouds, aboard the Carpet of Suleiman.'

Ad-Dimiryat flinched back, and his trunk lifted high overhead before writhing back down to lie in his lap. Breathing harshly, Ad-Dimiryat said, 'Then you condemn yourself from your own lips. You flew here by magic to loot the tomb of Suleiman himself.'

'I did not know that Suleiman's tomb lay in this country,' said Sinbad. 'Not until recently, that is. I came here by magic, it's true. First by flying carpet, and then when it came under attack and I fell into the water, I was helped by the people of the sea. On the isle of the queen of the serpents I gained a magical salve with which I walked across the remaining leagues. But I am not a sorcerer,' he added, 'merely a sailor whose voyages have a tendency to lead into hot water of a sorcerous variety.'

'You claim that you were not looting Suleiman's tomb?' asked Ad-Dimiryat. 'But my patrol says that you were found there, and they took the sword from you.'

'I took shelter in what I believed to be a cave,' Sinbad said, 'after I came to this land. I saw your patrol and they pursued me, so I hid in there. The sword I took to defend myself, but I was too weary to fight them off. Tell me, do they treat all visitors to your country in the same reprehensible manner?'

Ad-Dimiryat stroked his tusks. 'We are at

war,' he said. 'At war with the sultan, who usurped me using sorcerous weapons provided by an evil wizard. Malik Gatshan, that hypocrite, fights me, Ad-Dimiryat bin Shahrukh, rightful sultan of Djinnistan, with the sorcery he feigns to despise.'

'You're rebels?' It would explain why they were camped out here in the wilderness. And their wariness was that of outlaws. 'But who is this wizard who you speak of? I came to Djinnistan in search of a sorcerer. Ja'afar is his name. He abducted the sister of my caliph.'

Ad-Dimiryat started. He regarded him lugubriously. 'I believe that is the name of the evil wizard who aids our enemies. Of any Daughter of Eve, I know nothing. But Ja'afar dwells in a tower on a spur of rock outside the City of Jewels.'

Sinbad sprang to his feet. 'Then that is where I must go,' he exclaimed. He hesitated. 'With your leave, sire,' he added.

'You would go to the sorcerer's tower?' Ad-Dimiryat was astounded. 'It is many leagues across the Badiat Ealgim to Schadou Kiam. And you would have to pass by the city of my enemy before you could hope to reach the tower.'

He clapped his paws and djinn servants brought them food and drink. Sinbad sat down and ate hungrily. 'I must,' he said indistinctly. 'I must take Princess Abassa back to Harun al-Rashid. Do I have your leave to go?'

'I believe that you are no enemy,' Ad-

Dimiryat temporised. 'I shall not keep you here against your will. But you cannot cross the Badiat Ealgim by yourself.'

'Are you offering to help me?' asked Sinbad.

Ad-Dimiryat looked pensive. 'I told you that we are at war with the djinn of Schadou Kiam,' he said. 'We made an attack on the city only recently, but we were defeated, and many of us were killed. As matters stand our strength is not sufficient for another raid into heavily settled territory. We are fighting for survival.

'I am in a quandary,' he went on. 'I would not let a Son of Adam with whom I have shared salt set out on an impossible mission into enemy territory... and yet it is too soon for all-out war, which is what would transpire were I to send my troops with you.'

'I see your dilemma,' said Sinbad. He shook his head, lifting a protesting hand. 'Your hospitality has been like water for a man lost in the desert. I absolve you from any further obligation, but would ask if you could tell me the way I must go.'

'If you are resolved,' said Ad-Dimiryat, 'you will at least take this,' and he took from his men the scimitar of Suleiman that had been confiscated from Sinbad on his capture. 'Its true owner has no use for it, but you will need protection. Armour I would give you too,' he added, 'but none that we have here would fit you.'

Sinbad took the sword with gratitude. 'My

thanks, sire,' he said. 'Truly you are munificent. So where must I go?'

Ad-Dimiryat produced a jewelled dagger and scratched out a map in the grit. It showed the coast of Djinnistan, the Mountains of Kaf, and up on a vast plateau, endless deserts. 'This is the Badiat Ealgim, the Desert of Demons,' said the djinn, 'and this is the Desert of Monsters, which we call the Badiat Coldare.'

Sinbad nodded. He remembered Aladdin's words. 'And where is the City of Jewels?' he asked.

Ad-Dimiryat scratched a symbol at the far end of the Badiat Ealgim. 'Here,' he said. 'A long and perilous journey even for djinn. Only en masse were we free from attack.'

'What monsters dwell in the desert?'

'None know. They do not come out in the day. And no one who has ever been benighted in the desert has lived to speak of any encounter. All the survivors speak of is howls and snarls and shrieks heard at night, and djinn missing in the morning. Here,' he added, scratching in a tall hillock, 'is the tower Ja'afar has taken as his own.'

Sinbad gazed at the map. Without help, without the carpet of Suleiman, he would be beset with endless difficulties. Crossing this desert would be the first challenge. And it would be him alone. A single man in the country of the djinn. But—he examined the blade again, then sheathed it and strapped the sword belt round his waist—a man with a sword. And what more could he expect? This weapon would at the very least give him the edge on the opposition.

'My thanks, sire,' said Sinbad. 'With your leave I will depart.'

The djinn gave him a small sack containing food for the journey, then led him to the edge of the camp. 'If you follow this valley downwards,' Ad-Dimiryat said, standing with several sentries, 'it will debouch into a larger one heading east. Follow that and by nightfall you will be on the edge of the desert. I would send warriors with you, but...'

'Think nothing of it, sire,' said Sinbad. 'I understand that you are not ready to risk precipitating a war you cannot win. With this sword and these provisions, I shall prevail. Farewell, true sultan of Djinnistan!'

He flourished the blade, then sheathed it again and turned and began to make his way down the defile.

The wind howled among the peaks, and all that could be heard was its mournful soughing. Sinbad picked his way down the path between the great boulders. Back in Baghdad, a single one could have bought Sinbad an empire. Here, they were nothing more than obstacles. Sword in hand, he threaded his way through this bewildering labyrinth for several hours.

After much walking, he came to the end of the gorge, where it opened out into a larger valley. Here he sat down on an emerald boulder to open the bag of provisions, which proved to be something very like felafel of the kind he was used to from Baghdad. He mixed some of it with water from a brackish stream and rolled it into balls, which he ate uncooked. He had no way to fry them; not even scrub bushes grew among the emerald rocks. The result was a tasteless chewing exercise, but it filled his aching belly.

He thought he heard movement from further up the gorge. Dropping what remained of his meal back into the bag he turned, unsheathed the sword of Suleiman, and faced the path down which he had come. Still the wind howled, and he strained his ears in hopes of hearing the sound again, a stealthy footfall. But he could hear nothing.

After a while, he sheathed his sword and went on his way down into the broader valley. Halfway down a narrow path that led to the banks of a larger stream, he froze in his place,. The air high overhead was swirling into a vortex. It seemed horribly familiar. The howl of the wind resolved itself into a booming laugh, and suddenly, hovering above Sinbad, was an even more familiar sight.

It had a great, grinning, jowled, evil green face, a grossly fat body, great trunk like arms and legs. 'Hahahahahahahahahaha!' it roared. 'Hahahahahahahahahaha! O Sinbad! At last I have found you!'

4 THE SORCERER AND THE THIEF

Standing in the throne room entrance was a man Ahmed had last seen sleeping in the palace bedchamber in Baghdad.

Ja'afar was a tall, sepulchral man, whose censorious face was adorned with curled mustachios. His nose was long, his eyebrows slanted, his eyes were hypnotic dark pools. He wore flowing green robes, and a white turban adorned with a diamond aigrette. His hands were hidden by long sleeves that dangled at his sides. As Ahmed turned to run, he raised one of them and the sleeve fell back to reveal a slender hand that held a talisman in the form of a five pointed star.

'Stay where you are, thief!' he demanded. He stalked closer. 'As you see,' he added, 'I have another talisman, to replace the ring you stole from me, thief.'

'This man says he is no thief,' said Malik Gatshan. 'Aye, and no sorcerer. And indeed, no liar. He certainly is a liar, it seems! The punishment for any of those transgressions is dire, but a lying sorcerous thief... He will indeed be made to suffer.'

'Enough!' cried Nakeya. She produced the brazen vessel. 'Whoever you are, whatever magic you are capable of, know that we have magic as well. This vessel contains the marid Hadana, of the blood of Iblis, who is enslaved to Ahmed's ring! Come any closer, and I will call up the marid!'

Ja'afar halted in his tracks and regarded the vessel curiously. 'Who is this man, Ahmed?' asked Sir Acelin,. 'He is no djinn. What does he here?'

'This, sir knight, is the former Grand Vizier of the Caliph Harun al-Rashid,' said Ahmed in mocking tones. 'This is Ja'afar himself.'

Sir Acelin regarded Ja'afar. 'Then it is you who carried off the Caliph's sister,' he cried. 'Yield her to us at once!'

Ja'afar laughed incredulously. 'Would you carry her off to your draughty castle in the cold West? Have you come all this way because you have heard tell of her beauty? And you say that I carried her off?'

'You did!' Ahmed said. 'You came with your djinn to Baghdad and abducted her!'

Ja'afar turned to Malik Gatshan. 'Will you let these criminals insult me in your own throne room?' he demanded. 'I am not a patient man.'

Malik Gatshan lolled on his throne. 'The maiden says they have Hadana under their sway,' he said wearily. 'That's the trouble with sorcerers. They have that tendency to order we djinn around. All it takes is a talisman, a ring, or some such gewgaws, and knowledge of your name, and they can conjure one, imprison one, coerce one. It's all Suleiman's fault, of course. All we djinn wanted was our rights, but we were spurned in favour of you sons of Adam. And when we rebelled it was Suleiman who defeated us.

'Hadana,' he added musingly, 'I remember him. He inhabited the wastelands, roaming freely. He was always a great lover of female beauty. How did you imprison him? Or perhaps I can guess...' He turned his gaze upon Nakeya.

'That's no affair of yours,' the Abyssinian told him firmly. 'He is ours to command now. He has no option but to do as we tell him. And if any of you threaten us we shall summon him and command him to lay waste to your city and your people.'

Ahmed leant close to Nakeya. 'Remember,' he whispered, 'we can only call him a third time. Then he will be free. Don't let's waste the chance.'

'Waste it?' she murmured. 'This is our hour of greatest need. We have Ja'afar here with us. Surely the princess is nearby. We can call up the marid and use him to force Ja'afar to hand her over...'

Ja'afar was trying to listen. 'Sire,' he said in appeal to the sultan, 'what are they muttering? You have heard their own admissions that they are sorcerers, thieves, liars. Let them be tried and executed at once!'

'I am no sorcerer,' said Sir Acelin, gazing challengingly at the djinn guards. 'Nor am I a liar or a thief. I am a knight, a paladin of the Emperor Charlemagne—and it is you, Ja'afar, who is the notorious sorcerer.'

'He's got a point,' Ahmed said with a quizzical look at Malik Gatshan. 'You surely know that Ja'afar is a wizard! I'll be honest with you—it happens from time to time, you know—I'll be honest with you, we have found ourselves mixed up in magic far too much in recent weeks, but we're not sorcerers—and he is!'

'If anyone should be executed,' Nakeya added, 'it is Ja'afar. His crimes are without number, and sorcery is but one of them.'

Malik Gatshan laughed a little sadly. 'Well do I know of his iniquities,' he said. 'Alas, I am under his spell.'

'You?' said Ahmed. 'The great sultan of all Djinnistan, at the beck and call of a piffling little he-witch like that?'

'We made a pact,' Malik Gatshan replied. 'It was sealed with powerful spells and oaths. He has control over me. I told you we djinn are sadly prone to coming under the thumb of sorcerers.' He lowered his voice. 'Would that I could break free! But in the meantime, I do his bidding—and slay all other sorcerers who come my way!'

'But how did you find yourself in such a terrible position, sire?' Nakeya asked.

'Eh? What's that? Oh, ambition, my dear. Ambition.' The sultan looked remorseful. 'I bound myself to Ja'afar in return for his assistance in seizing power of the kingdom. With his aid I drove out the sultan Ad-Dimiryat and his loyal legions and assumed his place. I now rule over the City of Jewels and all of Djinnistan—barring those rebel controlled areas up in the Mountains of Kaf. I regret letting him talk me into such a degrading situation, but he is true to his promises. Only recently did we drive off a rebel attack on Schadou Kiam itself with Ja'afar's aid. So you must understand, my dear. It's a matter of politics. Much as I loathe and detest the fellow, I must do his bidding. And if he says that you are sorcerers and that you must die—sorcerers you are, and dead you soon will be.'

'You're forgetting something,' said Ahmed. 'We're not sorcerers, but we do have magical allies. The marid Hadana will come to our aid. Already he has fought djinn for us during our voyage. If you try anything, we will summon him up...'

'You can't waste our last chance like that,' Nakeya whispered.

'What other option do we have?' Ahmed whispered back.

Sir Acelin leaned over. 'The carpet,' he said. 'Let us fly out of here and go in search of the princess.'

Without further ado, Ahmed unrolled the carpet and ushered them to stand in the centre. He raised his hands high, preparing to speak the words, when Ja'afar cried out, 'Not so fast, thief.'

The sorcerer had planted one curly toed slippered foot on the edge of the carpet. 'I suggest you move yourself,' Ahmed said, 'if you don't want us to take off with you half on and half off the carpet. You'd make a very nasty mess if you fell from a great height.'

'There's no need to speak of such matters,' said Ja'afar, stepping fully onto the carpet. Ahmed and his two companions took an involuntary step backwards. 'Let us instead discuss what you want. Your infidel friend said that you wanted to carry off the Princess Abassa.'

Ahmed swallowed. 'We came here to bring her back to her brother, yes,' he said. 'Four of us set out. Sinbad was our leader, but we lost him.' His eyes narrowed. 'You sent that djinn, didn't you? It was Zoba'ah Abu Hasan, who helped you carry off the princess.'

'Sinbad, Sinbad,' mused Ja'afar. 'I know him of old. Time after time he visited the caliph's palace, telling us his wonderful and unlikely stories of shipwreck and adventure on the high seas. How fitting it is that the sea should have claimed that artful storyteller! But I know you, too, if not as well. I know that you are no hero like Sinbad. You hail, do you not, from Baghdad's fabled thieves' quarter? Ahmed, the notorious thief of the bazaar. What freak of chance dragged you into this bizarre escapade?'

'Don't listen to him, Ahmed,' said Sir Acelin warningly. 'He speaks with the tongue of the serpent.'

'You are a thief,' Ja'afar repeated as if Sir Acelin had not spoken. 'A rogue. You care for none but yourself; you are not a damsel-rescuing knight like this fellow. Again I ask you, what brought you into this?'

Ahmed shrugged. 'Well, Sinbad...'

'Sinbad is dead,' Ja'afar reminded him. 'He has no hold over you.'

Nakeya put a slender hand on Ahmed's arm. 'Ahmed...' she murmured.

'If you must know,' said Ahmed, 'I was only too happy to leave Baghdad. The guild was after me. I'd not paid my dues. Twelve dirhams I owed them. And the sheikh of all the thieves wanted upfront payment, or I would be fed to the Tigris fishes. So a jaunt across the seven seas with sailor-man Sinbad seemed like the best option.'

'I understand,' said Ja'afar sympathetically. 'But would it not be a better choice if you were to become sheikh of all the thieves? Would you not like to rule over your fellow rogues? Sit at the head of the thieves' guild, with all those dirhams and dinars yours to embezzle as you saw fit?'

Ahmed laughed. 'Well, of course. But that's never going to happen…'

'Can you be sure of it?' Ja'afar asked silkily.

'Don't listen to him, Ahmed,' Nakeya warned him. 'He's trying to corrupt you.'

Ahmed gave her a wry look. 'I was born corrupt, girl,' he said roughly. 'Just because I've knocked around with a disgraced nun and a knight who's lost his shining armour doesn't change that. I was born on the streets of Baghdad. Thieving was the only career I had open to me, and I had to steal the tools of the trade before I could follow it. I've always had my eye to the main chance. And right now it doesn't look like we've got many options here.'

'We have Hadana,' said Nakeya insistently.

Ahmed gave her a lopsided grin. 'But only I can control him,' he said, holding up his hand with the ring glittering on it. 'So what I say goes, doesn't it?'

Nakeya exchanged a shocked look with Sir Acelin. 'I can't believe I'm hearing this,' she said.

Ahmed turned to Ja'afar. 'I've listened to what you've got to offer me, and it sounds good, I must say. But you're not a charitable man. What do I have to do in return?'

'Come with me to my tower,' said Ja'afar. 'Come with me, and I will tell you how I intend to make myself master of the world. When I am mightier than the mightiest of caliphs, any favour I wish to grant will be possible.'

'Let's go there at once,' said Ahmed eagerly.

He intoned the words of power and the carpet shot over the heads of the djinn guards, and out of through the palace entrance, leaving Malik Gatshan and his warriors looking on astounded.

5 THE DESERT OF DEMONS

As Zoba'ah Abu Hasan bore down on Sinbad, the sailor drew his scimitar from its sheath. Laughing, the djinn tried to seize Sinbad, and the latter swung a wild cut at him with the sword that passed through Zoba'ah Abu Hasan's flesh as if through smoke. Despite this apparent failure to cause a wound, the djinn roared in pain, his great mouth yawning open to reveal rows and rows of pointed teeth.

He landed on his feet amid the glittering grit in front of Sinbad and produced a sword of his own from a sheath that hung at his side. Its blade blazed like a glowing ember, giving off heat like a scorching desert wind.

'So!' the djinn boomed. 'Thou hast some fight in thee, eh, Sinbad?'

Before his opponent could respond, he swung a blow at Sinbad's head but the sailor parried it forcefully. A deafening clang rang out across the valley. Sinbad followed this up with a savage lunge at the djinn's bare chest, but Zoba'ah

Abu Hasan leapt back, landing on his shoeless feet some yards away. Laughing maniacally, he ran straight at Sinbad, who dodged to one side at the last second and aimed a cut at the djinn's flank. Zoba'ah Abu Hasan spun aside, and Sinbad was forced to parry another blow. When their blades met, a shudder ran down his blade and he was forced to his knees.

'Yield, O Son of Adam,' the djinn said complacently. 'Thou canst not hope to defeat me.'

'You didn't kill me the last time,' Sinbad said, attacking the djinn in a flurry of blows that Zoba'ah Abu Hasan deflected with a negligent series of parries. 'What makes you think you can kill me now?'

The djinn ticked off points, parrying an attack as he enumerated each one. 'Because thou art alone. Because thou hast no magic to save thee. Because thou hast not called upon Hadana to attack me. I can only assume thou hast lost control of that most puissant marid. It is man against djinn. It hardly seems fair, somehow.'

Sinbad lunged and his sword point nicked the djinn in his chest, and green blood drifted smokily from the wound, but Zoba'ah Abu Hasan seemed unfazed. 'Besides,' he added, 'I have no wish to kill thee.'

Sinbad, panting, lowered his sword. He dashed the sweat from his brow. 'Then why do you attack me again? This is the second time, and you say you do not want to kill me.'

'Orders have changed,' the djinn informed him. 'Last time I was to kill thee and thou somehow escaped drowning in the ocean. This time, however, my master demands thy presence in his tower by Schadou Kiam.'

'Demands?' Sinbad asked, forcing the djinn back in a series of blows. 'He wants me taken alive?'

Again he wounded the djinn, but as he did so, Zoba'ah Abu Hasan's blade caught him on the side, a stinging, burning sense of pain. Glancing down he saw blood trickling down his side. Angrily, he swung a blow at Zoba'ah Abu Hasan and lopped off his hand at the wrist.

But Zoba'ah Abu Hasan laughed, and under Sinbad's astonished eyes a new hand grew where the old one had been. The djinn picked up his sword from the sand and renewed his assault.

'Alive,' he said, eyes flaming. 'My master would prefer thee alive. He hath a use for you, he says.'

Sinbad's foot twisted on a rock and he fell on his back, dropping his scimitar. Zoba'ah Abu Hasan loomed over him, sword held high.

There was a boom from the rocks above and a ball of green fire struck the djinn and sent him sprawling to the ground. Deftly Sinbad sprang to his feet and spun round, searching both for his scimitar and the source of the fireball.

Something metallic glinted in the green sand and Sinbad flung himself upon it, rolling.

Coming back up he saw several figures issuing out from the cleft by which he had entered the valley. Beast-headed, they carried swords and spears. One had a massive cannon slung over his shoulder. It was still smoking.

Zoba'ah Abu Hasan tried to get to his feet as the other djinn ran down the side of the valley to surround him, brushing past Sinbad as if the sailor was not there. Their leader, who carried the cannon, was a blue skinned youth with the topknot.

As the rest of the djinn came to surround him with their spears the youth trained the cannon on the prone, struggling Zoba'ah Abu Hasan. 'Stay where you are, lord of the wind,' he laughed wildly. 'Or I will fire again, point blank.'

Zoba'ah Abu Hasan laying panting on the ground, glaring up at his captors. Sinbad watched in astonishment. 'I thought Ad-Dimiryat was not going to help me,' he said, joining the djinn. 'Why the change of heart?'

The young leader of the djinn glanced at him. 'My father is not willing to send out his whole force,' he said, 'after our recent defeat. But after you had gone, he spoke with me about it, about how you would be going out into the Badiat Ealgim alone. He was concerned that he had sent you to your death. I offered to follow you with a few of the soldiers and keep you from harm. We had not thought you would have encountered trouble so soon in your journey. And from Zoba'ah Abu Hasan himself.' He laughed.

'Chortle all thou wilt, Al'Azraq,' snarled Zoba'ah Abu Hasan. 'Thy father lost his kingdom.'

Al'Azraq aimed the cannon right at the defeated djinn. 'You and your kind are all the same,' he said. 'Cowards! You would attack mere mortals passing through our lands. For that you will die!'

'What is this?' said Zoba'ah Abu Hasan. 'Thou thinkest I attacked Sinbad of my own volition?'

'Why else?' Al'Azraq demanded, lowering the cannon a little.

Zoba'ah Abu Hasan shook his head. 'I have fallen under the power of the sorcerer Ja'afar,' he admitted. 'He hath a talisman inscribed with my name. My will is not my own! Why would I, lord of the winds, trouble myself with one so insignificant as Sinbad?'

Sinbad snorted. 'You attacked me on the flying carpet and I was cast into the sea,' he said. 'If it had not been for the sea people, I would have drowned. I was forced to suffer a long journey both under and over the sea before I could reach Djinnistan. If I am so insignificant why did you try to murder me?'

'I tell you that I am under the spell of Ja'afar!' Zoba'ah Abu Hasan blustered. 'He sent me to slay thee. I thought I had done so. Then he changed his mind, wanted me to find thee, if thou still lived, and bring you to his tower. Until the talisman's spell is broken, I have no choice but to obey the sorcerer's orders.'

Al'Azraq spat. 'All djinn know that we are subject to sorcery. Suleiman learnt our weakness in the long ago days, and used it to enslave us. Those who rebelled against him were imprisoned, and even we who remained loyal to him can become slaves to sorcerer's whims. None of this justifies what you have done.' He levelled the cannon again.

'No, wait!' said Sinbad. He looked down at Zoba'ah Abu Hasan. 'You say that Ja'afar now wants me brought to his tower?'

Zoba'ah Abu Hasan nodded weakly. 'And I must! I am his slave!'

He struggled to rise but Al'Azraq jabbed at him with the cannon, looking up at Sinbad. 'What is it, son of Adam?' he asked.

Sinbad did not answer, his attention still on Zoba'ah Abu Hasan. 'This tower of Ja'afar's,' he said slowly. 'Is there a girl there? A Daughter of Eve,' he corrected himself.

'The princess Abassa is there,' Zoba'ah Abu Hasan replied.

'And you are under orders to take me to Ja'afar's tower, alive?' Sinbad asked.

'Aye.' Zoba'ah Abu Hasan nodded.

'Then we're both of one mind,' said Sinbad solemnly. 'I too want to go to the sorcerer's tower. Take me there.'

'Sinbad!' protested Al'Azraq. 'Are you offering yourself up willingly to your sworn enemies? I told my father I would protect you! What is this madness?'

Sinbad smiled at him. 'It could be the solution to all my problems,' he said mysteriously. 'Zoba'ah Abu Hasan, you say you're not a willing slave.'

'Only Ja'afar's sorcery makes me a slave,' Zoba'ah Abu Hasan replied. 'I begrudge his control over me, naturally, but what can I do? I must obey him. He wields the powers of Suleiman.'

'And if you were to do his will,' Sinbad said, 'if you were to obey the letter of his commands, would that be enough?'

'That would suffice,' said the djinn. 'All I must do is bring thee back to the tower, alive or dead.'

'And Ja'afar did not say that I could not be brought back with a sword at my side…' Sinbad probed.

'What are you planning, O Sinbad?' asked Al'Azraq.

Sinbad faced him. 'Your father himself said that crossing the Badiat Ealgim would be suicide,' he said. 'But what if I was to be transported across it by a djinn?'

Al'Azraq shook his head. 'We are not flying djinn,' he began.

'No, but friend Zoba'ah Abu Hasan is,' Sinbad said, indicating their prisoner. 'He is the lord of the wind.'

After a pause, Al'Azraq said, 'I think I see what you are planning, but it is dangerous, O Sinbad. I counsel against it.'

Politely, Sinbad dismissed the young djinn's concerns. 'Zoba'ah Abu Hasan, I will let you transport me to Ja'afar's tower. On the understanding that you leave me be when I am there.'

'I will not let you do this,' Al'Azraq told Sinbad insistently.

'Set Zoba'ah Abu Hasan free,' Sinbad directed. 'If he takes me to the tower, you will not have to risk your lives in the Badiat Ealgim.'

Unwillingly Al'Azraq motioned Zoba'ah Abu Hasan to rise. 'You cannot trust him,' he warned. 'And we are willing to die if you will kill the sorcerer who aided the rise of Malik Gatshan.'

'My mind's made up,' said Sinbad. 'Zoba'ah Abu Hasan will take me to Ja'afar's tower, won't you, Zoba'ah Abu Hasan?'

The djinn laughed with all his former good spirits. 'By all means, O Sinbad!' he said. 'I will obey my orders and thou—thou shalt do whatever it is thou wishest. Come hither.'

Sinbad approached him. Zoba'ah Abu Hasan scooped him up in his big hands and deposited him on his shoulders, where he sat clinging on like a child playing piggyback.

Sinbad peered round at Al'Azraq and the other djinn. 'Go and tell your father,' he said, 'that Sinbad goes to Schadou Kiam in style. Tell him I thank him for all his help, just as I thank you. Now I must take my leave of you, O prince amongst djinn! Farewell!'

6 UNDER JA'AFAR'S SPELL

The flying carpet soared high above the domes and spires of the djinn city, in the direction of the tower on the spur of rock. Ahmed sat cross legged at the front, ignoring the cold looks of two of his companions.

'You traitor!' Nakeya said in a low voice. 'You've betrayed everything Sinbad was working for.'

Ahmed gave her a testy look. 'And where is Sinbad now?' he asked wearily. 'At the bottom of the deep blue sea, nibbled by the fishes. No doubt monstrous giant one-eyed fishes, knowing Sinbad.'

'You owe it to him to complete his mission,' Nakeya opined.

Ahmed turned to gaze sardonically at her. She and Sir Acelin crouched in the middle of the carpet. Over them stood the brooding figure of Ja'afar, his solemn, dark majesty only slightly marred by the whiteness of his face and his tight lips, and the frantic way he clutched at his turban as the wind tugged at his garments. Nakeya was giving Ahmed a dark look in return. Her hand was on the brazen vessel, which she was caressing absently.

'You're so beautiful when you're angry,' he said.

'Never mind that,' Sir Acelin snapped. 'The girl is right. Why did you betray us? You vowed to pursue this quest to the utmost. Is your word nothing?'

'I'm think you're getting me mixed up with someone else,' said Ahmed. 'I didn't vow anything. I just let Sinbad talk me into joining him on this madcap venture...'

'The guild was after you,' Nakeya said with a snort. 'You owed them money, which is hardly surprising...'

'... and by the way, you don't think Sinbad embarked on the caliph's mission purely out of altruism, do you?' Ahmed added. 'He wasn't just talked into it, he was blackmailed. By Harun al-Rashid himself.'

'The caliph is a wicked, conniving fellow,' Ja'afar commented in sepulchral tones.

Nakeya craned her neck round. 'Is that why you rebelled against him?'

'I rebelled against him because he came between me and my love.' The expression on the sorcerer's brooding face was tragic. 'But I will be avenged on him and all his kind. Arabs! Those desert savages. We Persians should rule, not the sons of mangy camels.'

Sir Acelin shifted uncomfortably. 'You would rule them as a witch lord,' he said. 'Your power is not that of a man, won by the sword's edge, but of one who calls upon foul powers of darkness to gain his twisted desires. Do you truly believe that you can become ruler of the world with the aid of dark forces?'

'They only do your will because of the magic you wield,' Nakeya agreed, her hand still on the brazen vessel. 'They detest you, sorcerer. Given the opportunity, they will destroy you.'

'Nonsense,' said Ahmed. 'Ja'afar will conquer the world with magic, and when he rules it, he will make me sheikh of all thieves.'

'Why would you want to be a sheikh?' Nakeya asked. 'Responsibility's something you've always shirked. Why this sudden ambition?'

Ahmed frowned at her. 'Look!' he said suddenly. 'We're almost there.'

They had passed over the city and were now heading straight towards the tower. Ahmed commanded the carpet to reduce its speed, and with Ja'afar's aid he guided it in towards an open balcony partway up the tower.

'Be vigilant!' Ja'afar urged him. 'Head for that opening, or you will collide with the tower.'

The walls of the tower were daubed in smooth cream stucco. Wide windows looked out upon the city and the surrounding desert and mountains. A spire rose from the top, beneath which was a line of smaller windows like the many eyes of a spider. It tapered outwards as it went down, but even at the base there could only be enough room for a couple of small chambers. The foot of the tower stood upon a tumbledown rock face.

The carpet flew in through the arch and landed in the middle of a wide floor paved in marble, lined with exquisitely worked rugs upon which rested a tabouret and several chairs. Overhead was a ceiling ornamented with arabesques, and wall hangings and exotic weaponry adorned the walls. On the far side a wide stairway swept upwards out of sight, while another vanished into the depths of the tower. The chamber was surely too large to fit inside the slender edifice they had seen from the outside, Ahmed thought confusedly.

Ja'afar strode from the carpet, and went into the middle of the room. He clapped his hands. 'Some refreshments for my guests,' he called out to the air. Ahmed could see no servants, no one at all. Who was the wizard speaking to?

He held out a hand to assist Nakeya from the carpet but she ignored him coldly and instead took Sir Acelin's hand, moving away from Ahmed. The knight and the girl whispered urgently to each other but Ahmed could not make out the words.

Plates containing sweetmeats and smoking

slices of meat and exotic vegetables cooked in creamy sauces floated through a low doorway, followed by a tray upon which sat a tea set, from whose teapot spout wafted a plume of steam.

'Please,' said Ja'afar, 'sit down.' He indicated the chairs.

Grinning conceitedly, Ahmed sat on one. He looked at Sir Acelin and Nakeya, who stood close together like the most bashful of guests. The teapot rose into the air and poured a brown stream into a bone china cup that floated up into Ahmed's grasp. He sipped from it approvingly and smacked his lips.

'Won't you do what the nice wizard says?' Ahmed said to the other two.

Purse lipped, Nakeya sat primly down on another chair. Sir Acelin remained standing, hand resting on her shoulder. A tea cup floated towards the Abyssinian girl, but she brusquely waved it away. Ja'afar took his own seat and sipped at his tea.

'What wonderful servants you have,' said Ahmed. 'So quiet. So inobtrusive.'

'It is no matter,' said Ja'afar dismissively. 'A simple cantrip takes care of the whole business.'

'I must say you have a marvellous place here,' Ahmed said. 'Is this the kind of luxury I can look forward to when I'm sheikh of all thieves?'

'This is a mere shadow of what my loyal helpers can anticipate once I rule the world,' Ja'afar told him with sudden eagerness.

'Where are you keeping the princess?' Nakeya was keen to get down to business. Ahmed gave her a discouraging look but she ignored him frostily.

'Won't you show us round your tower?' the thief said, placing his empty cup on a saucer. It floated away the moment he had done so.

'Show you round?' Ja'afar said suspiciously. 'Why, yes, that can be arranged. But you cannot meet the princess Abassa. She is indisposed.'

'You mean you've got her locked up in your dungeon,' Sir Acelin growled.

'I have no need of dungeons to keep her here,' said Ja'afar with a laugh.

Nakeya got crossly to her feet. 'Come on, then,' she said, going over to the steps leading down. 'Show us round, sorcerer, if that's what you're going to do.'

Ja'afar smiled tolerantly, and went ahead of her, beckoning the others to follow. 'Down here you will find no dungeons, as you seem to anticipate,' he said, leading them down the wide, winding stair. 'Merely my workshops and the stairs leading down to the subterranean chamber in which I perform my rituals.'

'Where you summon up your djinn?' asked Ahmed. 'Why do you need to do that, when you've got a whole city of them out there?'

Ja'afar gave him an urbane smile. 'Alas, they are not all my slaves,' he said. 'Only those whose true names I know and who I can control with talismans will do my bidding. I summon them to my chamber of conjuration when I have tasks for them to carry out. Sometimes they complain or speak impotent words of rebellion, but if I carry the right talisman, I am the master. In the city I am more vulnerable, even with the talismans I bear upon my person.'

The workshop was a large, echoing, pillared room, again too large to fit within the slender tower they had seen from outside. Benches were dotted about the stone floor, and upon them lay various metal objects in the form of body parts; arms, legs, torsos, heads all higgledy-piggledy. In the middle, facing the balcony, was a large wheel shaped construction of metal, upon which had been inscribed a bewildering profusion of cabalistic symbols. A series of deep runnels led down it to its centre.

Nearby was a free standing shelf on which green glass phials sat, each containing some kind of viscous crimson liquid. Beside the shelf was an anvil, and a huge forge sunken into the floor, with a pipe to carry away the smoke and fumes into the roof. A hammer and a piece of beaten brass in the shape of a man's forearm lay beside it.

Standing in alcoves in the wall were almost a dozen fully assembled metal statues, wonderfully contrived to resemble human figures, so much so that it was only the dull metallic gleam that told Ahmed that they were not surrounded by silent, unmoving men. What was truly eerie was that not a single one of the metal statues —and Ahmed counted eleven fully assembled— had even the most rudimentary of faces; instead a blank oval took the place of a visage.

On one side of the room was another balcony like the one upstairs, looking out over the city. On the other wall was a door, which Nakeya tried. It was locked. She stared meaningfully at Ja'afar. 'This leads to your dungeon?' she asked.

Ja'afar laughed a booming, rolling, rich laugh. 'I have already told you,' he said, 'I have no dungeon. That leads to a spiral staircase the descends into the mountain itself. At the bottom is my chamber of conjuration. I would urge you not to go down there. It contains terrible dangers for such as you.'

'That sounds like a threat,' said Sir Acelin quietly.

'What need I to issue threats?' Ja'afar said. 'You are my guests. I hope that all of you will see the sense in joining me, as your friend has done.'

He led them back to the main chamber. Nakeya paused by the steps that led higher up the tower. Her brows were furrowed in thought. 'Where does this go?' she asked.

'My dear woman,' said Ja'afar, 'anyone would think you wished to purchase the residence. Alas, it is not for sale at the moment. But once I rule the world, I shall present it to you as a gift.'

'Where do these steps lead, wizard?' Nakeya repeated.

Ja'afar smiled. 'To my private chambers,' he said. 'I would show you round them as well, but unfortunately they are not fit to be seen by guests. I really must summon up a djinn or two to tidy them up, but whenever I do that I can never find anything. Certainly there is nothing of interest to you in there.'

'So,' said Ahmed, with a cough, 'you promised to tell me more about your plans.'

'Well,' the sorcerer began, 'you have already seen my main weapon…'

Nakeya crossed to the carpet. She picked up the brazen vessel and regarded it darkly. Sir Acelin joined her. He nodded meaningfully at Ahmed. She shrugged, and mouthed 'What choice do we have?'

She turned, opening the brazen vessel as she did so. For a moment nothing happened. His attention caught by her movement, Ja'afar turned to regard her. His mouth opened. Ahmed turned to see what he was looking at.

Smoke began to boil from vessel, hurriedly coalescing into a manlike form.

'This is Hadana,' said Nakeya. 'I cannot control him, only Ahmed can do that, with his ring. Ahmed the traitor! But I can unleash him. He will destroy everything in this tower, all of us. Perhaps he will destroy the princess, too. But he will destroy you, sorcerer, and that will be an end to your crazy schemes.'

'Crazy schemes?' Ahmed cried. 'Who are you to complain about crazy schemes! What are you trying to do? Did you really think I'd sold out? That was just a trick.'

Desperately he lifted his beringed hand and addressed the smoky form. 'Bismillah Alruhmin Alrahim!' Ahmed cried. 'Hadana, attack! Attack Ja'afar!'

'It is you who is the fool!' Ja'afar laughed. 'You thought you had beguiled me with your talk of joining me? I brought you here for one reason and one reason only: because you have that ring. My ring. And now I shall take it back. O ring!' he apostrophised the object. 'Return to your master!'

To Ahmed's horror, the ring that he had tried so hard and so many times to wrest from his finger sprang off it and leapt across the space between them, slipping itself neatly onto Ja'afar's outstretched finger.

'Long ago did we make our pact. At my bidding did he snatch the Carpet of Suleiman from the chapel in Abyssinia, and lured you away on a deadly quest into the desert. Lamentably, you suborned him with the powers of my stolen ring, but now my ring and my power over the marid has returned.'

The sorcerer turned. 'Hadana! Seize these recreants! Take them down to my workshop.'

'To hear is to obey, O sorcerer,' said Hadana.

7 HOW SINBAD CAME TO THE CITY OF JEWELS

Over the desert Sinbad flew, on the shoulders of the djinn. The wind whipped around him, stirring his threadbare tunic so goose pimples broke out across his flesh, and blowing stinging clouds of grit into Sinbad's face. He had to keep his eyes open to no more than slits. It was so loud he could barely hear what Zoba'ah Abu Hasan had to say.

'Down below is the Badiat Ealgim, which some call the Desert of Demons,' the djinn was shouting. 'Good it is for thee that thou cross it with my aid, O Sinbad. Wert thou to cross it on foot...'

'I know,' Sinbad shouted back. 'The other djinn told me. Something dwells there that even your kind fear. Something worse than djinn, if you don't mind me saying so.'

'I take no offence,' said the djinn. 'I am offended by naught—naught but that I am a slave. Wilt thou do something for me, Sinbad?'

'Name it,' shouted the sailor magnanimously, although he was in a poor position to be granting favours.

'Thou goest to fight Ja'afar, my master,' Zoba'ah Abu Hasan said. 'He hath a talisman with which he controls me. Thou wilt know it when thou sees it. It hangs on a chain about the sorcerer's neck, a circle of silver the size of a dirham, inscribed with runes and glyphs. Take it from him and destroy it.'

'I will try, O djinn,' shouted Sinbad. 'I will try. And this will free you? But how can I destroy it?'

'It is silver like any other kind of silver,' the djinn confided in him. 'It can be melted in a forge. That would destroy it, and free me from its spell.'

'Very well, O djinn,' said Sinbad. 'I shall endeavour to free you.'

'My thanks, O Sinbad,' the djinn replied. 'Bear in mind, also, that until the talisman is destroyed, Ja'afar will be able to control me. I will have no control over my actions, regardless of where my sympathies lie.'

They flew on. Sinbad contemplated this added complication. He had given his word—his word to try. But he would do what he could to free this djinn. Zoba'ah Abu Hasan was helping him. He deserved some kind of reward, and what reward most befitted a slave but his freedom? Yet it would be difficult indeed to take the talisman from the sorcerer's neck and to cast it into a fire hot enough to destroy it. Particularly if the djinn remained obedient to Ja'afar's orders. Ja'afar would not stand for it.

Through the storm of sand Sinbad made out something hazy and indistinct. It seemed to be the walls of a great city, lying amidst the sands in the shadow of the emerald mountains..

The distant city walls seemed to shimmer in the haze, and Sinbad looked again from shaded eyes, wincing as grit stung his hand. It could be no more than a mirage. He remembered the City of Brass. But that was a dead city, leftover from long before Suleiman was born. This was a city of the djinn. It existed by magic.

'I must tell my master that I am coming,' the djinn shouted over the roar of the wind. He began speaking as if to someone who was not there.

The sound of a hammer rang out in the still air of the workshop. Ahmed lay upon one spoke of the great metal wheel, hands bound to the rim, feet attached to the point where the spoke joined the hub. Nakeya, similarly bound, lay on one side, Sir Acelin on the other. Hadana floated above them, in his form of a devilishly handsome youth.

'Would you do the orders of that evil man?' Nakeya was saying to the marid, nodding her head in the direction of where Ja'afar stood at his forge, hammering at a sheet of brass that was slowly taking on a resemblance to a man's leg. 'His plots will not benefit the djinn.'

Hadana shook his head. 'You must know that I am a slave, like all djinn who enter into pacts with the Sons of Adam and the Daughters of Eve. Aye, you know it, and your companions know it, for was it not ye who enslaved me? And yet even ere that I was a slave to you, O girl. Bewitched by you. Enslaved by fetters of love.'

Ahmed felt her shift uncomfortably beside him. 'That's enough of that,' Nakeya said. 'Very well, it was we who enslaved you, but we had no choice. And if you are my slave, by bonds of love or of magic, then why have you bound me to this structure?'

'I have a new master now,' Hadana said. 'The master of the ring. I have no choice but to obey his orders.'

Ahmed cursed under his breath, and Nakeya turned to regard him. 'Are you regretting throwing your lot in with the sorcerer now?' she asked.

Ahmed sighed. 'I told you, that wasn't what I was doing at all. I wanted to get into this tower. Only here are we likely to rescue the princess from her dungeon.' From where he was pinioned he could just make out the door that led to the steps into the rock. Princess Abassa was imprisoned down there, he was sure of it. So near and yet so far. Impotently he rattled his chains.

Ja'afar ceased hammering and looked up. 'You must remain there for some while, my guests,' he said. 'Only once I have completed all my automata will the ceremony begin.' He looked up at Hadana. 'You will not speak to them!' he added. 'Return to your vessel.'

He lifted his hand and the ring glowed, and Hadana, with a last long lingering piteous look at Nakeya, evaporated into smoke and shot inside the brazen vessel which lay upon a nearby shelf.

'Ceremony?' Ahmed probed. 'What ceremony? What automata? You mean these statues? They move?'

'They will move,' Ja'afar temporised. 'Spirits will move them.'

'Not our spirits,' Sir Acelin growled.

Ja'afar shook his head in agreement. 'Not your spirits, no. The spirits in question have yet to be conjured up. But you will be instrumental in providing these automata with their true form, or should I say false seeming?'

Ahmed did not understand. 'What are you talking about?' he demanded. 'We'll do nothing to help whatever crackbrained plot you're hatching.'

'Oh, but you will,' said Ja'afar. 'You will not help voluntarily. All it will take is your blood.'

He took the brass sheet, which now had

been beaten into the shape of a leg, and fitted it to a half assembled metal statue—or automaton, if what he had said was to be trusted. Ahmed watched in perplexity. The sorcerer meant to animate the statues by summoning up spirits. And yet somehow the three of them were to be involved.

'What do you think this madman intends?' Sir Acelin whispered to him.

'He wants our blood,' said Ahmed with a shrug.

'He intends to use it in his foul sorcery,' added Nakeya.

'We cannot stand for such evil practises!' Sir Acelin said.

The note of a gong crashed out from the chamber upstairs. Ja'afar glanced up from his work on the automaton. 'Zoba'ah Abu Hasan?' he mouthed. He put down the brass leg and got to his feet. Without a word to his captives, he strode across the workshop and vanished up the steps.

'He's left us!' Ahmed said. 'How do you like that?'

'Silence,' Nakeya urged. 'Listen!'

From up above drifted the sound of voices. One was recognisable as the wheedling tones of Ja'afar. The other was deep and resonant, tolling like one of the bells with which the Christians call the faithful to prayer.

'Who is that?' Sir Acelin wanted to know. 'What are they saying?'

'Listen!' Nakeya repeated.

Ahmed and Sir Acelin did as she advised. Ahmed could hear little. He tugged at his chains. Then he craned his neck round to see what he could of the workshop. His eyes lighted on a prybar lying unheeded on a bench adjacent to the metal wheel. He lifted a fettered hand and reached out over the rim of the wheel.

'What are you doing?' Nakeya hissed. 'He's stopped talking. He'll be coming back down here. Stop that!'

Sweat broke out on Ahmed's brow as he stretched himself to the utmost. He was half on and half off the metal wheel now, hampered by the chains. But at last his groping fingers reached the handle of the prybar. He heard the thud of footsteps coming down the steps. His fingers closed on the handle of the prybar. Louder grew the footsteps. Still clutching the prybar he wriggled back onto the wheel and lay there panting, dropped the prybar beside him, then moved himself to cover it.

Ja'afar appeared in the doorway. Without looking at the prisoners, he crossed over to the automaton he had been working on and resumed his labours. Nakeya lifted her head.

'Who were you speaking to?' she asked. 'A djinn?'

She looked excited. Ahmed could not understand why. Ja'afar looked up from his work. 'A djinn, yes, another of my slaves.' Absently he caressed the coin he wore on a necklace. 'He told me tidings that will be of interest to you as well as me.'

'I heard you utter a name,' said Nakeya.

Ahmed looked round at her. Her face was flushed. Sir Acelin also looked excited. 'What have I missed?' the thief asked.

'Did you not hear?' asked Nakeya. 'Sinbad is coming. He is being brought here.'

'Sinbad?' Ahmed was astounded. A weight that had been crushing down on his shoulders suddenly lifted. 'Sinbad's alive? He's coming here?' He grinned savagely at Ja'afar. 'Hear that, wizard? Sinbad's coming. He'll soon scotch your cunning schemes.'

Nakeya shook her head. 'No, Ahmed,' she said. 'He comes here as a prisoner.'

'The girl is right,' said Ja'afar. 'Soon Sinbad will join you upon the wheel, and his blood and your blood and the blood that I collected in Baghdad will all be instrumental in bringing face and form to my conquering automatons, who will pave my way to the conquest of the world. But that you will never see, because by then you will all be dead.'

Sinbad had eavesdropped on the conversation between Zoba'ah Abu Hasan and Ja'afar with mounting horror. By now they were flying across the city he had seen on the horizon, which he recognised from the descriptions as the City of

Jewels, Schadou Kiam. Now that Ja'afar's voice was no longer rolling out of the ether, Zoba'ah Abu Hasan had begun flying in the direction of a tower on a hill outside the city.

'Zoba'ah Abu Hasan!' Sinbad said. 'What is that place?'

'It is the tower of Ja'afar,' Zoba'ah Abu Hasan said. 'I must take you there and hand you over to my master, bound, a prisoner.'

Cold chains appeared from nowhere, enmeshing Sinbad in their web. He struggled but it was futile. 'I must obey my master,' Zoba'ah Abu Hasan said remorselessly.

8 THE VIZIER'S PLOT

'I think we're owed a few explanations,' said Nakeya frostily. 'You say we'll be dead? You say you intend to take our blood? But what do you mean?'

Ja'afar laughed. 'I do not believe that I am under any obligation to betray my intentions. As I told you, Sinbad is now on his way. And when he arrives, my plans will be complete.'

'Your plan will never succeed,' said Ahmed, shaking his head. 'It's doomed to fail. Any fool could see that. Because there's just one thing that you've forgotten.'

Ja'afar had resumed work on the automaton leg. At this, he looked up. A scowl was on his hitherto imperturbable features.

'What arrogant yelping is this, dog?' he demanded. 'My plans are perfect, calculated to the last jot and tittle. I will make myself master of the world.'

Ahmed had no idea what Ja'afar's plan might be, except that it apparently involved automatons, not to mention, djinn. Nevertheless, he was pretty that if he kept the man talking, did his best to make him angry enough, he might let something slip. Anything could be valuable. 'That's the problem. You're hoping to achieve this by sorcery. Everyone knows that sorcery always has a sting in the tail.'

'Even Alexander the Great could not make himself master of the entire world,' said Sir Acelin, joining in, 'And he was no sorcerer.'

'Only Shaddad bin 'Aad succeeded,' Ahmed said, remembering the desolate wastes they had traversed west of Abyssinia, and the dead cities and palaces. 'And he came to a nasty end. Is that what you want? He made a pact with evil, just like you, and so his city was laid waste and his soul was carried off by the Angel of Death, never mind however much of the world he conquered.'

'I shall not fall prey to the fate of Shaddad,' Ja'afar assured him. 'None shall know that I am true master of the world, because I shall rule from behind the throne. None shall suspect me. And my puppets shall rule forever.'

'Your puppets?' Nakeya said. 'You mean these dolls of brass?'

Ja'afar's eyes narrowed. He went to attach the metal leg to the automaton. Now it looked like all the automata were complete. Without looking at the girl, Ja'afar said, 'You are perceptive, O Abyssinian. Perhaps there is more to you than meets the eye. How fascinating, to meet one so intelligent! Perhaps you could come to rival even I, given time. Well, I shall come to know you in the future. Or rather, your simulacra.'

He looked back at her, and gave a ghastly smile. Then he picked up an ornamental dagger from a nearby shelf and tested its edge. 'But you yourself shall not live long. None of you shall.'

'Because you mean to bleed us to death?' Nakeya said. 'But why? What will that achieve?'

'Mon Dieu! It is all a part of his foul sorcery,' Sir Acelin said disparagingly. 'Part of his diabolical magic. Never forget that your soul is now consigned to Satan, wizard!'

Ja'afar laughed. 'I am confident that I will be able to avoid Iblis' snares. But you too show surprising intelligence, infidel. Your blood shall bring life and semblance to my faceless automatons. Your blood. Sinbad's blood. And the blood of others far higher in rank than you.'

Ahmed wanted to try and tease out more clues to answer this riddle but before he could speak another clashing gong note rang out from the chamber above. Without speaking, Ja'afar turned away from the automaton and strode to the stairs.

The moment he was gone, Ahmed grasped the prybar clumsily in his fettered hands and began to force open a link of the chain. Nakeya and Sir Acelin watched in anxious silence.

The wind was growing louder, clouds of

desert grit blew around them, and the tower of Ja'afar was drawing ever closer. Now Sinbad could make it out fully, from its highest spire to its foot on the spur of the emerald mountains. He saw that, although windows and balconies were visible on its walls, the tower betrayed no sign of any doorway at its base. That should have come as little surprise, of course, Sinbad told himself reprovingly. A sorcerer who had power over the djinn, the marids and ifrits, would have no need to walk into his house like a conventional man. A simple spell could take him anywhere he wished to go.

And failing that, a djinn like Zoba'ah Abu Hasan could transport him to the far side of the world, if he so desired. Sinbad remembered his first sight of the djinn who now transported him, when he had been high above Baghdad, causing chaos with the wind of his passing, carrying with him Ja'afar and the princess. Even now Sinbad could picture the scene in his mind's eye, as clear as crystal. The exultant expression on the sorcerer's morose visage. And how the princess had looked.

Sinbad thought about this. There had been something strange about her expression when he had glimpsed it in that split second. Despite the rushing of the wind and the sense of impending disaster, Sinbad pictured it in his mind, trying to decipher it. What had been the thoughts passing through the princess'; mind?

The tower grew ever larger as they drew closer. Sinbad's own face was wracked with something oddly akin to terror. It looked as if Zoba'ah Abu Hasan meant to dash them against the cream stuccoed walls!

No! They were heading for a balcony partway up the tower. With incredible precision, Zoba'ah Abu Hasan shot in through the open window. He landed inside amidst a whirlwind that scattered rugs and tables across the marble floor of the chamber within.

The bonds that had pinioned Sinbad to the djinn had loosened. He leapt down onto the floor and tried to orient himself. Hearing footsteps from the far side of the chamber, he whirled around.

With a clatter, the broken link fell onto the metal surface of the wheel. Ahmed, his hands freed at last, turned his attention to the chains on his feet. It was the work of a scant few moments to open a link.

'Nakeya, you next,' he urged the Abyssinian.

'No,' she said firmly. 'Give Sir Acelin the prybar. You must find the princess. If what the sorcerer says is true, he will be bringing Sinbad down those steps any minute now.'

Sir Acelin turned his back on Ahmed and the thief slipped the prybar into his bound hands. With a grin at Nakeya, Ahmed jumped down from the metal wheel and made his way to the door that led to the steps downstairs.

The lock was a simple enough device, but he had no time to waste picking it, despite all his skills. He snatched up a chisel from a workbench and jammed it brutally into the mechanism, then twisted it to the right. He heard the rending sound of breaking metal, a resounding tinkle, and the door sprang open. It revealed a winding set of steps, leading down into the cold and the dark below.

After a brief search Ahmed found an oil lamp and lit it. Holding it high overhead so shadows danced and skipped about on the cold, oozing walls of the spiral staircase, he began to make his way down into the depths.

'Hurry up,' Nakeya said impatiently.

'I am working as quickly as I can,' Sir Acelin told her.

The knight was kneeling behind her, as she sat up on the wheel. He had the prybar inserted into one of the links of her chain and his sinews were standing out in his neck as he tried to turn it. And yet the chains were seemingly made of adamant. It was humiliating for the knight; a townsman like Ahmed could free himself from the chains but he himself seemed to lack the strength.

Again he twisted, calling upon God and his saints under his breath. Strength seemed to suffuse his entire being and with a sudden pinging sound the link broke. Nakeya stretched her freed arms out in delight. Grinning in his relief, Sir Acelin ducked under her arm, shuffled round and set to with the fetters shackling her ankles. As he did so, he averted his eyes from her legs which had been bared when she sat up.

'This is no time to be a prude,' she told him. 'At any other time I would appreciate your chivalrous nature, sir knight, but right at the moment...'

Stung, Sir Acelin flushed, and renewed his efforts more vigorously. Seconds later, the link snapped and dropped with a clatter to the metal wheel. Nakeya took the prybar from the knight and motioned for him to turn around.

'We should have freed you first,' she said, hearing distant noises from elsewhere in the tower. 'You may have a fight on your hands in no time.'

'Forget me,' said Sir Acelin. 'Where did that wizard put the brazen vessel? If you can find it, you will be able to call up Hadana. We will have need of djinn.'

'Hadana?' Nakeya spoke bitterly as she worked at his chains. 'Now that Ja'afar has regained his hold over him, Hadana will not obey our commands.'

'Not even yours?' Sir Acelin said. 'The poor fellow is clearly still besotted with you.'

Nakeya twisted the prybar and the link broke. Sir Acelin shuffled himself round so she could work on freeing his legs. She looked down at him, biting her lip.

'Do you really think that will work?' she asked nervously.

The sound of Ahmed's footsteps grew into a booming echoing as he made his way down the steps. The temperature became ever colder as he descended, and the air seemed dead, somehow devoid of all life. The lamp was his only source of heat; its handle was growing uncomfortably hot while his extremities were freezing cold.

Still the shadows danced on the walls. Again and again Ahmed thought he saw something moving out of the corner of his eye, but when he turned he saw only shadows stirred to frenzy by his own sudden movement.

The cold had been welcome at first, after the heat of the desert, but now it was growing unbearable. During their journey Sinbad had told them of a previous voyage, which had taken him to an icy land in the frozen north where he had sailed with the fierce Northmen, savage heathen warriors. Ahmed, a man who had lived most of his life in the Arabian heat, had shuddered at the tale, and hoped it had been only another of Sinbad's wild imaginings. Now he thought he understood just a little of what the sailor had undergone in the frozen north.

He stumbled suddenly as he turned the corner and the steps ended abruptly. Regaining his balance he found himself standing on the slimy, slippery floor of an artificial cave cut from the living rock. As he held up his lamp, he saw that the oozing walls were carved and daubed with strange cabalistic designs he recognised from the regalia of marketplace soothsayers and astrologers. Geometric shapes of a weirdly sinister kind adorned the walls, stars and triangles and complex sigils. This was like no dungeon he had ever seen before. And he was no stranger to incarceration.

He paused halfway across the chamber, looking down at the five pointed star painted on the ground, and wondered what it might mean.

Maybe the princess was imprisoned on the far side. He saw what looked like an archway in the opposite wall. 'Princess Abassa!' he called out softly. 'Are you there? Your rescuers have come, O princess!'

The arch contained a door. As the echoes of his voice died gradually away, he heard what sounded like something moving around on the other side of it. He crossed over, put the lamp down on the ground and studied the door. More symbols had been carved into it, another five pointed star, surrounded by a circle. Strange lettering—Hebrew, Ahmed guessed—had been inscribed between the points of the star. The door was locked from the outside with a bar. Ahmed realised that this could only be a prison. He wondered how the sister of the Caliph had coped under such appalling conditions.

Hastily he yanked up the bar and pulled the door open. It creaked dramatically, the sound echoing and re-echoing. Ahmed picked up his lamp and held it high, peering into the cell beyond.

Something moved, clambering up clumsily from a pile of dirty straw. Ahmed almost dropped the lamp. This was no captive princess.

The thing that faced him opened its jaws, revealing rows of serrated teeth, and let forth a roar that seemed to shake the chamber to its foundations.

9 IN THE PRINCESS' BOUDOIR

'Ja'afar!' Sinbad exclaimed.

The sorcerer stood in the archway leading to the staircase, a look of exultation on his morose face. He took a step forwards, hand raised a little.

'For a long time I have wanted you dead, dog,' he said softly. 'Even before that I resented you, begrudged your popularity in Baghdad. You probably don't remember me, do you? Only a minor court functionary, a lesser vizier, very much in the background when you graced the caliph's audience chamber with your presence and told your frankly unbelievable stories...'

'Talking of the caliph,' Sinbad began, 'or rather his sister...'

Ignoring the interruption Ja'afar took another step closer. 'All that time I was watching the caliph, witnessing his debaucheries and his depravity. All that time I was planning. Learning.

Studying. I spent time with sufis and dervishes, alchemists and astrologers, wizards and sorcerers, learning their forbidden arts. Learnt how to summon the djinn. I learnt how to travel to the further reaches of the world. That was how I came to know this land. It was here that I gained the ring that made me more powerful yet.'

He raised his hand, and Sinbad saw the silver band on his finger. He recognised it as the ring Ahmed had worn. The Ring of Ja'afar. He looked away in despair, his eyes falling upon something on the floor, amid the rugs and tables. A dulcimer. And beside it a carpet. He crossed over, kneeling to examine the latter.

'The Carpet of Suleiman!' he said, looking up accusingly at Ja'afar. 'And Nakeya's dulcimer. Where is Ahmed? And the others? They came here, didn't they?' He rose to his feet. 'Tell me where they are!'

Ja'afar laughed. 'You will be reunited with your friends in due course,' he said. 'For a long time I wanted you dead, dog, but now I have a better use for you. Did you come here seeking them? Or were you sent to kill me?'

'Kill you?' Sinbad rested his hand on the pommel of his scimitar. 'I'm prepared to do that, if necessary. But that wasn't why I was sent here. Where is Princess Abassa?'

Ja'afar looked surprised. 'My wife is in her chamber, resting,' he said. 'What concern is that of yours, dog? But we waste time.' He lifted up his talisman, and addressed the djinn who had been hovering nearby in silence. 'Zoba'ah Abu Hasan, I abjure thee in the name of...'

In a single fluid motion, Sinbad unsheathed his sword and swung it at the talisman in the sorcerer's hand.

Nakeya took up the brazen vessel. Absently she caressed it. It had been found in the desert, on their way to the City of Brass, she recalled. That thief Ahmed had appropriated it. But it had proved useful in the fight against her demon lover, Hadana. She nerved herself to open it.

She heard a distant echo of running feet from the steps down which Ahmed had descended. Sir Acelin called to her from the doorway. 'He's coming back! I can hear him!'

Nakeya set the vessel back down on the shelf. She was grateful for any interruption, however brusque; she felt nothing but anxiety at the thought of seeing Hadana again. The djinn who had seduced her. Who had fathered a child upon her.

Sir Acelin stood beside the opening, peering down into the darkness. A glimmer of light was shaking violently down there, growing brighter and more erratic as the thunder of footsteps echoed up from the depths. With it came a frenzied panting sound.

Nakeya crossed the chamber and came to Sir Acelin's side. 'I hear him too,' she murmured.

'He sounds to be in trouble.'

'That is nothing unusual,' said Sir Acelin gravely. 'Should we go down to see what is the matter?'

'We would be bowled over in the rush,' Nakeya commented. 'I wonder if he found the princess.'

Her nostrils twitched as a fetid odour wafted from the archway. Mingled with the echoes of Ahmed's running feet was a heavy, measure tread, and the ground beneath their feet began to shake. Something was following Ahmed, coming after him.

The yellow glow of the guttering lamp came into sight. Moments later Ahmed turned the corner. He was staggering, bedraggled, smeared with slime, fouled with cobwebs, his skin a mass of cuts and bruises. In his hand was the oil lamp, still glowing despite the rapid ascent, and on his face was a look of desperation.

Ahmed whirled round as the light from the arch fell upon him, and flung the lamp down the steps out of sight. There was a dull whoomph! a wail of pain, and a roar of flame that died suddenly. The sounds of pursuit started up again, and Ahmed turned and ran up the few remaining steps into the light.

'Coming…' he panted. 'It's com- coming…! It's… it's horrible! Coming after me! I set it free and now it's coming after me!'

Sir Acelin seized him as he charged into the

workshop. Ahmed struggled in his grasp. 'What is it?' he demanded of the scrawny little thief. 'What did you set free?'

'And where is the princess?' Nakeya asked.

Ahmed spun round as the heavy tread of the thing that had been following him grew louder. 'I don't know where she is,' he stammered, eyes wide as he peered into the blackness. 'Unless that's her.'

'Talk sense, man,' said Sir Acelin curtly. 'That's no princess. It must be some kind of, of...'

'Some kind of monster!' Ahmed wailed. 'Where's your sword? You'll have to fight it.'

Sir Acelin shook his head. 'I lost my sword when we were aboard the carpet,' he reminded him. 'It's somewhere at the bottom of the sea.'

Ahmed ran out into the workshop, looking frantically around him. 'There must be some sort of weapon here!' he said. Still the tread of his pursuer grew louder, echoing up the steps. His eyes fell upon the brazen vessel. 'That's it!' he said. 'We'll fight fire with fire!'

He snatched it up. 'Don't be a fool!' Nakeya said. 'We can't control... him,' she added in a dying fall as Ahmed opened the stopper.

Once again, smoke began to billow out of the vessel, coalescing with remarkable speed into the form of a saturnine youth, who folded his arms and gazed down at them. 'Who freed me from the vessel?' he boomed. 'I know you have no way to command me. You have liberated me!' His green glowing catlike eyes focused on Nakeya, and his expression softened. 'O my true love!' he cried. 'You have called me unto you. Come to my arms!'

He swooped down on her. She stumbled backwards, shaking her head. 'Listen!' she cried. The sound of the approaching monstrosity was growing even louder. It sounded as if it was about to turn the corner and climb the last few steps. 'A monster threatens us! Please, for the love you hold for me, save us!'

Even as she spoke the monster burst into the light, bounding up the steps on all fours, a dark fiend that was all wings and horns and claws. Its warty skin was blackened and smoking from where Ahmed's oil lamp had exploded upon it, but it seemed undeterred. On its cherubic face was an eager expression.

Reaching the top of the steps the monstrosity slowed to a halt. It saw Nakeya first.

'Mama,' it croaked. 'Mama!'

A sword leapt from the wall bracket where it hung, landing in Ja'afar's grasp in time for him to swing it to counter Sinbad's blow. The clash of steel on steel rang from the walls of the chamber.

'Not so fast, dog,' the sorcerer said with a sneer. 'You may have learnt how it is that I control my djinn, but you will never destroy the talisman.'

'You enslaved him! Man of evil! Abductor of

women! I shall drag you back to Baghdad to meet the caliph's justice.' Sinbad swung his scimitar as the djinn looked on in silence.

Ja'afar parried the blow and again steel rang out in the chamber. He lunged at Sinbad, the point of his sword nicking Sinbad's cheek so blood ran freely. Somehow Sinbad knew that the sorcerer was playing with him. He had no intention of killing him, but he would protect his amulet.

Sinbad lunged in return and the sorcerer deflected the blow with a superb circular parry. As Ja'afar tried to follow this up with another cut, this time to his other cheek, Sinbad leapt back deftly.

'You've not spent all your time studying black magic,' said the sailor grudgingly. 'You wield that blade with real skill.'

Negligently, Ja'afar leaned on his blade. He was not even out of breath. 'I summoned up the sprits of the master swordsmen of history to instruct me in the art. I wonder where you learnt to fence. Some back street in Basra, I'll warrant.' He leapt back as Sinbad swung his blade again, then parried, running his blade along Sinbad's edge and almost flipping it from the sailor's grasp.

Sinbad dodged another lunge then seized hold of a wall bracket to swing a savage kick at him. Ja'afar stumbled backwards to evade it, but the heel of Sinbad's bare foot caught the sorcerer a glancing blow to the chin. He staggered confusedly into the middle of the chamber, where Zoba'ah Abu Hasan watched the fight as a man might watch two battling stag beetles.

Sinbad let go of the wall bracket and landed close to the stairway. Ja'afar ran lightly towards him, his brandished blade a weave of steel. Sinbad jumped to one side, and rolled across a rug until he came to rest beside the pillar that divided the steps going upwards from those leading down.

'Dog!' laughed Ja'afar. 'Do you think to…?'

He broke off, cocking his head. Sinbad stared at the sorcerer in puzzlement. Then he heard it too. From the chamber below came a terrible clamour of shouts and screams. Above it all boomed a toad like croaking that seemed, for all the world, to be saying 'Mama! Mama! Mama!'

'The fools!' Ja'afar raged. 'Somehow they have released it!'

'Who has released what, sorcerer?' Sinbad demanded. 'What in Allah's name is going on?'

'I thought I had them securely fettered,' Ja'afar muttered. 'Zoba'ah Abu Hasan! Keep this man here! I must go below and see what is happening!' Without another word, the sorcerer brushed past Sinbad and ran down the steps.

The sailor turned to see Zoba'ah Abu Hasan floating towards him. He turned and ran—but not down the steps. Up them.

'Return, O Sinbad!' Zoba'ah Abu Hasan's gusty voice came from behind him as he ran, but he did not heed it.

At the top of the steps, Sinbad found himself in a lushly appointed, dainty little antechamber. Two doors led from it, while the steps continued upwards towards the spired roof of the tower. 'Princess! Princess!' he called out. 'Princess, where are you? I've come to rescue you!' Sword in hand he approached the nearest door.

'Sinbad!' groaned Zoba'ah Abu Hasan from the stairs. 'Return to me!'

Sinbad had no idea how he would deal with the djinn, but time was of the essence. He tried the door and it was locked. He shoulder-barged it and it burst open.

A cloying cloud of scent met him as he staggered into the chamber beyond. It was very plainly what could only be described as a boudoir. From somewhere within floated the distant chords of a lute, although no lutanist was visible. A large bed took up one side of the room, while silken drapes hung from the ceiling in profusion. A dressing table loaded with unguents and creams and perfume bottles stood before a massive mirror.

Sitting before this, a rabbit's foot held to her cheek, looking frostily at Sinbad in the mirror, was a singularly beautiful woman clad in revealing silks and satins. Kohl black hair swept down over well-formed shoulders. Sweet, carmine red lips were pursed in disapproval., slender eyebrows were lifted in surprise at this outrageous intrusion.

Sinbad had seen her from afar at occasional court functions. Princess Abassa, sister of the Caliph Harun al-Rashid, wife of Ja'afar, watched him in sphinx-like silence, only her heaving bosom betraying her anxiety.

'Make haste, princess!' Sinbad gripped his sword and looked back over his shoulder in the direction of the steps. 'Come with me! I'm here to take you back to your brother!'

When this elicited no immediate response, he looked back. The princess had dropped the rabbit's foot and was still watching him in the polished surface of the mirror. She swung round in her chair.

'Now why in the name of Allah would I want to do that?' she demanded, in a rich, throaty voice that was full of music.

10 ABASSA'S TALE

Hadana swooped down. 'Oh my child!' the djinn roared. 'O Shaqi! My child, and behold, my one true love! Mother and father and child! United at last!'

Ahmed and Sir Acelin exchanged bewildered looks.

'This,' said Hadana proudly, addressing Nakeya while indicating the hideous, wart riddled gargantuan baby, 'is Shaqi. Our child.'

Nakeya moaned. 'No, no, it's impossible!'

'What is all this?' Sir Acelin asked. 'What in the name of Christ is this monstrosity?'

'It's hideous!' Ahmed declared.

Shame in her eyes, Nakeya drooped. 'I told you how I was seduced by this marid,' she muttered. 'How I was cast out of the convent by the Mother Superior when it was seen that I was big with child. Before I was sold as a slave, I gave birth…'

'To a child half human and half djinn?' asked Ahmed. 'Is that possible?'

They heard a clatter of running feet from the stairs, and Ja'afar burst into the chamber.

Sinbad was impatient. 'Make haste, your majesty,' he said. 'There's a djinn right behind me, and I've come all the way across the world to rescue you. There's no time for games.'

He strode over. She rose to her feet and gave him a frosty look.

'Take your filthy hand off me,' she said as he grasped her arm. Her eyes narrowed. 'Don't I know you from somewhere?'

'I'm Sinbad,' he said hurriedly. 'The sailor. You've probably seen me at your brother's court. The caliph sent me to bring you back after Ja'afar abducted you. I've come a long way and I don't know what's become of all my companions, but there's a flying carpet downstairs and we can use that while your brother's distracted, get back to Baghdad...'

The door opened silently, and Zoba'ah Abu Hasan entered. 'Sinbad!' he boomed. 'You must come with me!'

'No, wait!' said Princess Abassa sternly. 'I would speak with this worm.'

Sinbad turned deftly, scimitar at the ready. 'Don't try to stop me, Zoba'ah Abu Hasan! Under other circumstances we might have been friends...'

'I must do my master's bidding until the talisman is destroyed!' Zoba'ah Abu Hasan said.

'You told me you would destroy the talisman!'

Princess Abassa tapped a slippered foot. 'If I might be permitted to speak,' she said.

Sinbad and Zoba'ah Abu Hasan fell silent. 'Of course, your majesty,' Sinbad said courteously. 'But we must make haste. Once I have despatched this djinn...'

'Enough!' A small vertical line had formed itself in the creamy perfection of the princess' brow. 'You are here to rescue me, you say?'

'Yes, your majesty,' Sinbad said. 'Now hurry downstairs before Ja'afar returns with who knows what monsters...'

'But what if I don't want to be rescued?' the princess asked.

Sinbad gaped at her. 'Don't want to... be rescued?' he whispered. 'But... but you must!'

'My thanks,' she said, 'for telling me what I must and must not do. As it happens, I do not wish to be rescued, not by a salty rogue with a penchant for unlikely tales, nor even by an eligible, handsome fellow of good birth and breeding—which you are not, Hinbad or Sinbad or whatever you call yourself. As it happens, I have already been rescued from a terrible fate, and once is enough for me.'

'Rescued?' Sinbad looked at Zoba'ah Abu Hasan as if for help but the lord of the wind said nothing. 'But you're still in Ja'afar's clutches. Who...? How...?'

'It was Ja'afar who rescued me,' the princess

said simply.

Sinbad put a hand to his brow. It was hot, almost feverish. He could feel himself developing a headache. 'No, you've got this wrong,' he said. 'Ja'afar abducted you from Baghdad, from the caliph's palace. Zoba'ah Abu Hasan, surely you can confirm this!' He appealed to the djinn. 'After all, you were instrumental.'

'I was summoned to aid my master in a daring rescue attempt,' said Zoba'ah Abu Hasan. 'With my assistance he rescued his one true love from her brother.'

'Rescued her from her brother?' Sinbad said. 'Why should she be rescued from her own brother?'

The princess looked away. 'What can I say but that my brother was... jealous when he learnt that I was in love with the grand vizier?'

'You're in love with Ja'afar?' Sinbad demanded. 'But what... why?' He broke off, confused. Sheathing his sword, he waited for an explanation.

'I do believe that is none of your concern, sailor,' she told him. 'Ja'afar was urbane, witty, sophisticated, intelligent, well read, handsome, and possibly the only true man in Baghdad, if not the entire caliphate. It was only natural I should fall in love with him. Besides, he was the only man at all I knew well other than my brother. No other men were allowed anywhere near me. And my brother came to regret allowing even the grand vizier into my presence.

'We used to meet in secret,' she went on, as the distant sound of what might have been a fight drifted up from somewhere below. 'In the darkest of night, in a bower in the palace gardens, with only the song of the nightingale to keep us company. In the end, Ja'afar told me that he could not bear this secrecy any longer, that it was against all honour. He resolved to ask for my hand from my brother. I warned him against it, but he persisted. Of course, Harun spurned his request, even planned to have him removed from office and executed on trumped up charges. But Ja'afar's own spies caught wind of the conspiracy, and before Harun could make his move to rid himself of his grand vizier, Ja'afar and I made our own counterplot.

'As was his wont, my brother went out into the city that night in disguise, and Ja'afar had him arrested in a low drinking den and cast into gaol. Then he made himself Caliph and attempted to have Harun executed alongside some gutter thief. When I heard of this plan, I was troubled, and remonstrated with him, and in the end, he resolved to keep him imprisoned in a room in the palace, nameless and unknown. But somehow my brother and the thief escaped, and for a long time we heard nothing of them. Alas, Harun returned, with his low companion, and using sorcery, had my Ja'afar flung to the very edge of the world. It was here that he found himself, in Djinnistan, although I knew nothing about it at the time. And it was all to his betterment, since he was able to enlist the aid of Zoba'ah Abu Hasan and the djinn, after helping foment a revolution.

'Then he returned to Baghdad. Here I had been kept under house arrest by my lecherous brother, who, now he thought he had rid himself of his rival, spent every day attempting to, to force himself upon me!' A pensive look crossed her attractive face. 'And soon we shall return, and with his magic Ja'afar will replace my brother and his court with automatons and rule from secret. And leading the automata will be you, Sinbad.'

She turned to Zoba'ah Abu Hasan. 'Take him to my husband.'

'You fools!' Ja'afar cried. 'What have you done?'

'And what have you done?' Nakeya countered. 'This is my child, so Hadana tells us! Why have you been keeping him prisoner?'

She crossed over to the monstrosity. Sir Acelin and Ahmed both tensed as if to spring to her defence. But when she laid a maternal hand upon its warty skin, it gurgled with delight. 'Mama!' it said, fawning. 'Mama!' Hadana joined them, smiling proudly.

'How touching!' sneered Ja'afar. 'I found this gruesome urchin roaming the land of Alzanjabil

Alakhdar. How it came to be there who knows, but no doubt after it was born it naturally gravitated to the country of the djinn. It was instrumental in my war to place Malik Gatshan on the throne, slaying many djinn in the fight, but it proved to be too destructive. I have had it confined below ever since, and now you have been so foolish as to release it.'

'It doesn't seem so fearsome now,' Ahmed ventured. 'Not now it's found its mama.'

At that moment, another figure appeared from the arch leading to the stairway. Zoba'ah Abu Hasan carried the struggling figure of Sinbad. Behind them trotted the princess Abassa.

'This crude fellow broke his way into my bedchamber,' she said, giving Ja'afar a disapproving look. 'What do you mean by it, my husband?'

Ja'afar was immediately cringing. 'O my love, my sweet, my little nightingale!' he said. 'I did not realise.. that is to say... Zoba'ah Abu Hasan!' he stormed. 'I told you to take Sinbad prisoner.'

'To hear is to obey, O master,' said Zoba'ah Abu Hasan, who had been eyeing Hadana and his child curiously. 'I bring him to you.'

'You were tardy enough about it!' the sorcerer barked. 'To permit him to force his way into my dear love's boudoir! You shall suffer for this!' He looked more closely at Sinbad. 'And the fellow still wears a sword!' he added, striking his brow despairingly. He reached up and snatched the weapon from Sinbad's side, then flung it across the workshop. 'Must I do everything for myself?'

'I know what you plan,' Sinbad said. 'I shall stop you, mark my words!'

'How could you?' Ja'afar sneered. 'On the contrary, you will aid me.' He lifted the ruby ring, and brandished the silver talisman. 'Djinn! Do my bidding! Take these sons of Adam and bind them to the wheel!'

In less time than it takes to tell, Sinbad lay beside his companions, bound hand and foot. But still he was defiant.

'Are these statues your automatons?' he asked, indicating the statues. 'You surely don't think the citizens of Baghdad will mistake them for their rulers?'

Ja'afar hauled on an iron lever and the wheel began to turn, slowly at first. A metal projection jutted out from it, and every time it brushed up against one of the metal statues, there was a shower of sparks and the statue would whir jerkily into life, before stilling again into immobility. 'How you confound me, Sinbad! But you are mistaken if you think they will see these iron statues. Since my love has been as indiscreet as to tell you something of my plans, I might as well let you know your own fate. With my sorcery I shall transform them into exact simulacra of Harun al-Rashid and his cronies.'

He lifted up one of the green glass phials

and shook it so the red viscous liquid swirled around inside. 'This contains blood leeched from the caliph by one of my imps. Each one of these phials contains blood from one of the caliph's officers or nobles. The blood will be deposited into the centre of this wheel. And with it will go your own blood and that of your companions.'

He gestured at the runnels that led down into the hub of the wheel. Sinbad saw now that pipes led across the stone floor from the base of the hub, each one connecting with a different statue. If blood ran down the runnels into the hub it would ooze out of the pipes into one of the statues.

He remembered what he had heard from the rug merchant on his return to Baghdad. The man had spoken of *the blood drinking ghoul who terrorised the nobles and princes of the land.... Almost all of the nobility have reported waking up with strange incisions on the body still sticky with blood—as if some foul creature had been feasting on them in the night!* Somehow Ja'afar must have been responsible. He had kept the blood fresh by some sorcerous means and now meant to use it in his foul alchemical experiments.

'It will be piped into one of the automatons and they will be transformed by my spells into an exact reproduction of its original owner,' Ja'afar added; 'exactly the same but bound to do my will. And your simulacra will lead the invasion. The caliph will hardly suspect Sinbad and his heroic companions!'

He broke off in dismay at a whistling roar from outside. There was a hot waft of brimstone. Then something slammed into the tower wall beside the balcony with enough force to make the entire tower shake.

11 UNDER ATTACK

'What in the name of Iblis is happening?' the sorcerer shouted.

Ja'afar clutched onto his turban and turned to gaze out through the opening at the desert city beyond. What he saw outside made him gasp out loud. He ran forward onto the balcony, gripping onto the balustrade. Princess Abassa went to join him, trying to haul him back inside.

Managing to sit up, Sinbad saw that the air outside was crisscrossed with streamers of smoke. Although he could not see the fighting, the sounds of battle that had previously been audible on the edge of hearing from the city were now much louder.

'Who's fighting who?' Ahmed wanted to know.

Sinbad twisted round. The thief lay on the spoke of the wheel currently furthest from the balcony, and could see nothing. 'I think it must be Ad-Dimiryat,' he said. 'Finally he has mustered his forces and made an attack.' As the wheel continued to turn, and Princess Abassa tried to persuade Ja'afar to come inside, he related his recent adventures.

'If only I had a sword,' Sir Acelin muttered to himself, struggling with his bonds. 'I cannot bear the thought of dying like this, a sacrifice to a paynim idol.'

'I can't bear the thought of dying,' Ahmed told him.

Another stray shot struck the tower and again the chamber shook. Wailing and gurgling in fear, Shaqi leapt up onto the wheel, nuzzling Nakeya affectionately. He was a very big baby, roughly the size of a well fed desert lion, and Nakeya had to struggle to keep him at bay.

'Mama!' he grizzled. 'Mama!'

The two djinn swirled around in the air, as if straining at the leash to join the fight that was unfolding down below them. At last Ja'afar came back inside the chamber, Princess Abassa clinging to him.

'The rebels attack,' he told the chamber at large. 'Malik Gatshan's forces fight them in the streets. But it seems that their main objective is this tower.'

'What do you expect?' asked Sinbad. 'After all, it was you who provided Malik Gatshan with the wherewithal to take over Djinnistan. Those rebels are led by the rightful sultan.'

'Enough!' said Ja'afar scornfully. 'This only makes the ritual's completion all the more urgent.'

Disengaging the princess, he produced a long, wicked bladed dagger from his belt. 'And the first whose blood I shall spill,' he went on, 'will not be Harun al-Rashid's, will not be Ishak's, or any of the other nobles, but you, Sinbad!'

He halted as Shaqi bawled at him from where he lay cuddled up to Nakeya. 'What is that cursed babe doing there?' he demanded. 'Hadana! By my ring I command you! Remove your brat!'

The marid swooped down and carried the protesting baby away. 'Mama!' Shaqi wailed. 'Mama!' He fought in his father's grasp as Ja'afar advanced on Sinbad.

Sinbad also tried to struggle, but he the chains had him pinioned. 'What do you mean to do, drain me of all my blood?' he demanded wildly.

'Only a few pints will be sufficient to imprint one of the automata with your features and persona,' said Ja'afar, his face bland, the blade lifted high, waiting for the turning of the wheel to bring him round. 'It will be enough to leave you feeling drained, ha-ha, but not enough to kill you. Of course,' he added as he held the blade poised, 'I shall have to kill you later. I cannot risk the possibility of you turning up in Baghdad as the real Sinbad. That might just give the game away.'

'Do you really think this is a game, wizard?'

Sinbad asked in horror.

Ja'afar laughed maniacally and nodded. 'Aye. Whether it is a game of chance or of skill still remains to be seen. But I play for high stakes,' he added, as Sinbad came within reach. 'The highest!'

He lunged. As he did so, a whistling noise grew louder, followed by an explosion as some kind of missile struck the side of the tower. This time the entire chamber shook as if in an earthquake. The wall containing the balcony fell away. Spiderwebs of cracks opened up across the floor and ceiling.

A large piece of stone fell with a crash on the wheel and abruptly it stopped turning. With a snapping sound the rim broke, in just the spot where Sir Acelin was bound. Suddenly the knight's arms were released. Wonderingly he sat up and started trying to free his legs.

At the same time Ja'afar was struck by a falling fragment. His dagger came stabbing down, not into Sinbad's arm but into his ribs. Blood gushed out, flooding the runnel, and Sinbad cried out in pain.

Sir Acelin heaved at his bonds, ignoring the rain of stones from the unstable ceiling, and the uproar of fighting that was now coming from directly below the tower, as if the spur of rock had been surrounded by struggling djinn. With a metallic snapping sound, the knight's bonds broke, and the knight leapt down from the wheel.

With the princess' aid, Ja'afar pushed himself back up. The gory spray had subsided. Sinbad lay back, breathing shallowly, face white. But the runnel was scarlet with his blood and it was now trickling into the hub. Desperately, Ja'afar dabbed at it with the hem of his robe. 'Too much,' he muttered. 'Much too much.'

'Step away from the wheel,' Sir Acelin demanded.

He had found Sinbad's scimitar—the sword of Solomon!—and now held it levelled at the sorcerer. Absently Ja'afar looked up. 'Fool,' he muttered. 'You do not know what you do. Sheathe that weapon.'

'It seems it lacks a sheath,' said Sir Acelin, 'and yet I will sheathe it in your black heart if you do not set Sinbad free.'

He turned to where Ahmed and Nakeya were bound, and with a couple of swings of the scimitar he freed their hands. At once they both began unloosing the bonds that kept them bound to the hub. The stone that had struck the wheel seemed not to have harmed the mechanism beyond stopping it from turning. The metal pipes were shaking as if Sinbad's blood was now flowing through them.

'Only thing for it,' Ja'afar muttered obsessively to himself, picking up the phials containing the blood of Harun al-Rashid and his courtiers. 'If I add this, maybe each automaton will adopt a different aspect...'

He approached the wheel, and took out one of the phials. Sir Acelin swung at him with his sword, and Ja'afar staggered backwards. The phials fell to the rubble littered floor and smashed.

'Brute of an infidel!' Ja'afar cried. He lifted high his ring and the talisman. 'Zoba'ah, Hadana! Slay him!'

The two djinn swooped down on the knight. He whirled round, scimitar held high, and parried their attack. Ahmed and Nakeya, now free, clambered across the broken wheel to where Sinbad lay, blood still seeping from his chest.

Ahmed withdrew the knife and flung it away. Ja'afar seized him and tried to wrestle him away. The two men fell to the ground, struggling amidst the wreckage. Nakeya, ignoring them, knelt beside Sinbad, cleaning his wound as best as she could. As she did so, she became aware of a large, gurgling presence. She looked round and heard a cry of 'Mama? Mama!'

Sinbad's eyes cleared. He looked weakly up at Nakeya. 'The automata?' he whispered.

The metal statues stood motionless in the alcoves. In the rubble strewn space beside the forge, Ahmed and Ja'afar were fighting for control of the knife. Silhouetted against the ragged opening in the wall, Sir Acelin battled the two djinn. Nakeya looked more closely at the automata. They were beginning to change somehow, the metallic skin flushing with a crimson hue. When she told Sinbad what she had seen, he tried to raise himself up onto his elbow, but she gently pushed him down.

Sir Acelin was wearying. The two djinn, under Ja'afar's sorcerous control, fought inexorably, both wielding magical blades that ran with flame. The knight was unused to wielding the weapons of the Saracens, but this scimitar seemed to possess uncanny powers. Hardly surprising, considering where Sinbad had found it. He thrust, hewed, and lunged with it, wounding both of his opponents more than once.

By now they were fighting amidst the wreck of the balcony. The desert sun glared down from the naked sky. Glancing over the edge, Sir Acelin could see a throng of fighting forms in the dust far below. Some of them were trying to ascend the creamy flanks of the tower towards them. The city itself seemed to be the scene of fierce fighting.

Princess Abassa shrieked. Ahmed and Ja'afar were struggling in the orange glow of the forge. As they did so, Ja'afar snatched the knife from Ahmed, but lost his grip and it went clattering away across the stone floor. Ahmed threw himself full length and tried to grab it but it struck the lip of the forge and bounced over the edge, vanishing with a hiss into the glowing coals.

Ahmed rolled over to find Ja'afar looming

over him, a blacksmith's hammer in his hand. He swung it at Ahmed, but the thief rolled again, and as the sorcerer stumbled, overbalanced by his swing, he pushed himself up with one arm and aimed an almighty kick at the sorcerer's behind. Ja'afar, screaming and scrabbling at the very air around him, fell over the lip of the forge pit and vanished into the burning orange glow.

Princess Abassa, who had been watching the fight in horror, ran sobbing from the workshop. Black smoke blazed up thickly, then drifted away in the suddenly silent air of the chamber.

From outside came the sound of fighting djinn, but the clash of blade on blade within the chamber had ceased the moment the sorcerer's body vanished into the fire of the forge. Ahmed turned to look in the direction of the balcony.

Sir Acelin stood, scimitar in hand, as the two djinn knelt before him in supplication.

'We are free,' Hadana boomed.

Zoba'ah Abu Hasan nodded. 'The talismans that made us slaves were destroyed in the fires of the furnace, along with the sorcerer.'

'Then...' Ahmed said in wonder, looking round the chamber. 'That means we've won!'

Nakeya grinned from where she knelt with Shaqi at Sinbad's side. Then her face fell. She pointed in horror.

Ahmed whirled round. Where the automata had been were now a series of identical figures. A dozen or more simulacra of Sinbad stood there.

Each one carried a scimitar. Each one lifted its head that bore Sinbad's handsome visage. Each one stirred into life and strode jerkily towards them.

12 AN ARMY OF SINBADS

At the foot of the tower was a scene of chaos, as djinn fought djinn. Many of them had the wings of bats, while some had four arms, two like that of a man, the others like a lion's forelegs. All were clad and accoutred for war, with blades and cuirasses of brass.

Ad-Dimiryat's forces had circumvented the city, striking directly at the tower that they knew to be the source of Malik Gatshan's power. The desert trek had been arduous, and many djinn had been lost en route. Now they were fighting on two fronts, with a contingent led by Al'Azraq bombarding the tower before attempting to scale the spur upon which it stood, while a larger force led by Ad-Dimiryat himself kept advancing forces from Schadou Kiam at bay. The fight had spilled over into the City of Jewels itself, and Malik Gatshan himself had come from his palace to direct the proceedings.

Lines of djinn fighters clashed in the sandy stretch between the city and the rocky spur,

Ad-Dimiryat's rebels, armed with sword and lance, battling Malik Gatshan's elite ifrit forces, the 'Abna' Ablis, who rode upon fire breathing lions. Bat winged djinn stooped on the attacking forces, some plucking Al'Azraq's men from the rock spur as they scaled it and hurling them into the abyss. But Ad-Dimiryat's forces had grown since Sinbad had left him, and he had a troop of flying djinn himself, who now flew up to battle Malik Gatshan's aerial forces.

Halfway up the cliff beneath the tower of Ja'afar, Al'Azraq stood on a ledge flanked by several of his picked djinn, searching for a route up. High above them the tower was dimly visible, and they were perturbed by the distant clash of blade on blade that filtered down to their ears, audible even over the roar of battle.

'Did Sinbad reach the sorcerer's tower after all?' asked his lieutenant. 'It seems that fighting is going on in there.'

Al'Azraq nodded grimly. 'So it seems. We must hope our bombardment did not affect him adversely. Well, what matters is that Ja'afar is not able to come to the aid of his puppet sultan.'

Down below, Ad-Dimiryat's forces were pursuing back Malik Gatshan's retreating lion riders. They found the gates of the city shut against them, and began to fire upon the walls with their cannon. Ranks upon rank of Malik Gatshan's djinn infantry issued forth from a sally port and set upon the rebels' left flank, and Ad-

Dimiryat's forces were swiftly divided.

Leading the new attackers was a tall figure in glittering armour. He was little more than in insect from Al'Azraq's viewpoint, but the djinn lifted up his cannon in both hands and fired it with remorseless accuracy.

It hit the infantry commander and the djinn exploded like a firecracker, showering the sand with body fragments and sending his ranks into disarray. Under cover of the confusion, a group of Ad-Dimiryat's fighters gained entrance through the sally port. Moments later, after a swift, brutal, decisive action, the main gate was in the hands of the rebels.

Now more forces from the direction of the palace were seen to be deployed by Malik Gatshan, and the streets of the city closest to the gate became a chaos of struggling shapes. Dust rose from the streets, and smoke joined it to as some of the buildings were fired by the rebels. Soon little could be seen of the City of Jewels but the fog of war, and above it the flying djinn fighting out their own aerial combat.

All was confusion. The fantastic city of Schadou Kiam was ablaze, its domes and spires and minarets growing black in the flames that licked them. For a moment, Al'Azraq spared a thought for the innocent djinn citizens caught up in the fighting. But he quashed the thought as unworthy of a djinn warrior, turned, and gestured upwards.

'We go on!' he declared to his warriors.

'Mountjoy and Saint Denis!'

Sir Acelin gripped the scimitar in his hand. He wore only a tunic and hose, having lost his armour long ago, but his fair hair, confined by a fillet, streamed behind him as he ran towards the advancing automata.

He vaulted the broken wheel, dodging past Sinbad, seeing Nakeya and her overgrown offspring crouched nearby, and landed by the forge, where Ahmed stood weaponless. Thrusting him to one side, Sir Acelin brandished his blade at the nearest automaton.

It was an eerie sight. Sinbad's well known features regarded him with all his customary warmth. Sir Acelin knew that handsome visage very well, that small, neat beard, those dark, piercing eyes that always seemed to be gazing into distant, unseen horizons. Each one of the automata resembled Sinbad as Sir Acelin had first met him, clad in his Saracen garb, with turban on his head, white shirt and tight dark trousers. Each one was identical with the one closest to him, who held a sword in his hand, a Saracen blade, a scimitar like the one that Sir Acelin wielded. But it was not Sinbad. None of these simulacra was Sinbad. Sinbad lay behind Sir Acelin, on the wheel, pale and bloodless amidst the rubble of the sorcerer's tower. Sir Acelin feared that the sailor was dying.

The automaton met his attack with an effortless swing; it met Sir Acelin's edge with a clash that rained the stone floor with sparks. The knight staggered backwards a short way, then ran at his opponent with a wild shout, swinging his sword at that turbaned head. But the automaton's scimitar was there to meet his blow, parrying with mechanical efficiency, and this time following up with a swift, clinical chop that slashed across the knight's unprotected ribs so crimson spread through his white linen tunic.

Sir Acelin barely noticed the pain. He lunged at the automaton, but this time another simulacrum of Sinbad was before him, attacking from his right. As Sir Acelin's blade rattled impotently from the metal torso of the first automaton, he felt a fiery thrust into the small of his back as the second automaton attacked.

'Don't be a fool, Sir Acelin,' Ahmed cried.

He seized a length of metal from beside the forge and ran to the knight's side. But as he did so, more automata with the face of Sinbad marched to attack him and he found himself surrounded by flashing blades, cutting and thrusting at him with remorseless efficiency. Ably he defended himself with the steel rod, but he was soon surrounded.

'Help him!' Nakeya begged Hadana. 'If ever you loved me, help Sir Acelin. And Ahmed too!'

Hadana strode across the workshop. Zoba'ah Abu Hasan joined him, blowing a gust of wind that sent automatons tumbling like ninepins. Ahmed stood surrounded by prone automata. He turned to run but halted unwillingly as he felt a hard, cold, metal hand close around his ankle. Looking down he saw a prone Sinbad clutching at him—but it was not Sinbad, he reminded himself, it was one of the automata.

He lifted his steel rod and brought it frenziedly down on the grinning automaton, bashing and bashing at the sorcerous contrivance until it loosened its grip. He went staggering across the workshop.

The rest of the automata had risen from where they had fallen, and now they advanced in a solid line, scimitars flashing as they came. Sir Acelin came to meet them but this time he was joined by the two djinn. And now, crawling rapidly across the stone floor, red faced and bawling, knocking automata aside, came Shaqi.

Nakeya shrieked and jumped down from the wheel. Ahmed seized her as she tried to go after her son. 'He seems to be doing pretty well for himself, girl,' he said, gripping her struggling form.

Hadana laughed exultantly. Side by side they fought the unfightable automatons. Only one had been put out of action, that despatched by Ahmed, and even that one still lived, struggling round the floor with its skull stove in. Zoba'ah Abu Hasan's winds could knock the Sinbad automatons off their feet, but soon they rose again, swords whirling. Sir Acelin was fighting in the middle of them. He made better progress: his sword cut through the metal of the automata as if through water, but even lopping off metal limbs did not halt them; they kept coming despite wounds that would have slain a man of flesh. The automata were inexhaustible. And the knight was tiring.

A scimitar slashed his breast. More scimitars rose and fell, and rose again, bloodied, as the knight sank to his knees. Vainly he hacked with his sword at iron legs, but then another blade swung down, lopping off the hand that held it so hand and scimitar went bouncing off across the stone floor to land in the shadow of a pillar. A second followed it, and his head was half severed from his neck. He went down amidst a whirlwind of bloodied steel, and he did not rise again.

Nakeya sobbed and buried her face against Ahmed's chest. Clumsily he tried to comfort her as the djinn began to retreat across the workshop, fighting a desperate rear-guard.

'These things are unbeatable,' he said in horror. 'We can't stay here…!'

A hand rose to clutch at his wrist, and he looked down to see Sinbad's pale, anaemic features gazing up at him.

'How did you free the djinn?' Sinbad asked in a breathless voice.

'What?' Ahmed said, shouting over the clangour of blade on blade. 'I don't know, I pushed Ja'afar into the forge...' He stared at Sinbad.

'The heat must have destroyed the talismans controlling them,' Nakeya said in sudden realisation.

'But what talismans control the automata?' Ahmed said.

'It must be this,' said Sinbad, weakly slapping the metal of the wheel. 'Help me up! We must destroy the wheel.'

Ahmed and Nakeya helped him off. 'How can we destroy this? Ahmed said. He slammed a fist down on the wheel, then winced, and sucked at the heel of his hand. 'It's solid metal!'

Light glimmered in Sinbad's eyes. 'Suleiman's sword! Surely that will destroy it if anything will! Where is it?'

Ahmed shook his head. 'The knight had it. Sinbad... he's dead. The automata killed him.'

He pointed across the workshop to where Sir Acelin's body lay. In the shadows nearby lay the fallen sword. Sinbad cursed. Between them and it stood the automata, battling the djinn.

It was at just that moment, as if in answer to a prayer, that a blue skinned djinn with a black topknot climbed in through the balcony, followed by several more rebel djinn. 'Al'Azraq!' Sinbad hissed. 'Help us!'

'Sinbad!' Al'Azraq cried. 'You live!'

'Never mind that!' the sailor told him. 'You and your djinn! Join forces with the others and fight off the automata! We need to be able to get hold of Suleiman's scimitar!'

Under his breath as Al'Azraq and his fellow djinn added their force to that of the two already fighting the automata, he muttered, 'I only hope this works...'

Although the metal men showed no sign of being forced back, they were sufficiently occupied fighting their new foes for Ahmed to sprint forward, dodge round two of them, and snatch up the sword from beside Sir Acelin's brutally butchered body. Turning on his heel, he shouted across the room to Sinbad; 'Catch!'

He threw the scimitar of Suleiman over the heads of the embattled djinn and automata. Sinbad thrust up a weak hand, and seized the sword by the hilt. Staggering and groaning weakly, he turned, and brought the blade slicing down into the metal of the wheel.

The automata began to slow, their movements becoming more and more uncoordinated. As the wheel began to melt, the automata slowed to a stop and one by one fell with a clatter to the floor.

Helped by Nakeya and Ahmed, Sinbad crossed over to the closest automaton. With a kick, he turned it over. A blank face of metal, lifeless and inanimate, gazed up at him. Sinbad stared unspeaking down into that visage for a long time.

EPILOGUE

Malik Gatshan's crimson face gazed down at the square. The eyes rolled in their sockets, the mouth hung slack. The neck terminated in ragged flesh, and the entire head stood on the top of a pole by the palace gates.

Inside the palace, Ad-Dimiryat sat upon the throne, Al'Azraq and his men stood beside him. Upon the mosaic floor stood Sinbad, still looking weak, and Nakeya and Ahmed. With Nakeya was Shaqi, and both Hadana and Zoba'ah Abu Hasan stood with them. Between them was Princess Abassa. She had been found after the battle was over, hiding in her boudoir, in tears.

On a plinth before them lay Sir Acelin's body, clad in mail and with the scimitar Sinbad had found in Suleiman's tomb.

'Djinn will transport the hero's remains back to his homeland,' said Ad-Dimiryat, reaching the end of a long address. 'He was a courageous man, who shall never be forgotten by the folk of Djinnistan. And so shall all of you be honoured.'

'I think we'll have to be getting back home

ourselves,' said Ahmed. 'We have to get the princess back to the caliph.'

Princess Abassa gave him a cold look, and turned to the djinn sultan. 'Sire,' she said formally, 'as one royal person to another, I beg of you a boon. Do not let these common folk carry me back to my brother. I have suffered at his hands, seen my husband slain. My life is a bleak one, and for what reason? Only because I fell in love. Only because my brother was jealous and seethed with unseemly lust. Is it fair, is it just, that I should be borne back to him like some kind of prize of valour?'

Ad-Dimiryat's elephantine features regarded her gravely. 'I would not wish such a fate upon anyone, princess,' he said with feeling. 'Sinbad, my djinn will also carry off you and your friends to your home if that is what you desire, but what do you say to this? Will you insist on my djinn taking Princess Abassa back to suffer indignity at the hands of her brother?'

Sinbad was torn. 'I was sent to Djinnistan with this sole objective,' he said, 'to bring back Princess Abassa when Ja'afar abducted her. Men have died in the quest, and we have suffered much. Would you deny me the right to fulfil the wishes of my caliph?'

'But you were told to bring back an abducted princess,' said Ad-Dimiryat. 'I see no such person here. Instead I see a young woman who has suffered just as you have suffered, who came to this land in the hopes of living a happy life with the one she loved.'

'Who plotted to take over Baghdad with those automatons!' Ahmed said. He turned to Sinbad. 'You know I don't care much about the caliph or high politics. But you told him we would bring her back, and I don't want you to come back empty handed. Not after all the trouble we've been put to.'

'But can't you see?' Nakeya said. 'You can't drag her off to Baghdad, to suffer who knows what fate at your caliph's hands. She came here because she loved Ja'afar. People can't choose who they love.'

She exchanged a look with Hadana, then reached down and petted her son.

Sinbad nodded slowly. 'Nakeya's right, Ahmed,' he said. 'If we were to take the princess back to Baghdad, it would be we who would be the abductors. No, this will be one time when Sinbad does not succeed in his quest. Perhaps now the caliph will leave me be, and allow me to settle down in Baghdad as I always wanted rather than sending me off on another mission to the ends of the earth! And you can come with me, Ahmed, and get back to some honest thieving.'

Ahmed looked stricken. 'I don't know that I want to go back,' he said, 'considering the fix I'm in with the guild. I owe them money, you know. A lot of it. And look'—he gestured at his tattered robes. 'I have not a dirham to my name.'

'I'm not a poor man,' said Sinbad. 'I think I owe it to you to help you out.'

'What will you do, if you don't go back with Sinbad?' Nakeya asked the princess. Abassa looked uncertain.

'The princess will be welcome to remain here at my court for as long as she wishes,' said Ad-Dimiryat. 'But you speak as if you do not mean to join him.'

'I do not,' said Nakeya. She smiled at Sinbad's look of startlement. 'It has been quite an adventure, O Sinbad, but I will not return to Baghdad. It was never my home. I was a slave. The caliph said I would be set free if I helped you obtain the carpet.' She laughed. 'I did that and much more. I think I can count myself free now. And in this country I have found my child and his father.' She turned to Hadana. 'Things between us have not always been as good as they could be,' she went on, 'but we have both known slavery and both known freedom. Now it is time we learnt to live with each other. For the sake of our son.'

Ahmed turned to Sinbad. 'It looks like it's just you and me, sailor-man. So, hi-ho, it's off to Baghdad, is it? To an uncertain future. Where I'm in a spot of bother with the guild of thieves, and you will be in trouble with the caliph. But what of the carpet? It's no more than a rug now that I've lost the means to control it.'

Laughing, Sinbad shook his head. 'We need

no carpet when the magic of the djinn will whisk us away to Baghdad in the twinkling of an eye. Trouble will never leave us, thief, it's in our nature. But all that matters is that we have the guts to stand up to it. Farewell, Sultan of the Djinn, and thank you for your aid. It would be a long voyage without your magic. Farewell!'

THE FANTASTIC ADVENTURES OF SINBAD

Sinbad And The Great Old Ones

Sinbad sails the seven seas in his struggle to foil the evil magician Abdul Alhazred's plot to summon up the Great Old Ones and unleash upon the world the Age of Cthulhu...!

'If you grew up with the Harryhausen 'Sinbad' flicks and were a fan of HP Lovecraft, this is the book for you...' Vulpine from Innsmouth
'Strange and interesting...' Brian Chrisman
'Highly recommended!' Amazon Customer

Shipwrecked while escorting the Princess of Serendip to her bridegroom, Sinbad the Sailor discovers that she has been abducted by the wicked magician, Abdul Alhazred, who plans to sacrifice her in an attempt to open the dimensional gate and summon the Great Old Ones—demonic gods from beyond the stars.

Accompanied by a motley crew of alchemists and slave girls, princes and policemen, Sinbad sets out to foil the evil sorcerer's plot. The journey will take them from lost desert cities to mysterious jungle islands, and from the streets of Samarkand to the fabled Plateau of Leng, until at last Sinbad alone stands between the peoples of the Earth and slavery to the forces of cosmic evil...

SINBAD AND THE GREAT OLD ONES is a must for all fans of sword and sorcery, Lovecraft's Cthulhu Mythos, and the swashbuckling Sinbad films of Ray Harryhausen.

Sinbad And The Viking Queen

Given the task of escorting an emissary from the Emperor Charlemagne, Sinbad is dismayed when his dhow is attacked by Northmen—savage pagan pirates who sail the northern seas, slaughtering and pillaging. But these warriors, and their queen, Helga Hammerhand, have a different mission—one for which they require Sinbad's services, willing or otherwise.

As a prisoner, Sinbad joins them on a voyage into the frozen north, far beyond their own country of Frostheim, in a desperate search for the land at the back of the north wind. Through seas of monsters they sail, but once the channel of the sea serpents is passed, what horrors will they find in the lands beyond? And will Sinbad ever escape? Or is this his final voyage?

Printed in Great Britain
by Amazon